Surprise Attack!

Tor felt a rush of heat and saw red light through his arm and eyelids as the weapon bloomed up and out in a sudden, huge ball of roaring white fire that set the center of the valley ablaze, instantly roasting the crowd, the assembled Peshtak, and the Domesman.

Tor looked up, stunned. Turning, he found the guards by the shelter had been blinded by the flash and were standing in burning grass, holding their faces. Tor raced through burning leaves and grass and felled the seven guards with swift strokes of his new axe. The front of the shelter was smoking and flaring, and he could hear a shrill voice inside screaming. He dashed around to the back, encountering three Peshtak, killing all three in a whirling flurry.

He ripped mats and bark from the rear of the shelter, hacking through saplings and bindings. Diving in, he felt a knife bite into his right arm. He whipped his axe around again in the smoky dark, felt it slice deep, and resheathed it. In the smoke he saw a woman lying bound. He slipped his arm under her shoulders and ran out the hole in the rear of the shelter.

The Dome in the Forest

Paul O. Williams

A Del Rey Book

BALLANTINE BOOKS • NEW YORK

A Del Rey Book
Published by Ballantine Books

Library of Congress Catalog Card Number: 81-66660

ISBN 0-345-30087-4

Manufactured in the United States of America

First Edition: December 1981

Map by Chris Barbieri

Cover art by Ruth Sanderson

To David and Mary

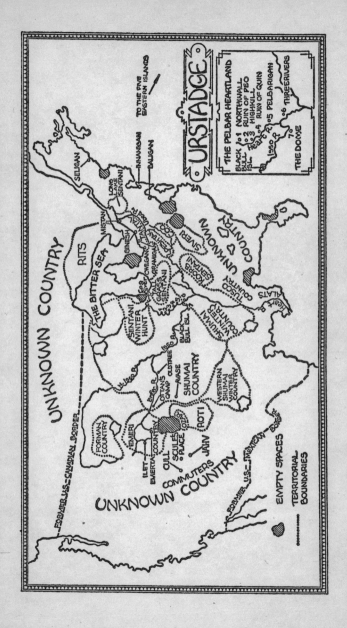

1

IN the darkness, the sound of rain slowed, and high on Gagen Tower on the river wall of the city of Pelbarigan on the Heart, the first signs of light made the two guardsmen restless. They hunched against the chill in their sweeping raincapes, standing as much as possible under the weather canopy. Fires had been burning near the bank for some time now, and shadowy figures moving among them, as the dim cloud-filtered dawn began slowly to grow.

The taller guard yawned, ran his hands through his hair, and said sleepily, "The Shumai and Sentani are up early. What goes?"

"The Shumai are taking some of the starband to the empty place southwest of here."

"To the empty place?"

"Yes. It is almost the spring equinox. For many years now some of the Shumai have gone there every equinox, spring and fall, to see the rising of the great rod from the earth."

"What? Where did you hear about this?"

"Last night. I was down there. Hagen the Shumai was talking about it. Winnt the Sentani is going out of curiosity. The Shumai insist that there is a rod of shining metal that rises out of the ground on a hillside near the edge of the empty place. A hunter first saw it by accident some years ago. Now a group of them always goes back and watches it. Always at the equinox. It never fails."

"Huh. Does it ever come between times?"

"I don't know. They think not. I'm too sleepy now to think much about it. Besides, I want to get out of this incredible rain. Will it ever stop? I wonder why we have no flood yet."

"Not much snow in the north this year, I hear. But

look. Even in this dim light you can see the river is bank-full."

"I wonder where the next watch is. It is time for bed. Look at the light coming now."

The smaller guardsman picked up her short-sword and buckled it on, murmuring, "I hear our replacements coming."

The two new guardsmen emerged onto the tower platform and saluted, sleepily but in good form. "Where is Ahroe?" the taller guard asked.

"She is going with them. Down there. To see the rising of the rod."

"Ahroe? Why? Does that mean Stel is going?"

"Yes. Both. Ahroe is a representative to see this thing. A guardsman. The council thinks we should be aware of it. And Stel—well, with her going, they felt it a courtesy to let him go as well."

The tall guard laughed. "She will take good care of him anyhow," he said as the two night guards slowly descended the winding stairs.

Below, on the bank, Hagen held the hand of Ahroe's son, Garet, as the boats were launched. The boy was about eleven, and unhappy to be left behind. Stel laughed as he squatted down and kissed him on the forehead. "Be good," he said. "Don't beat Hagen up. Don't tear down the city. Learn well. We won't be long. If you were three years older, perhaps you could come."

Garet frowned deeply and pushed out his lower lip. "Come, Garet," said Ahroe. "Give us a guardsman's face."

He tried, but the result was comical. No one laughed at him, though.

"Garet," Hagen began gently. "We will take a walk up to the blufftop to see them go downriver. Come, now. Let's get you a coat."

Ahroe quickly pushed off the arrowboat. They paddled out to join the Sentani flotilla, shuddering a little in the chill rain out on the water. The Sentani starband, orderly as usual, had already formed their pattern of boats. The Shumai running hunters knew little of boating and had no formation. But they were eager, since it was nearly time for the rising of the rod, and they leaned into their paddles. Tor, their axeman, stood in the middle of their largest canoe, slim and broad-shouldered. He shifted easily with the rocking of the craft, as his paddlers drove their blades into the river, catching the rhythm of the long strokes they would use all day. The strange fleet moved downstream through the gray spring morning.

At the third promontory on the bluffs, the prescribed place, the guardsmen on the tower sent along the long, haunting notes of departure and farewell from their great trumpets, and the paddles of the whole group were held up momentarily in reply. The rain continued, and the rhythmic paddling became almost a hypnotic relief from it, something to keep one occupied and warm.

They paddled with only one break, at noon, until after dark, then drew the boats well up onto the west bank, away from the river. Here there were no bluffs, and the water stood back into the trees on the shore.

Two Shumai hunters had gone ahead, running, three days earlier. They had a giant fire going, with large pieces of wild cow sputtering on it. There was not much singing, though, or celebrating. After they all ate, they crawled under the boat shelters, bone weary with paddling, and settled for sleep.

"Will there be a flood?" Ahroé whispered.

"Perhaps a small one," said Stel. "But the starband said there was not a great depth of snow up north near the Bitter Sea. I think we will not have a big one."

"I didn't think I'd ever say it nine years ago, but it is good to be traveling again."

"With you. Come closer. Are you fully out of the rain?"

"Come on, Stel. Kiss me once, and let us get to sleep. Do you think there is anything to it? This rod?"

"Of course. I wonder what."

"We will see. There will be a long run. Good night." Ahroé settled herself, her graceful wrist thrown across Stel's shoulder. He didn't move until she slept deeply, then he gently put her arm into her sleepsack and drew it around her.

Morning came gray and dripping. The band lifted the boats even farther, just to be safe, and set out in the dawn, chewing more wild beef and trotting slowly, gradually picking up a good morning pace through the bottomland, then up onto the higher land, prairie and grove, away from the river. The whole landscape was sodden, but the high goose flocks going northward in their great, sinuous Vs, sounded wildly cheerful, calling their thrilling sounds down through the spring mists.

The noon pause was a long one, not because the mixed band of Heart River peoples were exhausted, but because they knew they had a long run that afternoon. The wet ground had made some feet sore, though, and many tried to dry their soft running boots a bit by the three fires, kneading them to keep them supple. In all, twenty-one Sentani had joined the twelve Shumai. Stel and Ahroe were the only Pelbar. They had another twenty-two ayas to run that afternoon and evening. The great rod was due to rise the following morning.

Afternoon grew very long for the two Pelbar, who had lost their running hardness, and they lagged back, over-taken near sunset by two small bands of young Shumai coming from elsewhere to see the rod. Ahroe was espe-cially chagrined to see the young men move by so effort-lessly and on down the trail ahead. Stel cared little for such things. Running was not a matter of pride for him, but of getting somewhere. His curiosity alone urged him on, and the pleasure of renewed freedom in the open country.

Well after dusk the two saw the circle of fires ahead. It was a large one. Nearly two hundred Shumai had gath-ered to see the rod. The Pelbar soon discerned that it had become for the Shumai a sort of spring rendezvous before the summer dispersal to follow the herds of wild cattle westward.

A holiday atmosphere prevailed, with music and some group dancing. A large wild bull had been roasted whole over a great pit, and all were invited to carve off meat as they wanted it. The appearance of the Sentani and finally the Pelbar couple gave the gathering the sort of family feeling that the Heart River peoples increasingly enjoyed since the great fight at Northwall over a decade earlier had ended the hostilities among the three cultures.

Stel, who was musical, could already hear that Sen-tani improvisations, which were done in a regular pro-gression, with variations, were influencing the wilder Shumai music. He even heard some Pelbar melodic pat-terns, and soon had joined a group of instrumentalists, contributing flute music to the ensemble of strings.

Behind him, Winnt, the Sentani from Koorb, sat with Ahroe. His son, Igna, lay by them, under his furroll, done in with the long run. Winnt was plainly lonely for Ursa, his Pelbar wife, whom he had married at the end of the time of hostilities, just before the great battle at Northwall. Ahroe's Pelbar manner comforted him. Besides, she was the only Pelbar woman other than Ursa who had traveled far from the three stone Pelbar cities spaced out along the Heart River: Northwall, Pelbarigan, and Threerivers. Ahroe and Stel had been through the western mountains several years earlier, and they carried themselves with the same detached nonchalance that most of the outdoor people did, watchful and quiet, sturdy and able to face crises squarely, peaceful as they were.

"What do you think it is, this rod?" Winnt asked.

Ahroe shook her head. "Who knows? It clearly has something to do with the time of fire, since it is in the middle of an empty place. Perhaps it is some mechanism left by the ancients, working without direction, in response to some sort of inner controls. They were very accomplished before the time of fire."

"But to leave something to keep working for eleven hundred years?"

"Yes. That is hard to imagine."

Tor, the axeman, walked by with a slab of meat on his smallknife. Seeing them, he paused and squatted down. "They say that all this rain has exposed the structure under the rod. It is only last year that we saw there was one. Now the land is sliding away and a great part of the ancient building sticks out from the hillside below the rim of the empty place."

"Stel said there must be some structure," Ahroe commented.

"This is a great one, and not a ruin. Surely it comes from ancient times. It seems of artificial stone, very sturdy, but it will not last long now."

"Why?"

"The end already protrudes. It has long pilings of artificial stone and square stone boxes on the ends. If the erosion continues, it will wash out and tumble down."

"The rod comes from this building?"

"From the top. They say you can see now where it is fastened on. A box protrudes from the far side, too, but we can't see it because it lies out over the empty place."

"With all this rain and erosion," said Winnt, "perhaps

it will wash out all the poison, down to a level where one can safely walk on the empty place."

"Perhaps. But not yet. Already, though, the grass and weeds of last year have moved down the slope. The empty land is shrinking. But the edge growth is wild and twisted, as I have seen before, for many arms." Tor stood and stretched. Starting to go, he turned back to them, his axe on his hip swinging and slapping him. "One other thing. They say you can see now that the end of this structure is higher and rounded, like the ruin near the river at the great bend."

"A dome," Stel mused. "A great dome, then."

"A dome. There is one at Koorb, tumbled and burnt, but not in an empty place, so it can be viewed. It is almost gone now, but it is what the Sentani call a dome—like the one at the great bend."

"It is like a man's skull, a great piece of head bone, so Konta says."

"We will see in the morning."

"It is going to rain again, I think."

"I fear so. I hope we moved the boats high enough. I want to be off to Koorb, eh, Igna?"

The boy said nothing, though he was awake and listening.

"If it does rain, there is an outcrop with an overhang a short way south," said Tor. "Some of the people are already moving their furrolls there."

"Thank you, Tor," said Ahroe. "I am limp as a rabbit-skin, as they say in the west. We appreciate your friendship."

The axeman paused, embarrassed. "Ahroe, I am not friendly for this reason, but I am wondering if I can ask something of you and Stel. It is a big thing. I had not wanted to. It is about Tristal, my nephew. I must wait here for him. He was to arrive with the Zar Reef Band, but they aren't here. I fear it is because of his running, which is not much. He is my brother's son, but my brother and his wife died in the wild fire that burnt so wide a stretch of the tall grass prairie south near the Oh, and Tristal was left alone.

"He is fourteen. I am sure that he will not be able to make the run westward—he should be here by now. Since he isn't, that simply means he isn't able. The wild ones have passed early this year, and we have to move.

It is hard on Tris, too. He is thin—well, scrawny. But he is a good boy. I have often thought he needs more of a settled life until he matures and his chest deepens—if it ever will.

"Is there a chance that there might be something for him to do at Pelbarigan? I know some Shumai have worked for the Pelbar, and there is quite a colony now near Northwall, farming—may they be forgiven for that —and cutting wood."

"I am sure he can do something," Ahroe returned. "He can live with us, too. We are outside the wall now, and Hagen is with us."

"Hagen?"

"He is a Shumai, an old man I traveled west with. He is like my father."

"Like a father? He lives with you now always?"

"Yes. Right now he is looking after Garet, our son. He seems to have no needs himself, but he needs people to take care of. After all, it is not work that your nephew needs. He needs somebody to love him."

Tor snorted. "A Shumai man may like that, but he never needs it."

Ahroe unexpectedly reached out and patted his leg as he stood there, then smiled and laughed outright. "All right, Tor. But I have seen Shumai who like it so much it is hard to tell that they don't need it. Now I think I will go get Stel, if I can tear him away from his music. It is time to sleep. Right? Where is your outcrop? Are you coming, Winnt? Is Igna asleep?" But she didn't pause for an answer, and the two watched her walk away, stiff-legged from the run.

The two men looked at each other. "She is some woman," Winnt said.

"For a Pelbar."

"For anybody. She will be good for Tristal, I am sure. And Stel will be better."

Tor reached down, and they touched right palms. Then the axeman picked up his furroll and walked lightly toward the outcrop.

AFTER some rain in the night, the early dawn brought gray sky, sodden ground, and a wet breeze, but no more rainfall. The whole gathering of people stirred and arose early, without fires or food, walking out and up to the rim of the westward hill that marked the edge of the burn, the empty place from the time of fire.

As the light grew, Stel and Ahroe saw a desolate wasteland, much more gullied than the empty places of the west, with the typical glassy surfaces where the land had been melted into a solid surface, but here cut, carved, rain-tumbled. Not very far down the slope ahead of them, the dim outlines of a building from ancient times, of artificial stone, called concrete by the Commuters, protruded from the hill. It had its back to them. The dome at the end already hung outward over empty space, its pillars reaching only air.

As morning slowly increased, about the time of sunrise, if there was one, a square slid open in the dome, small and far, and a long rod slowly rose, higher and higher, into the air. The top was crooked and looked somehow disrupted, as if some odd piece of metal were fused to it. At last it stopped rising. Then, when it revolved slowly, an awed murmur went through the crowd. It stopped again. Then it revolved in the opposite direction and slowly sunk back down into the dome. The small square shut again, sealing so that its location could not be easily seen from the hilltop.

No one moved or spoke for a long time. The whole appearance of the rod could not have lasted more than four sunwidths on the Pelbar clock. Ahroe looked at Stel. "Someone is in there," he said.

"Or a mechanism."

"Perhaps. But what if someone is in there? We ought to know."

8

"How? Look. It is an empty space."

Stel's eyes narrowed, but he said nothing. "Stel," said Ahroe. "Stel. You mustn't think of going there. Look at what is happening to Stantu, the Shumai at Northwall. Look at the Ozar. It makes a slow death."

Stel put his arm around her. "I wonder," he said. "There may be a way. But not today. We will discuss it at home."

"Yes, Stel, I know that rimes well with dome."

He laughed. "I think I ought to sketch it out, providing what dimensions I can sight from here. Look. Some of the people are going already."

Tor strolled over to them. "What do you think?" he said.

"We aren't sure," said Ahroe. "Stel's first reaction was that there were people in there. But they would have had to be in there from the time of fire, and that is some eleven hundred years. We know that would be impossible."

"Do we?" Stel asked. Then he looked at the expressions on the others' faces. "Yes, we do," he added.

"There's one more thing about Tristal," said Tor.

"Yes?"

"He has a dog. He is inseparable from her."

"A Shumai dog? One of those horses?"

"She is big, all right, but very gentle. Could you stand a dog around?"

Ahroe looked at Stel, catching from his expression that he thought it would be amusing. Being so long behind walls, the Pelbar had few pets, and those were small and generally functional, like the message birds that carried word from one city to another.

"That will keep Hagen busy hunting," Stel said. "Surely we must have the dog. She will be all right."

Tor put his hand on Stel's shoulder, as the Pelbar squatted down, sketching. "You are good people. I will wait here for him, then bring him to Pelbarigan." He looked down to where Stel had begun to draw. "That is very good. You have made it just like the real thing. It juts out so much farther this year. Look how the mud has slid from under it. I fear that another wet year like this one and the whole thing will collapse. There is something new, too. That black stain near the dome. I never saw that before. Look. It oozes out of the earth."

They looked and saw a stain, appearing viscous and shiny, below the dome. Tor shrugged. "Well, I am not going out there to taste it. So now you have seen it. The rising of the rod. It surely is strange. Are you going today?"

"Yes. When Stel finishes."

"Good-bye for now, then. I must run south and see if the Zar Reef band is coming." He gave them the farewell gestures and left, his double-headed axe slapping on his right thigh as he ran.

The room glowed yellow. It was square, lit by a long strip running overhead. Around a long table of worn, painted metal, eight people gathered, thin and slightly hunched, dressed in single garments like body stockings, but looser, mostly dark, charcoal gray. On one wall a large screen marched with arrays of glowing dots. Viewing it, a man, old and dark-skinned, said, "The comps are preparing to raise the wand. We will have time for your report now, Susan, since you insist on it."

He looked over at a small, ancient, slightly fierce-looking woman, who sat more hunched than the others.

"How much of it? It all would take some time."

"Just summarize for us. We all know the history."

"So you think. Humoring me? Very well, then. I'll—"

"Tell me, Susan the Wizened," said a short, heavyset man with brooding eyes, "why did you take the last name of Ward—and so recently. Are you the warden in this prison? The wizened warden of a hidden prison?"

"Quiet, Butto, please," said another woman, young and extremely beautiful. "Let's get on with it."

Susan cleared her throat. Then she laid aside her ancient dulcimer, of real wood, lovingly patched with plastic. Her thin body seemed sturdy, but hung loosely on a skeletal frame. In ancient times she, like Royal, the other old person, would have been called a black. The rest of the principals, who were all gathered in the room, as well as most of the comps, were white.

"It is all rather sad," she began. "You must agree not to interrupt."

"Yes, we agree," Royal sighed.

"Well, then," said Susan. "Suppose we start with a bit of the official history. Here. I'll throw it up on the screen."

She touched a series of squares on the table, and a printed text flashed up on the wall:

After much discussion, the original council arrived at the decision that the proper work-level ratio would be maintained with twenty principals and thirty components. The decision as to which people would become components appeared to be a hard one, since they would be assigned the menial labor of the dome and levels, but a battery of intelligence and adaptability tests was developed, and the top twenty were picked to be the principals. Surprisingly enough, the others agreed fairly cheerfully, knowing as they did that the future of mankind in all probability lay in their hands. They volunteered to be the components and willingly submitted to the necessary drug program to guarantee that their personalities would not vary from the calmness and steady resolve that would be needed to maintain the dome and levels at peak efficiency. This ratio has been carefully and scientifically maintained ever since, and it has produced so smooth an operation that it is proof of the wisdom of the founders, and of their purpose and policies. It is therefore hoped that future generations will also see fit to follow the wisdom of just proportions, and that the geneticists will so plan their operations.

"I'm sure you are all familiar with that text," said Susan, drily. "After Royal suggested that I do my independent investigation of our history, in order to keep me out of his way, I found how wrong it is. The more I have looked into this whole question, the more fascinated I have become."

"Yes, yes. What did you find?"

"I have found enough laminated documents and tapes to indicate that a cell of the chief scientists decided privately to lessen the population to fifty. Naturally, they— the chief scientists—were all included. But they carefully calculated the available resources, biological and chemical, and, knowing the pool of recyclable material, including organics currently involved in being humans, they then quietly decided on the right human mix, for race balance, education, and stability, and set about to murder the rest. Apparently it was not easy. They had a good deal of trouble with some unstable, that is, unwilling, types, especially a group led by someone by the name of Sheela Winehimer, who was a lab technician in the original drug-manufacturing facility. At one point there was a sharp fight. The record said it took place on level three, southwest quadrant. I went there and found the evidence in the walls, even though it had been repaired.

"So we began our history with a mass murder, and—"

"As man has always done, and always will," said Butto, shaking his head.

"You've been reading that poet, Jeffers, again," said another young man, Dexter, with some sarcasm.

"To continue," interrupted Susan, mildly, "with another of our myths. The official history has it that the geneticists brought down the size level of the comps immediately. Actually the comps were the same size as the principals for some centuries, and the decision to miniaturize them had its origins in a secret liaison between one geneticist and a comp. This disrupted the rigid social structure and caused a rebellion. Miniaturization was undertaken to insure that this would never again happen."

"A liaison? But the comps are sterile males. Surely—"

"They weren't always. They were of both sexes, and they cohabited for a long—"

"Nonsense. Look. The signals from the comps are coming in," said Zeller, a brown-haired man with a long face.

An array of lights changed and marched on the screen, forming columns of numbers. All turned to view them.

"There, then. It is the same. Heavy radiation every way the scanner turns. It is hard to believe. If there were only some way to check it."

"We cannot send someone out. None of our protective suits can long sustain anything like that radiation. We cannot sacrifice someone."

"Look, though. As usual the separate air intake shows no radiation, in fact less background than usual."

"It is the weather, the rain. No dust blows up into the air."

Eolyn, the beautiful one, spoke up, in a voice surprisingly deep and full, especially for someone so thin. "Ask for the view-window report, please, Royal. Let us see how the comps read the weather and scene."

Royal touched several buttons. A voice came from the ceiling, and at the same time what he said printed in light on the wall: "The view is the same, but the gullies are all deeper. The marker gully has deepened by ninety-seven centimeters since last measure. That to its north approximately 120 centimeters. The glassy surface is crumbling off. Rain is not falling now, but much rain has fallen. The landscape still shows no sign of life. If the slope of the dome erodes like the view slope, then the dome is eroding out."

With that last sentence, another young woman, Ruthan, drew in her breath sharply. Eolyn frowned at her slightly.

"Our danger grows," said one older man.

"The dome has lasted and will last. It must last. We may be the last men on the planet. The last life. We must outlast the radiation. The rain will help. It will wash away even the deeply radiated soil."

"It never has."

"Time for the other reports," said Royal. "Zeller, give us supply."

Zeller touched another square of buttons. As arrays appeared on the screen he intoned, "Algae, normal. Power, normal. Air reconstitution, normal. Organic recycling, normal, except for the very slight seasonal lowering. We must insulate better so that will not recur. Hydroponics, normal. Seed preservation, normal. Tungsten-recovery project, 40 percent. Freon concentration, satisfactory. Presence of unwanted organics, zero. Oil-supply level . . ."

As Zeller paused, all looked up. They were stunned. Royal raised his hand. "Touch in the numbers again, Zel."

Zeller did, but the result was the same. "Perhaps there is a malfunction in the sensors," Royal remarked.

"We can test it," said Zeller. "I will ask for pressure and flow from the upper chamber to the fabric room. It will be easy to return."

Zeller sent the commands with rapid fingers.

On the screen a row of zeroes showed.

"The lower chamber will tell us," said Zeller, nervously. "The circuit is separate. Perhaps a malfunction."

Again he touched the numbers. Again a row of zeroes registered on the screen.

"The ancients," said Butto, "never intended that tank to last so long. It has given way. We have lost our oil supply."

"Internal repair flows have repeatedly been pumped in, though, even as precaution. Every care has been exercised," said Zeller.

"Internal repair does not preserve structure," returned the prophetic Butto. "All breaks down eventually. Outside supply is needed. We are a seed in an impervious shell, eating ourselves. Now even the shell is beginning to crumble. We must grow or die. Better for us to die if we will so devastate the earth again sometime."

"You are a poet, Butto," said a comfortable-looking old man with a shock of white hair. "Your views are broad, interesting, and nontechnical. Zeller, what are the implications—"

Thornton Cohen-Davies was interrupted, though, by the appearance through the sliding panel of a red-haired girl, thin and slight, with a strange, rapt face. She was waving her arms slowly in the air, moving around the room, making soft barking noises. She circled the table twice, as the council grew more impatient. Then she stopped by Royal, reached over his shoulder, and touched his button panel so rapidly her hands seemed to blur. The screen awoke in a pattern of dots, and as she continued to command the lights, they formed a giant bird, with a long neck and wide body, flying with great wings. The group recoiled in astonishment at so grotesque a creature. Butto suddenly erased the light sketch and muttered, "No one, even an unbalanced child, should be allowed to distort nature so. The birds of the tapes are creatures of perfect beauty—not this terror. Look at the distortion of the mind."

Celeste, the child, again reached over Royal's shoulder, again touched the button panel rapidly. All looked up, and saw her create a sinuous moving V of tiny crosses, and send it across the screen wall. It was followed by another. Celeste's eyes were enraptured as she watched. Butto again moved to erase, but Royal had blocked his signal. Butto rose and strode from the room with a strangled growl.

Royal looked at Celeste and said, "My child, put it in

memory, and play it to your own screen. We have a serious problem we must discuss. Do you understand? Now go. We must continue." He rose and gently urged the awkward girl from the room. Zeller continued to test the oil supply on the screen. The lights said there was none. All sat silent.

"What do you suggest, Zeller?" said Royal.

"Further inspection, using comps."

"Will you lead it?"

"Of course."

"We will finish the council later, at 3300." They all rose to leave except Cohen-Davies. He sat at his place, then called back the bird creature Celeste had put on the screen and sat musing.

The full-voiced woman, Eolyn, stopped at the sliding section and watched him. "What, Thor?" she asked.

He shook his head. "I don't know. I seem to remember something. It is from the destroyed memory programming. What if? . . . Perhaps if I look at this long enough."

"Celeste can't speak, but she surely uses the light array with skill. Perhaps she will be of technical use yet," said Eolyn.

"With more skill than any of the rest of us," the old man replied. Eolyn left him sitting in the yellow light contemplating the great, ungainly bird, flying nobly and slow, across the wall screen, outlined in points of light.

Outside, Susan, returning to her room, stopped to watch Butto's back. He seemed more hunched than ever. "Butto."

He turned. "Not now. You keep adding to my misery, Warden."

"Butto. No more drugs now. You don't need them. You have the strength to face facts."

"Are they facts?"

"Yes, of course. I will show you the data."

"No. Never mind. Was that all?"

"No. That was just a little. But one thing I learned was how dangerous it has been in our past to use too many drugs to control our behavior. You mustn't."

"We always have."

"No. Not always. There have always been periods of drugs and periods of character. One of our finest periods, a brief, golden age, came under the leadership of a man who called himself, of all things, Benjamin Jefferson.

When he was Chief Principal, we for once composed music that rivaled that of the ancients. We still recite some of the poems of the time, and our only three dome novels come from a four-year period immediately before that era ended. In fact, one novel of which you surely have heard, *Curious Rats and Bumptious Foxes,* was really spoken by a comp, though he conspired with Jefferson to have it read out by the Chief Principal to give it stature."

"A comp? That? A good book. I have listened to it at least three times. What happened?"

"Well, this is a pretty dull place, you know. The drugs dull us to it. Without them there was some raving boredom, and that resulted in a rebellion of comps. More killing resulted, and a renewal of drugging."

"Well, doesn't that show that drugs are necessary? Man's destructive tendencies have to be curbed."

"Oh, Butto. A case might be made for the notion that the great increase of drug-taking by the ancients, in their last days before the holocaust, might have had something to do with the dreadful urban environments they created for themselves. The drugs served in part to shut out of consciousness the world that they had created. They continued the tradition here. After all, they manufactured some of the drugs. In ancient times, some people even took drugs to wake up or go to sleep."

"What's wrong with that? Isn't it evidence of man's superior control over his own awful tendencies? We can't depend on our moods or the accidental conditions of our miserable bodies."

Susan looked at him. "Butto," she began, but he turned away. She watched him slouch down the hall, then turned to her own far chamber and habitual reclusiveness.

Butto reached the stair landing and looked back, a deepening frown on his face. He descended to level two and the drug lab, deftly mixing several chemicals on a spoon, while watching the door. Then he suddenly licked the crystals off the spoon, plunged it in the ultrasonic cleaner, racked it, and left. As he continued on down the stairs, he touched out a private code to several comps on his belt communicator.

Reaching level seven, he picked his way through the storage piles toward a far corner, which he had whimsically called the Room of the Dark Nine, a place unfrequented, supposedly, by any but Butto and his eight favorite comps. He was alone. Quickly shucking off his body suit, he sat naked in the lotus pose, tugging his heavy legs into place. His finger reached out and touched the walls into light and life, playing for the ten thousandth time the tape of jungle life before the time of the holocaust. As the drugs took hold, he watched the shadows and movements grow angular. His face drifted into rapture as the purple leaves of understory plants waved. Great insects flew with burring sounds. Small birds, aqua and jade, flitted from leaf to leaf, and the filtering light from above, barely sifting down through the great, hairy, blue-leaved trees, flicked and shaped on the forest floor.

Butto knew it was time for the snake, the great jewel-backed one with the quadruple tongue, gliding, with its thousand tiny legs, across the ground. Butto loved to watch it slide its bulk across a decaying pink log, resting for a moment on the crumbling curve, as if on another, greater snake, its scales scattering fire in honey droplets, eaten by the scrambling fuschia beetles. Then the snake glided on, at last, the line of its body diminishing, the arrow of its tail tip twinned, each point barbed with light. Yes, the earth before the nuclear war had been beautiful.

"We do not deserve," Butto said aloud, "another chance outside. We would do it again. We are loathsome, never lovely like that snake. Even the leaves in hydroponics are green—ugly and mutated." Once again, Butto intoned the poem of Parker Steinberg, of the fifth generation of the dome and levels, a doleful recounting of man's evils and the longing for natural peace above ground. As he chanted the hexameter couplets, surrounded by the images of the moving purple leaves, Comp 9 and Comp 11 joined him. They too were naked, and they took up the chant mesmerically with him, repeating the verses over and over. The two comps were only about 130 centimeters tall, and slightly built. Their faces seemed glazed over. Their hands were scarred, and their bland eyes hung in their cheeks like unripe plums, unmoving and docile.

Zeller ran every check he could think of, and each showed the oil had drained from the tank. Though not as great a catastrophe as the recent fall of a floor, killing sixteen of the fifty making up the population of the dome and levels, this too was a major disaster. The oil had been used sparingly, to synthesize food when necessary, to provide fabrics, to mold the plastics that formed almost everything in the contained culture.

Meanwhile, Thornton Cohen-Davies let the image of the bird play on the great screen of the decision room. He was troubled and puzzled. His function had long been that of Humanist Memory. He had been one of three whose task it was to go over and over the life of the ancients, as it had existed before the nuclear disaster, remembering and preserving, sorting and reminding. The other two, working at the time in genetics, had died under the sudden collapse of level five, far end. What was it about this bird? Surely it was unreal, nothing like those on the tapes he had seen. But it reminded him of something. What odd feet—like those of the fabled alligators that had haunted the bayous of the south before they had been boiled like jellies in the consuming fire.

Was he getting senile? Had his long-trained memory failed him? This was what he was for—knowing all about that bird, if it were a bird. A thought crossed his mind. Celeste, who had not spoken since a shock she had had in the genetics lab as a small child, was strange. She communicated largely through the machines, and with them she was superb. Her mathematical and conceptual abilities belied her ungainly walk and long, knobby legs. Her math was graceful and mature.

Cohen-Davies touched a code, and a voice said, "Comp 14."

"Are you still in decontam? This is Cohen-Davies. I have some instructions for you."

"Yes, Principal Davies. I am nearly done. Comp 19 and 3 have gone. I am alone."

"Put your communication in 25-7 mode then, please."

"Yes, Principal."

"Now then, Bill, listen. Did it really look the way you said out there?"

"Yes, Thor. All desolate and forbidding. Is that what you wanted?"

"No. Celeste has light-drawn a bird. Let me project it to your viewscreen." He pushed a button.

"Ugly thing. She certainly has a wild imagination. I

guess it helps keep her sane down here—without interference, that is."

"Yes, Bill. Think. The thing haunts me. I think I should know about it. Has it ever had a reality?"

"How would I know? I've never seen anything like it, of course."

"Could it be possible that Celeste has gotten outside the levels. Could she have seen anything outside, perhaps?"

"Very unlikely, Thor. The alarm system would have sounded."

"Perhaps, with her vast knowledge of the whole network, she found a way to silence it. What do you think?"

"I doubt it. But if she had entered the dome, a very faint radiation would still cling to her. The best thing would be to pass a counter near her—soon, before the radioactivity could be dissipated. If she had, too, there is the additional danger of unwanted organics."

"Yes. I don't want her in trouble. Could you, discreetly, make such a test? I will bring her by you in level two, far wing, at 3250. Is that acceptable?"

"Yes, Thor. Will do. Can you be free for a game later?"

"Perhaps. But let us settle this first. Now off. Someone comes."

Eolyn's approach slid the partition aside and she reentered. Celeste's bird still played on the wall. "Shut it off, Thor. It has upset Butto again, I know, and he has disappeared. I fear he is getting dangerous and will need mind-washing."

"That is pretty hard to do to him now. It's drug residues, I think. And he is the only one we have left with any knowledge of genetics since the floor collapsed."

"But I am worried. He seems to have a following. We are so few now. If he really convinces a body of us that all mankind ought to be eradicated, they may try it. We need to nullify that in advance."

"Perhaps you are right. Well, I must go. I want to communicate with Celeste."

"Would that such were possible."

"I would like to get her hand-pollinating again. It seems to soothe her. She even hums a little to the flowers."

"Poor Celeste. Damn her."

Cohen-Davies left, passing down the dim, yellow-lit

corridor. Later, as he and Celeste moved through level two, they passed the small, inconspicuous Comp 14, Cohen-Davies' secret friend, whom he had lifted from his partial chemical lobotomy, lessening it slowly through counterdrugs, a private endeavor. They had been friends now for some years, playing electronic bridge through their own encodings, making remarks to each other, even finding a way to laugh electronically, sending the secret impulses from the spacious, file-filled quarters of Cohen-Davies on level one down to level five to the sterile cell of Comp 14, or Bill, as Cohen-Davies called him.

As Celeste and Cohen-Davies continued walking, a thin electronic whine told him that Celeste indeed had been out into the dome, how he could not imagine, because only the comps went there, due to the constraints demanded by radiation protection and freedom from microorganisms. The levels had long been pure.

Cohen-Davies abruptly turned the girl and marched her to the deserted gen-lab. She was frightened and sought an array of electronic buttons. Cohen-Davies made sure they stayed out of her reach. He sat her down on a lab table and said to her, not unkindly, "Now listen, Celeste. I know you have been in the dome." She winced. "I will not tell. But you are radiation-contaminated—though only slightly. There will be organic contamination, too. We must decontaminate you quietly, so no one finds out. All right? Do you understand?"

She took his hand. He touched his belt communicator, and Comp 14 appeared and led her down the corridor. Soon he showed her how to make it seem, as was appropriate, that she was leading him.

Cohen-Davies sat musing. Perhaps she had reached the window. Perhaps there were such things as those birds. If that were so, then all the earth outside would not have been destroyed. Surely the birds would have to fly from somewhere to somewhere. Her second electronic picture indicated a flock of them. My God, what would that mean? But what of the radiation? Surely the rod had read that faithfully. They had run many tests on the equipment—at least all they could without risking exposure. If they had only had a real nuclear scientist with them at the time of the blast so many centuries ago. To be cut off without one, to have built knowledge here, in this prison, with the skills of drug technicians, engineers, and chemists. Well, they were fortunate enough to have survived at all. So much depended on them.

Then Cohen-Davies had another thought. If the birds survived, perhaps men did, too. Perhaps it had all been a waste. He began to laugh. He couldn't stand that thought. But they had never picked up a single radio wave. The organic scanner of centuries ago had never found animal heat, even on its most sensitive settings.

Cohen-Davies put in the code for Eolyn. Her face appeared on a private screen. "I would like to confer with you," Cohen-Davies began. "But I must ask your attitudes. Would you be averse to my telling you a thing about Celeste that—" Eolyn's face contorted with impatience. "—that might amuse you?" Cohen-Davies said. "No. I see not."

"Thor, this is no time for amusements. We have just lost our whole oil supply. And that insufferable girl. She should be converted to a comp. No. I am serious. She is damaged. We have so few people, and now no real geneticists. What will we do? What is it? You are not telling me something."

Cohen-Davies shrugged. "Signing off," he said. Then he sat, tapping his fingers for a time. Turning, he touched Bill's code again.

A voice said, "Comp 14."

"Bill, how good a view is there out the window in the dome?"

"Not very good. Except for the optics. The scanner."

"Ah. I know nothing of it."

"It lets you enlarge portions of the view. You can even freeze them on the screen for study, or store them. But we never do. There is nothing to see. Dirt and sky. Sometimes moving clouds."

"Can you enlarge a small thing?"

"Oh, yes. If you want to look at gullies."

"Thank you, Bill. Signing off," said Cohen-Davies. He sat for a time, tapping his fingers again. Was it possible that Celeste could even work the scanner? No, that seemed hardly credible. He rose, sighing, and then stood, absently, thinking.

Meanwhile, on level three, near side, Ruthan directed the pollination of the new tomato crop, three rows, set in organic slurry, propped with hydrocarbon rods, with spring clamps. Each blossom was touched with a pollinating rod by hand, delicately, between dips in the starting solution. The deft comps could do many blossoms so carefully and well that each bore a perfectly round fruit under the shimmering bluish light strips. The paste from these tomatoes was cubed in with the protein from beans and rodents, then flaked for use with soy. The soy was a luxury, taking so long to mature, but it also grew easily. With slight individual care, for which labor was simple, soy produced bountifully. Genetic selection had bred beans double the size of the ancient ones.

Ruthan loved to chew them dried and raw, tough and resistant as they were, but she took care to let no one know. The custom and prejudice of the dome and levels called for eating processed food almost exclusively—so processed that its individual components were completely shrouded. Ruthan had heard rumors of the reasons behind this policy, but they were so macabre that she shivered whenever she thought of them.

The beans on the south side lengthened up the wall and started on the ceiling strings, reaching for the light. It was time to prune them back, taking each clipping carefully and tossing it into the funnel that fed the salad-cube processor. Soon she and the comps would train the vines downward again, slipping new light strips into the arbors so they were fed light from both sides of the vines. She thought of Dexter. It was pleasurable but also disconcerting. She would have to depress her feelings with drugs soon, ridding herself of tendencies toward ancient and useless strains of behavior. But still, what else did the dome and levels offer? She would think drug therapy over.

Dexter, meanwhile, in his quadrant on level five, was in charge of the rodentry, the only source of animal protein. He needed no comps since the whole operation slid smoothly along automatically, though occasionally he borrowed from the comp pool for general cleanup, or for company as much as anything.

At this moment he was not thinking of Ruthan. He stood on his hands, almost perfectly motionless, the knotted muscles of his arms tense but controlled, not yet trembling. Perched high, on each of his feet, a white rat hunched. Dexter was trying to convince another to climb

to them. They had rehearsed it endlessly, but so far only
the two had learned.

Dexter sighed, looking directly into the rat's wobbling
nose. "Come, Betsy," he said. "Come on now. Like last
time. That's right. Hands on my arm. That's right. Good.
There is a food cube up there. You'd better get it before
Minerva eats it. Come on, now."

Betsy's paws trembled. Her nose touched his arm, but
she withdrew her pink paws to her chest and sat, slightly
humped, looking at Dexter's arm, which had begun to
shake slightly.

"Come on, you little slime," Dexter said, in soothing
tones. "Put those hands back up there before I grind
them off and make a bracelet out of sections of your
bones. I will string a length of your useless rat gut around
old Cohen-Davies' neck for a bauble."

Reassured by Dexter's gentle voice, Betsy put her
paws back, then ran up his arm and sat on his head, her
naked tail dangling down in front of his nose.

"Up now. Good Betsy. Up my back. That's it, you
ground grubber."

She began to stretch up, but Juno suddenly raced down
his right leg and confronted Betsy with a squeal, teeth
grinding. Dexter collapsed in a heap of laughter, dumping Minerva. Betsy scurried to the gate of her cage.
Where was Juno? Dexter realized that he lay on top of
her, and when he got up, he saw she was dead.

He stroked her, then picked her up and strode over to
the vats. With two slices, several deft strokes, a twist, a
cupping hand, and some jerks, he had gutted her, thrown
the guts into the organic recycle, stripped off her skin,
put it through the hair recovery feed, then took the
hairless skin, peeled and trimmed the central square, recycled the rest, and dropped the meat and bone into the
pickling tank in preparation for protein processing. The
square of skin he placed against the roller and, touching
the button, fed it into the curing mechanism.

Then he dipped his hands and held them up to the
ultrasonic air flow. Turning, he saw nine ranks of cages,
all occupied by white rats, large as cats, staring at him
accusingly and silently. He bowed.

"I'm sorry, my friends. Juno had no business running
beneath me. I regret her demise as much as you—yes,
surely more, since you have expended no energies trying

to train her. Now then, Minerva, Betsy, into your cells."

He directed a small sonic herder at them, touched the activator, and steered them back into their own enclosures. Their weight tripped the doors—open, then closed. All was well again. Dexter, jumping, caught the trapeze he had mounted from the ceiling. "Now," he said, "for my next act, I shall imitate the great man-apes of the ancients. Here, my lovelies. Watch this swing." The rows of pinkish, quizzical eyes followed him, having forgotten Juno.

Dexter swung, again and again, expertly, finally reaching to touch his toes to the low ceiling, which was, like the rats, yellow in the bands of sodium strip light. He swung back again, then up, flipped, and landed on his feet. He turned and bowed again. From the upper tier, nine rats, all in a row, each with a blue mark on its cage door, clapped front paws repeatedly but listlessly.

Dexter shook his head. "Such an audience. Well, ladies and gentlemen, I leave you to your own contemplations. I must depart. Cohen-Davies is training me in the ways of the ancients. When he ages to oblivion, I must be stuffed full of their trivia. After all, today the Dow Jones averages are up several points." He laughed and left the room doing cartwheels, the sliding panel barely opening before he passed through. The lights dimmed automatically, and a new food block descended. Soon the rows of rats munched quietly, with rapid teeth, to the accompaniment of ancient music, an electronic Unfinished Symphony.

Deep in level six, in a dim corner of the genetic-breeding cubicle, known as the Brat Shack, rows of glassy tubs sat covered, with slight bubbles seething through them. The atmosphere lay warm and humid. A pulse bumped gently and steadily, coming from a device with no other purpose than to produce it, slow and reassuring. In the tubs fetuses swam, growing slowly, tube-connected, some tiny and fishlike, others larger. These were now the charges of Butto, since the true geneticists had died in the collapse of the floor.

The panel slid. Celeste entered, as if stealing up on them. In the dim light she peered at each vat. Were they to be human? Surely that one was not. Look. Instead of tiny hands, curved claws lengthened. She drew in her breath. In her silence and isolation she still came back to this place of shock and horror. Celeste squinted with aversion into another vat. The slowly turning flesh dollop swam in a solution of the wrong color. It seemed to turn stiffly, to gather bubbles. No. Surely it was dead. So Butto knew nothing at all of this work. What would they do? She could not explain. Every time she tried to open her mouth to speak of it, her voice rebelled—ever since she had been down here and seen them making a comp. It wasn't as it should have been. It wasn't genetic transformation. Drugs, a slight struggle, violent malformation, and stunting of the body surgically—all whirled before her eyes. They didn't know—not only Butto. None of them. The old skills had lapsed. She had checked the tapes in the privacy of her own chamber once she had trained herself in the codes. If they knew, what would they—a sound. Celeste shrank down under a tub frame.

Butto entered, sweating and naked, a strange gleam on his dark face. Three comps followed, naked too. Butto looked at the tubs, one by one, forty in all. "Comp 11," he said.

"Yes, Principal Butto," the comp muttered.

"Tub fourteen has gone bad. Recycle it. Wash it, first. Filter the fluid. We will irradiate it for reuse."

"Gone bad, Principal?"

"Do not ask. It was the geneticists. It is not my fault. They themselves had lost the skill, had forgotten the meaning of the tapes. It is all hit or miss now. Well, it does not matter. Better that we all die than that we so destroy the world again."

"Yes, Principal. May we see the stars the next time?"

Butto whirled on him. "Never refer to that anywhere else. Never."

"Yes, Principal. I am sorry, Principal."

"We may see the stars, but only through the leaves. At 8900."

"Yes, Principal."

"You are free for 1250 after you flush fourteen." Butto spun on his heels and left rapidly, his buttocks jouncing slightly.

The two comps, both small and spindly, wheeled the tub to the drain, pumped off the fluid, then whirled the tub-stand section over to the disposal and dumped the mass of flesh out of it. Celeste heard a slap and plop as it slopped into the wide tube leading to organic recycle.

"He was good this time," said Comp 9.

"Yes. Better than pleasure. I want to see the stars, though."

"It does not matter."

"No. Nothing matters. Butto is right. And he will see to that."

"What? I don't understand."

"Nor do I. I am only a comp, as you are. Let's go to the dinner chamber. Comp 15 will be there. He will tell us about the dome."

Celeste remained crouched for some time after they left. The slight bubbling sound continued, as did the pulse. She squeezed her eyes shut. Her tongue seemed to swell up and cry out by itself, but she made no sound. She would get out into the dome again. What did it matter now? Since the floor accident, everything had gone wrong—more wrong than before. If she only had a father. The ancients had fathers and mothers. She had tried to make Cohen-Davies one, but he had not understood. And if even he had not understood, then who could? She would return to the dome, then, and the door she had found—or a better one. The sky had been so gray and the air so chill. But the lines of birds really flew there. If she went soon, it would be the dark cycle. She would take her ultrasonic pointer and an exercise robe. She would take extra shoes too, one pair inside the other. And now that Cohen-Davies had had her decontaminated, she knew how to do that herself, too. No one would know.

TOR had not run south. He waited near the dome, being troubled and feeling a need for thought. Two days after the others had gone, he lay at ease by the fire. The running band had been angry with him, though they were

silent and subdued, knowing his need as an uncle to care
for his orphaned nephew. But Tor was an axeman, and
one of the best. They felt his staying behind was a be-
trayal, somehow, despite the circumstances. Yet they always had been a loose and voluntary organization, and
he knew where his primary duty lay, in spite of his own
desires. The band would be passing the great south curve
of the Isso by now, Blu leading them. Tor tried to take
life as it came, though he was uncertain of his next
moves. He knew he couldn't bear to stay at Pelbarigan
with Tristal. He would go on alone, perhaps finding his
band. He loved the open, the shock of hunting, even the
endurance of hunger, so long as it didn't get too bad.

But everything was in flux. All but the old Shumai had
given up spears now—since the fight at Northwall over
a decade ago. Now they all carried bows—mostly
modeled after the Pelbar longbow. Perhaps he would
have to learn that, too. It was clear that he would be no
match for one, even though it seemed somehow unmanly
to stand way off and kill with something like that.

Still he had another reason for not going—a nameless
sense of something he could not pin down. It seemed to
hang about this place like a vapor. Tor was always
thrown off balance by his own peculiar way of simply
knowing things, or sensing them, and waiting for them to
grow in his mind into some semblance of clarity. He
would fall into silences even with his men. Ideas would
emerge from him without forethought. He suspected his
men had left with Blu as willingly as they had because
they saw that mood on him. More than once it had saved
them, when he made some quick discernment—as it did
with the best axemen—and they knew they had to
value Tor even though his mysteries frustrated them.

Late in the afternoon, Tor heard a far, faint quavering yell. He stood and returned it, filling the near woods
with his half-human wail. They were finally coming,
then. He would have meat for them anyway, seven
chucks, all axe-killed. It was far from a useless weapon
if you could throw it well.

Soon a row of figures appeared, trotting very slowly. It
was Legon, with his wife and three others from the family—two young men and an older woman—and last of
all Tristal. The boy looked faint. Beneath his weakness,

though, Tor could see a quiet Shumai determination. Perhaps all was not bad with him.

Tristal sank unashamedly down by the fire without spreading his furroll as Tor greeted them all. "Don't mind Tris," Legon said. "He has been sick. Still is. A fever. Chuck, huh? Well, I could use some of that. Frey, can you serve us some? Ama, would you serve Tristal?"

"I will take care of him," said Tor. He sat by the boy. Yes, there still was fever. Tor gave him a tarred wicker cup of warm broth, with fat pieces of meat and wild onions. Tristal had trouble swallowing it, but seemed eager for it anyway. He clung to Tor's leg, and the axeman could see he didn't even know he was doing it. Cutting off chunks of chuck, Tor fed the boy, piece by piece, as the others settled down for the evening. Then he put the boy into his furroll and fed the fire, smoothing out his own roll next to Tristal's. Ama was disappointed.

As the fire died down, Tristal stirred restlessly. "Where is Raran?" Tor said.

"She will come. She was off hunting when we left. She will find us all right." Before long, as Tristal said, the great dog glided into the firelight and sat by the boy, who reached out his hand to her. Raran then touched her nose to Tor, then to Legon and Frey, and finally returned to Tristal and thumped down with a sigh on the other side from Tor. Soon Tristal faded into sleep. Tor lay awake a long time thinking. Three times high flocks of geese went over in the night, their barking honks coming down from the darkness.

"Tor," said Legon.

"Yes."

"He is a good boy, Tor. You will be proud of him. He learns things. I have never seen anything like it. You tell him once and he not only knows, but he thinks out beyond you. He is quiet, but you will see. He will be there when you need him."

"Good. I am glad. Thank you, Leg."

"Let him rest here awhile. He has been very sick. He will be all right. We will go in the morning."

"Yes. All right. I am in no hurry. I am going to take him to Pelbarigan."

"There?"

"Yes. For the summer. A Pelbar couple has agreed.

They were here to see the rod. An old Shumai named Hagen lives with them. Old friends."

"Stel and Ahroe."

"You know them?"

"Only their story. They have been west beyond the great mountains, far beyond Shumai country."

"They?"

"Yes. They are Pelbar, but there is some steel in both of them. I am glad for Tristal. That will be good."

No more was said, and soon Legon was asleep. There it was again, in Tor's thought. Something impending. Well, he would be ready for it, whatever it was.

In the morning, Legon and his party left, running north around the empty place, eager to head west. Tor and his nephew waved, with Raran undecided as to what to do. Soon she returned to Tristal and sat down by him, curling her rump against his leg.

Resting, Tristal recovered rapidly. Tor built a brush screen under the outcrop to help hold the warmth, and watched the boy with a yawning nonchalance. He wanted no anxiety to show. He knew Tristal felt bad about keeping his uncle from the run westward. The first night cleared, and the two played a leisurely star-naming game, but it was hard to play with only two. Soon, Tor asked the boy to name the stars he knew. They climbed to the ridge above the outcrop, and Tristal pointed and named half the heaven.

"Enough," said Tor. "I think you know them all."

"Not the dim ones."

The next night, Tristal was restless. He asked his uncle if it would be all right if he took a walk. Tor shrugged, glad to see him recovering.

In her chamber, Celeste keyed the code for structure, then followed the sequence until she was calling up on the screen details of the dome that were not open information. What was that, then? Another door? It ought to open into earth—but perhaps not now, with all the erosion. Tracing the path to it on the screen, she calculated then nullified the alarms, all for only a few time units, determined by the moments she planned to pass each point. Then she took one look around her chamber and left.

When she arrived at the door, she seared the seal

away with her ultrasonic pointer. The door swung outward. Unlike the last one, this portal was low in the dome, quite near the dimly seen earth outside. She would not need a rope. Looking down, Celeste squeezed through the door, holding it so it would swing shut. Then she dropped to the ground, hitting with a faint thud. It was mud. She had felt nothing like that before—a cold grime. She was the first, then, of all the people to leave the dome and levels after the ancient blast. A surge of pride fought against her fear.

Ahead of her a hill stretched up, and she labored, slipping and struggling, to climb it. She soon grew filthy and regretful. No, she would not return, not with Butto presiding over his monsters. Somehow she would manage to live—at least for a while—out here, where there were no sounds of the discarded sacks of flesh. Nor was there Dexter, fumbling and ironic, coldly personal. She could always go back later.

As she neared the hill crown, her hand grasped something. She stared. A plant. She scrabbled up farther. Soon she came over the lip of the hill and into many plants, dimly visible, wet for some reason. She swished her hands through them, washing herself. So this is what it was like to be out on the earth. What was ahead? It looked like a forest on the audi-visi tapes. All this, then, lay outside? Celeste laughed bitterly. A whole world grew out here, just out of their vision, out of the range of their sensing equipment. What of the radiation? What if it killed her? What would she do, anyhow? If so many plants lived, if the strange birds flew, could she not make a place for herself? She stumbled ahead, feeling her way, falling occasionally over rocks, once skinning her knee. High overhead, she heard the birds calling down. So they were there. She was in the world of real birds.

After a while she realized she was lost. She had no idea which way the dome lay. She knelt down. What would she do? Well, the sun would come, and she would find her way. What was that? A sound ahead. She set her ultrasonic pointer low and unleashed a brief pulse. She heard a strange cry, shrill and pained, then a voice.

"What is it, Raran? Are you all right? Here, lie down. Let me look at you." Celeste heard a slight whining, then a growl. Perhaps an animal growl, she thought. An animal? But the voice was a human voice, one she could understand though the speech was thick and different. The growling continued. Celeste felt a wave of fear. She turned to run, started to thrash through the bushes. Suddenly she heard a rush, and something hit her hard in the back. She went down sprawling. Turning over, she saw, dimly, a snarling animal face, and felt its warm breath. She shrieked and covered her face as she heard running footsteps.

"Raran, Raran! What is it? Here. A person. Raran, get back, go on now. Now!" The dog reluctantly pulled back, but sat alertly looking.

"Who are you?" Tristal asked, drawing his knife.

Celeste opened her hands and saw him dimly over her, then shrieked again and covered her face. Tristal sheathed his knife and knelt down by her. "What is the matter? Come now. No one is going to hurt you. Sit up here and let me look at you. Are you all right?" He lifted Celeste up against him and patted her back, then, feeling her strange cloth mantle, added, "Are you Pelbar?"

Celeste opened her mouth, trying, trying again to speak. Nothing came.

"Don't be afraid. Raran won't hurt you. Come here, Raran. Shake hands." Tristal patted the dog's leg. "Shake. Come on, now, shake." Raran lifted a paw and gestured repeatedly forward with it, and Tristal took Celeste's hand away from her face and placed it around the dog's paw. She shuddered.

"You are all bones. Please come now. You can't be left alone. Come back to the fire and meet my uncle. Come." He hauled her upright. She slumped against him, feeling helpless, crying to herself soundlessly.

"What is your name?" Tristal asked, kneeling again. "You will have to walk yourself. I have been sick and am not strong enough to carry you. Besides, you are nearly as tall as I am. Can't you walk?"

Celeste stood again. She opened her mouth, but nothing would come out. Nothing. She tried and strained. Nothing. She leaned on the strange boy with the thin, hard arms. He supported her until she recovered her composure, then he took her hand, and the three figures moved ahead through the darkness. She wondered how he saw, how he made his way. She lurched against a tree as they walked and stumbled down the hill. She stopped and felt the bark, then freed her hand from Tristal's and felt it all around.

"What is the matter?" he asked. "You can see, can't you?"

Celeste took his hand again. Yes, it was clear to him she could see. They moved forward again, through branches that slapped at her face. The great dog brushed and bumped against her side as she walked, and she could hear its puffing breath. Good God, why had she come out here? Was this what people had outside? How could they stand it—the danger, the wet, the cold, in company with beasts?

Far off she could see a flickering light. Tristal paused. "Now," he said, "Night Girl—I shall call you Night Girl since you won't talk—I'm going to yell for my uncle. I will be loud, but don't be frightened." Celeste only partly understood. Tristal cupped his hands and sent out a long, quavering Shumai yell, rising and holding, followed by a short one. Celeste felt her hair rise in terror. She clung to Tristal.

From the distance a similar yell was returned, almost an echo, but deeper. Again, Celeste felt a chill of fear. But Tristal merely remarked, "He will meet us. Come on again." Another yell came, nearer, and Tristal answered. Soon footsteps swished in the brush, and a great body surged dimly through the dark. A broad-shouldered man towered over her.

"What on earth?"

"I found her in the brush. She will not or can not talk. She is all mud and wet. She has strange clothes on. What'll we do?"

"Hello," said Tor, stooping close to her and speaking very slowly. "Do you understand? Raise your hand if you understand." Celeste raised her hand slowly. She could make it out, though his talk seemed thick and twangy.

"Come with us, then. I am Tor. This is Tristal, my nephew. What's your name?"

Celeste tried to open her mouth, then opened it wide, but nothing would come out. Tor stooped very close, looking into her face. She saw his blond beard and drew back, then reached out and touched it gently. Tor laughed.

"I'm going to carry you to the fire," he said, again very

slowly, and swept her up and walked off toward the distant light, Tristal following. Soon the dog trotted ahead of him, and Tor had to chide her to keep out from under his feet. Celeste put her head against his shoulder. He was wearing a sort of hairy covering. She buried her nose in it. It smelled sour. Or was that the man? She could not remember that anyone had ever picked her up this way before, though as a child she had been soothed often enough by the rocking machine. It was a pleasant sensation, though his nearness was frightening. Soon she clung to Tor, finding she enjoyed his bulk and solidity.

As Tor carried Celeste into the circle of firelight, she became aware of a new sensation—the acrid smell of woodsmoke, which she had first whiffed on Tristal. The axeman set her down gently in a pile of leaves near the outcrop, where the reflected heat of the steaming and blazing logs formed an island of domesticity in the great, cold night.

Celeste looked at the fire, astonished. What was it? The flames, like the light from the pool of water in the dome and levels, flicked up and down, rose, throwing heat, consuming the round cylinders into blackness, then crumbling away. Tor tossed a few more small logs on, sending a rush of sparks upward, swimming the air like motes in the eyes, then disappearing. Celeste blocked her face, then looked again, feeling added heat.

"Strange," said Tristal.

"What?"

"It seems as if she has never seen a fire before. It is a fire, Night Girl, a fire. Move your head like this if you know about it." Tristal nodded.

Celeste looked at him, not moving her head, but with an expression of slight contempt.

"She thinks you are patronizing her, Tris," said Tor. "Of course she has seen a fire. What strange clothes. What is she doing in Shumai country? Maybe she is a Pelbar from Threerivers. I've never been there, except to go by."

"No. They dress like the others. She is entirely new. Perhaps she came from some real distance, like the mouth of the Heart, and separated from her people. Perhaps it is warm there, and that is why she has no proper coat." Tristal felt her ankles, above her doubled dome slippers. "She is cold and wet, as well as muddy. We have to wash her and give her clothing."

Celeste drew back, frowning.

"Don't offend her, Tris. Look, Night Girl, nod your head if you understand. Do you?" Tor towered over her, bearded and furred, his long-handled axe on his hip. She looked up with wide eyes, then nodded, slowly.

"All right. See that skin of water near the fire? It will be warm. We will sit with our backs to you. I want you to take off your clothes, wash yourself from it by unfixing the stopper, then get into that furroll. Then make some sound—here, knock with that stick—and we will wash and dry your clothes. Then we will go away again, and you can put them on. Do you understand?"

Celeste nodded again, slowly. She desperately didn't want to do what he suggested, but he clearly wished it. He was by far the biggest person she had ever seen. Even Dexter seemed small and thin by comparison. She had dropped her pointer somewhere and had no way of disagreeing. Tor and Tristal walked over to the edge of the outcrop and sat down, backs to her. Celeste saw rocks and sticks she could use for weapons, but shivering with cold and fright, she did as Tor said and stripped off her dome clothes. Her white, thin body gleamed in the firelight as she watched the two conversing quietly, backs to her. She saw Tristal hold up the knife blade he was whittling with, and saw Tor move it aside so the boy could catch no reflection of her in it. She washed in the warm water, amazed that they simply let it fall on the ground and soak in, then realizing that, of course, an endless supply of water fell as rain and flowed in the streams outside the dome and levels.

No one had purified this water. What of the radiation? Well, it seemed not to harm them. Running to Tor's furroll, Celeste put her long, thin feet down into it, then wormed down herself until only her head protruded. It was soft and smelled unclean. Then she reached out and knocked on the rock with a stick. Tor strode over and looked down at her, hands on his hips, and laughed.

"You look like a mouse in his little hole, all right," he said. Then he quickly knelt down, took her head, and kissed her on the forehead. She felt his rough beard brush into her face, then leave. Her heart surged with the shock of his sudden face. A kiss. No one kissed in the levels, but she had seen it on the tapes. Cohen-Davies had given her a disquisition on kissing once, and offered, laughingly, to show her how the ancients did it, but when she expressed willingness, he explained that it was an antisocial habit not suitable to their survival in the dome and levels. The geneticists were against it, as it led to the emotional interrelationships that complicated their attempts to purify and preserve the human strain for the future.

But Tor had stood up immediately and watched Tristal go down to the stream below to rinse the mud from her bodysuit and exercise robe. The boy had dropped a fabric shoe, and Tor took it after him, leaving Celeste alone by the fire.

What a marvel—right outside her lifelong home. She could hear the fire rumbling and snapping, and the wind in the bare branches above made a hollow sound she had never heard. A few plants had started to sprout from the cold earth, and below the fire she saw a small, white flower with many petals and dark, broad, scalloped leaves. She wanted to go to it, but she was naked in the furroll. She never remembered seeing anything so simply beautiful. Below it she saw more blooms, but they were very dim in the night. As Celeste thought of the implications of where she was, and what it was like, her emotions of wonder and terror nearly overcame her. She cried into the edge of the fur, trembling and hunched, looking up to see the man and boy near her. Her clothes were draped over a branch propped near the fire. A misty rain had started and beaded Tor's hair and beard, gathering the fur coat on his shoulders into points at the hair tips.

Tristal knelt by her. "Don't worry," he said. "We will do everything we can to help you. We will take you home. Are you hungry? Let me give you some chuck soup. It has onions and five boiled May apple bulbs in it. You might like it." He brought a pitched cup of steaming soup close to her and set it down so she could reach it from the furroll. Then he wandered off with his back to her.

Tor called him from the far side of the firelight, putting his arm around him. "Good. Leave her alone. Let her get used to us. We will take her to her people, whoever they may be. Even this food is probably very odd to her." Tristal wanted to watch her, but didn't dare.

But he did turn and say, "Night Girl, you will like the

soup. Just try the broth first. Tor made it for me. I have been sick. It is easy to eat." Tor nudged him in the ribs, and they sat down across the fire from Celeste. Tristal began to sharpen his knife, but Tor made him put it away.

Celeste first smelled the soup. It was strange and sharp, as animal as the fur her whole body nested in. It would be her first food outside the dome. She cautiously sipped, and a deliciousness she had never experienced suffused her mouth. Yet it was hot, almost burning; dome food came out of the autoserve at 28 degrees, measured and unvaried. The heat hurt her lips, but the meat and onion flavor surrounded her tongue like a narcotic, spinning her senses loose.

She drank the whole cup, then banged her stick and held the empty cup out. Tristal took it and refilled it for her. Again she drank, catching small bits of meat in her teeth and feeling them as she chewed each thoroughly. She suddenly felt drowsy, settling into the furroll and sleeping almost as if drugged.

Tor and Tristal played a quiet game, the Shumai rhythm game called "Na, na," glancing at the girl occasionally. Finally Tor rose and took down her clothes, folding them and putting them by the girl's head. She woke as he stirred the fire. Some of the rain had turned to wet snow in large flakes, and the sparks rose and swarmed into the quietly falling white. Celeste was momentarily confused and disoriented by the contrary swirls, fire and dim flakes. What was this?

Tor gazed down at her. "It is snow. It is only the rain now cold enough to freeze. Do you understand?" She nodded. "Get dressed," he continued. "Tris and I will turn our backs again. Then you can come out and touch the snow if you want, or you can go back to sleep."

Celeste did dress, shivering in her smoky clothes, then walked from the outcrop and held out her hand to the snow, which lumped and melted as it touched her warm skin. What of the flowers? She went to them, knelt, watched the snow slowly piling on them, weighing them down. Were they to die, then?

Tor came behind her. "Don't worry," he said. "They are bloodroot and are used to it. Snow falls on their blooms nearly every year. It will melt and they will spring up again."

She turned to him, frowning. Could this be so? He held out his hand, and she took it to pull herself up. She held his hand, feeling its hardness, its calluses, and its size, which was larger than Royal's, than Dexter's even. Was he a mutant? No. He was too much like her, and his parental gentleness was a dimension new to her.

"Better go to bed," he said. "Tomorrow we will take you to your people, whoever they may be."

She did go, crawling back into Tor's furroll, while Tristal slid into his and Tor piled leaves between the two and wormed his body down into them, calling Raran to nest with him. The big dog did, but kept a front paw across Tristal. Soon they all lay quietly, breathing slowly and evenly. The dog sighed like a human. The fire died down, and Celeste stared up in amazement at having stepped with scarcely a thought out of one world and into another, wholly different one. She breathed in the damp of the spring coldness, watched the falling snow, and finally sank into a deep slumber, resolving that she would not go back. No. Who knows what they would do to her for her disobedience and initiative. Surely they would not believe what she saw unless she took it with her, and then they would be in a fury about her introduction of radiation and organic life into the pure dome and levels, preserved, but for her, for more than a millennium now. Almost her last thought before sleep was another remembered image —Butto, sweaty and naked, and his comp friends, emptying the dead fetus down the recycle tube with a wet, slopping sound. She shuddered involuntarily. Tor, feeling her movement, put his hand over and smoothed her hair in the dark. No. She would not go back.

She woke when Tor stirred and rose in the morning. She saw they lay in a hollow, among trees. In the rising light, she saw each branch and twig covered with thick, white snow, even now beginning to melt and rain down in the brightness of a blue day. She cried out with the strangeness and beauty of it. Tor turned and looked at her, smiling at her wide eyes, then went to the fire to rebuild it. All his motions were smooth and sure, seeming slow but deft, as if he had studied and perfected them in advance.

Celeste stood, shivering in her robe, and slipped on her fabric shoes. She went to the fire, held out her hands to it, drew them back from the sudden, fierce heat, then held them out again. The strange wildness of everything around her amazed her like a dream. Tor dropped his coat over her shoulders and cinched its belt around her waist. It seemed to swallow her.

He laughed. "Well, waif, now you are added to Tris, maybe I should start a nursery." She frowned. "Well, you understand, anyhow," he added. "Now, go sit on the fur-roll again. We have to make you some kind of shoes if you have to walk in all this wet."

She did as he asked, and, taking a piece of hide with hair on it from his backsack, he knelt at her feet and made some quick measurements as she felt an odd shiver of unwonted intimacy. Then he sat against the rock and cut out a rough pair of soft boots with a sharp knife from his underbelt.

"Wake Tris, Night Girl. He will have to sew these for you while I get some food ready."

She had to reach across the dog, which lay awake but at ease. Raran let out a slight, throaty growl, and Celeste jerked back. Tor rose and stood in front of the dog. Raran rolled and wagged, groveling at his feet. Tor held her collar. "Now wake him."

Celeste reached across again and shook Tristal by the shoulder. He came awake only slowly, eyes puffed, looking around as if he had forgotten all about last night, amazed at the presence of the girl.

"Raran has been growling at our Night Girl, Tris. Better teach her she has another master."

Tristal rolled over by the girl, then patted his lap. Raran instantly came over and put her head on it, tail down. "Now, pat her," he said to Celeste. She reached out a hand, and the dog again began a deep murmur. Tris jerked her collar hard, and the dog only pushed her head up against his leg harder. "Now," he said again, and Celeste, full of fear, put her hand across and touched the dog's head, then stroked it, feeling its smooth warmth, softer than sleep covers. The dog's eye rolled up at her. She saw the long mouth, with jutting, blunted canine teeth, and behind them rows of pointed molars, exposed by a drooping, black-scalloped lip, which hung open as Raran panted slightly. She seemed swept up in momentary vertigo. It was a beast. She sat touching a beast whose head alone lay longer than Dexter's rodents.

The sudden newness rolled away from her, but she

drew back, covering her face with her hands. Smelling dog on them, she wiped them on Tor's coat, only to have Raran put her nose back into her palm, wetting it with mucus, then licking the fingers with her long tongue. Celeste stood, holding up her hands. Would she ever get clean? Raran stood in front of her, now wagging her long-haired tail. Celeste ran to Tor and clung to him.

"Raran is only a dog. You don't know much about dogs, either? What are we to do with you? Don't worry. We will take you home today." She only clung harder to him, opening her mouth, trying to talk again, feeling his bulk, his warmth, his encircling arm.

"I . . ." she said. "I don't want to go anywhere. I want to stay with you."

Tristal looked up from his sewing. "She does talk. She sounds like a Pelbar, I think. Doesn't she?"

"Strange. Yes, she does," said Tor. "We will talk in Pelbar dialect, then. Is that better? Are we clearer?"

"Yes. A Pelbar?"

"You are not Pelbar, then?"

"No. I—I—"

"It doesn't matter. But I know you won't want us calling you Night Girl, for lack of a better name. What is your name?"

"Celeste."

"Celeste, then. Not a Pelbar name. Are you sure you don't want to go home?"

"Never. No. I want to stay with you. Out here."

"Out here? We aren't going to stay out here, Celeste. We are going to Pelbarigan. Want to come with us?"

"Pelbarigan? Yes, take me. Pelbarigan?"

"It is a city on the Heart River. A Pelbar city. You don't look in shape to run, but you can walk. It will take us several days. Will you come with us then?"

Celeste nodded, wondering what she was committing herself to. Instinctively, her hand reached for her belt entry array, to see what Pelbarigan was in central memory, but of course the unit wasn't there, and she felt only Tor's heavy belt. Turning, she saw Tristal working on her behalf, shoving a broad steel needle through the leather of her new boots. He smiled at her shyly, saying nothing. His hair glistened. It was much blonder than Tor's, but like Tor's was bound in a single braid behind his head.

She had never looked at Tristal closely, and now saw

his eyes in their washed blueness, frank and silent. Again she felt the shock and wonder of newness. No one in the dome and levels looked like that. All darkness had been flushed out of him. But he was truly a savage, without her careful education, surely without real technology, as he worked his heavy needle quickly, a bead of bright blood on one forefinger.

Tor handed her a pitched bowl of stew, thick and creamy, of the same things as that of the previous night. She ate it eagerly, looking up at a squirrel leaping through the high limbs, scattering clots of snow. She paused, her spoon near her mouth. Tristal watched her guardedly. A woodpecker knocked on a tree down the valley, and she whipped her head toward the sound. A vague thought formed in Tristal's mind, but he kept it to himself.

He finished the boots by midmorning and knelt down and slipped them on Celeste, leaving her inner slippers inside them, showing her how to tie them.

Tristal muttered something to Tor about going up the hill before they left and set out with Raran through the rapidly melting snow. With a slight detour, he went to the place where they had encountered Celeste. A small box gleamed in the melted snow. Tristal took it up carefully, turning it over and examining it. He put it in his bag and continued on up the hill, soon finding himself staring down and out across the empty place to the silent, snow-topped dome. He looked a long time. He was sure Celeste came from the dome. He would not tell Tor, lest his uncle would try to return the girl and poison himself on the empty place. What of Celeste? Would the poison affect her? Did she wash soon enough? Was it a short enough distance to traverse it safely? How could he warn her without revealing that he knew her origin, which she plainly tried to hide? Well, he would let it go for now.

Before noon they left for the river. The going was slow, Celeste finding it hard to press on. She had exercised regularly, on level one, far end, using all the prescribed forms, but it surely had not prepared her for life outside in the wild. She strove to keep up, but the two Shumai had to move very slowly, never saying anything to her, remaining gentle and silent. She found she didn't feel very well, either. Perhaps it was the food, the excitement, the flood of differences. In part it may have been her fear of this universe of newness. She gritted her teeth and continued.

By nightfall, though, she was so exhausted that she fell asleep immediately by the fire Tristal built while Tor wandered off into the brush, returning a short while later with two rabbits on his belt. He had skinned the animals out of Celeste's sight, so as not to alarm or disgust her, and, with his back to the girl, he cut them into a seething pot, adding the wild bulbs they had dug as they walked. But Celeste lay fast asleep, only her dark hair visible at the mouth of Tor's furroll.

The next morning found Celeste feeling even worse. She struggled up and walked until nearly noon, but then Tor cut some saplings with his axe, made a litter, and put her in it. He and Tristal carried her until late afternoon, when Tor, looking at his nephew, decided that the boy too had had enough. They went on, Tor dragging the litter, Celeste looking back at Tristal's face, watching his quick motions, noticing his fatigue, realizing he bore it with scarcely a thought and no protest. She thought that passive and didn't admire him for it.

The following day Celeste seemed weaker and feverish. Again they carried her, striking the river in midmorning. They took Tor's canoe out of the tree where the Shumai had hung it, soon spinning out onto the broad stream.

Now she looked back at Tor, who watched her with a worried look as he stroked upriver. She showed scarcely any interest in the great stretch of water, after an initial alarm, and he knew from this that she was very ill. Their hope would be to get her to Pelbarigan as soon as possible. Celeste slept fitfully. She was unable to hold down the food Tristal fed her, holding her head in his lap.

Once when she awoke, she saw only darkness, then small points of light above her. She cried out in fear, sitting up, then felt Tor's hand on her ankle, as he said, "Lie down, little one. We are going to Pelbarigan. Lie down and look at the stars. Look. Do you see the curves of the great snake reaching across the south? If you watch long enough, you will see a shooting star stretch its light across the whole sky. But you can sleep if you want."

Later she awoke again. The stars had all moved. Raran lay by her, and she realized that Tristal too lay asleep in the bow of the canoe, curled ahead of her. Tor stroked steadily behind her, and when she stirred, said, "Look again, little one. See? Above you is the crown of stars. There are eight of them, and their names are Ivi, Odu, Ictu, Nod, Efen, Assu, Mok, and Orau. You will learn them when you learn our star game."

"Where are we?" she whispered.

"Somewhat south of Pelbarigan. Soon the sun will rise, and you will then only have to turn your head to see the towers of the great stone city where they will care for you far better than we can."

"Tor."

"Yes?"

"You have been working all night as well as all day?"

"No. It is play, Celeste. For any Shumai, to be out in the air, or under this heaven of stars, with friends, and traveling, is the true flame of life."

"I don't understand. It is all so strange."

As if to add to the strangeness, in the dim and growing light, the long horn of Pelbarigan's Rive Tower sounded, stretching mournfully toward them, then throwing itself out across the river again and again from each jutting promontory of the limestone bluffs. Tor took up the long bull's horn he had left in the canoe and sounded a return, round and long, then resumed his paddling, as did Tristal, now roused and sighing once, in the bow.

Celeste tried to raise herself but lost interest. Tor turned the canoe around, slowly, so she could have a look at the city in the dawn, then continued north to where four guardsmen waited on the bank for them, eventually taking the craft and drawing it up onto the sandy landing slope. Ahroe was one of them.

"Ahroe," said Tor. "This is Tristal. Where is Stel? He was right. This is Celeste. She is from the dome."

"What? You knew?" Tristal said.

Tor laughed. "I'm afraid being outside has been too much for her. She is very sick. Can you care for her?"

Ahroe's smile faded, and she sounded the notes on her side horn for more guardsmen. "Tor," she said. "Why aren't you a father? You must have paddled all night. From the dome? Amazing. You must tell us. Come to our place. We have a bed for you, and one for Tristal. Stel will feed you, and you can sleep. The guardsmen and I will take care of the girl. Celeste? Celeste will rest. We'll give her a nest." Stooping, she said, "Hello, Celeste. I am

Ahroe. Welcome to Pelbarigan. You will be fit again soon enough."

Celeste cried out and held out her hands to Tor, and he knelt by her and lifted her up against him. "You mustn't worry, chipmunk. They will take fine care of you. Better than we did. You will be inside again. I fear our treatment of you has not done you any good. Ahroe will watch over you. See? She will be like your mother. Tristal will be your brother. They have everything you need, not just a fire by a rock and a dirty furroll, with chuck stew to eat. Now, kiss me, and I will go take a rest. I don't mind running all day and night, but this boat work makes my bottom sore. Come, kiss me."

Celeste put her mouth up to his beard, but she didn't know how to kiss. Tor chuckled and kissed her forehead, then let her back down. Then he stood and stretched, dusted his hands on his pants, and strode with Tristal toward the small house of Stel and Ahroe, which lay outside the walls, up toward the bluffs. Raran walked undulantly alongside the boy. Celeste turned her head, watching him, as the guardsmen lifted her onto a litter, picked her up, and walked toward the main gate, with Ahroe alongside, holding the girl's hand.

 IV

ZELLER sat at the control table. Eolyn stood nearby. He opened the switches to the electronic callers. "Comp 2, Comp 4," he said, evenly.

"Yes, Principal Zeller."

"Have you checked level-six storage for hydrocarbons?"

"Yes, Principal. There are few. We have piled them near the riser."

"Few? Did you dismantle the ancient computer banks for plastics?"

"Dismantle them? Oh, no, Principal. Did you want us to do that?"

"Yes, of course. Get on it right away. Have 3, 7, 8, 9, and 10 help. Where are you?"

"On our level, awaiting orders, Principal."

"You were to call in when you finished."

"Were we? I am sorry, Principal. We will go."

Zeller switched off the caller, looked at Eolyn, shaking his head, and said, "I surmise that they have never even looked into level-six storage. They are still on their bunks, chanting Butto's poems. He has infected them. All the efforts we have gone through to sort out the microorganisms in this structure, and Butto himself is an infection, even though he excludes many of the comps from his approval."

"Well, what do they have to hope for? What would you do as a sterile midget?"

Zeller blushed. "We all have our places in the preservation of mankind on earth."

"You would have made a good politician in ancient times. The fact is, we have the better places. But the whole thing seems to be coming down on us now, and fast."

"What do you mean?"

"Where is the next generation? Now our geneticists have been killed, Butto is running the Brat Shack. I was down there 1200 ago. Have you seen it? He is raising monsters. He hasn't had a successful infant yet, comp or principal."

"Why hasn't this been reported?"

"Butto has shrouded the information, I assume. But truth to tell, the last geneticists weren't doing very well, either. Celeste is our youngest, and she is fourteen. And look at her. She is a genius with the machines, but she can't talk."

"She once did," Zeller mused. "I wonder what happened. She certainly has responded to her environment."

"Don't be bitter. None of us chose it."

"We will have to go back to ancient breeding."

Eolyn shuddered. "Not I. Who would there be? Ruthan, me, and soon Celeste. Can you save a race with three women, one unwilling, one a bit odd, and the other perhaps normal?"

Zeller pondered. Then he laughed, held out his arms

to her in mock pursuit, leered, and said, "Well, it would be worth a try!"

She laughed but didn't move. Zeller was disappointed. "By the way," he remarked, "where is Celeste, anyhow?"

"In her chamber, I think. She is often reclusive. She has called me now every once in a while for some time, just to print out little inconsequential remarks. She doesn't even wait for a reply, or acknowledge my replies when I make them."

"All by caller?"

"Of course. What is the matter?"

Zeller frowned, then touched a code to Celeste's chamber. "Celeste, this is Zeller," he said. They looked up at the print monitor. Soon the letters began to appear.

"Yes, Zeller. I am monitoring you while listening to a tape. This is important to me. Would you mind calling me later? Thank you."

"Celeste, Celeste," he repeated.

On the screen the words typed out, "I know you don't want me for anything vital, Zel. Please let me try to work out this calculation from the tape. Thank you."

"We'd better go to her chamber, Zel. Those are the identical words she wrote out for me at least four cycles ago, with the name changed."

Zeller rose quickly and ran out of the control room and down the hall. Celeste's chamber door had been uncoded and would not respond. He inserted the master code which he knew as levels engineer. The panel still didn't slide. "Our electronic wizard has superceded the master code," he said to Eolyn.

"What will you do?"

Zeller took his belt caller and touched the code for the duty comp. "Yes, Principal Zeller," it said.

"Report to level one, south sector. Bring Comp 28 and a complete tool kit."

"Now?"

"Yes, now."

"Is it important?"

"Yes, God rot you. I'll give you about 25 to get here or I'll decommission you with a pulser."

"Yes, Principal. I hope you can find one that works."

Zeller switched him off, shaking his head. "I've never seen them this way. The chemical balance fed them must be altered. It begins to include hostility. Who is in charge of that?"

"Butto."

"Him again. We'd better get Royal to do it."

"Royal would feel it demeaning."

The comps came down the hall, trotting with their tool kits. "Open that slider," said Zeller. His hand held a pulser. Eolyn had never seen him with one before, and she wondered what was happening.

The two set to work, slow and fumbling. They could not seem to coordinate their hands and the tools, and dropped things constantly, but finally the door glided open. The room was empty. Zeller strode across it, his eyes quickly sweeping over Celeste's complex reply system. He keyed a code on her table. Above, the monitor wrote out, "Yes, Royal, this is Celeste. I am indisposed now. Too much exercise, I think. I was in the pool for 300 with Dexter, swimming steadily."

"How did she expect to get away with that? Suppose Royal called her when Dexter was there?"

"How often are we together? It is more of her irony. We depend on machines, and she has fooled us with her knowledge of them."

"What does this mean? Where is she?"

"She could be anywhere—even out in the dome, knowing her."

Zeller called ten comps, equipped them with heat sensors, and sent them off to comb the dome and levels for Celeste. He also called the principals generally and announced her disappearance. They assembled in the control room.

Zeller was nervous. He called the searchers. "Any luck? Where have you searched?"

"All of levels four, five, and six, Principal. But we have not found her yet."

"They are all on their bunks in level five," said Royal, checking a monitor on the wall.

"Then they haven't looked at all. Royal, you will have to take over their chemistry. Something is wrong. They won't do anything. The whole dome and levels will break down."

Butto rose. "I resent that. That is my charge, and it has been done correctly."

"Then why are they in their bunks?"

"I will see to them. You are not to touch their chemistry."

"Are not? That is not a statement in accord with our system of government, Butto."

"No, but neither is your interference. I will see to them at once." He strode out. After a few moments, Zeller followed.

"Royal, I suggest that you re-alter their chemistry without telling Butto," Eolyn said. "Have you been down to the Brat Shack lately? He is growing nothing but mistakes. We will die out."

Royal shook his head. "After all these years, all the successes, all our own discoveries here in the levels, must it finally peter out like this? We will have to make some quick revisions. After the fall of the floor, the old laws of the dome founders do not hold true. We have lost too much skill, too much knowledge. It was foolish to invest certain branches of knowledge in only one or two individuals."

"Who would have thought, in this controlled environment, that they would meet with an unexpected accident?"

"I suppose it was correct to lower the population to fifty. The levels would not have sustained the original 276. But that made things precarious. How did we lose our skill with drugs? They worked well for so long, even reconciling level members to learning skills they might have no native interest in."

"Perhaps the effect of the drugs changed."

"Perhaps. Well, we have two immediate problems. We have to find Celeste and restore the order of the comps." Royal punctuated his remarks with two long fingers, dark and straight. Then he saw the odd look on Thornton's face.

"Well, what?"

"I suppose you will laugh. But do you remember, Eolyn, when I called you about Celeste? You were angry, so I shut off the conversation?"

"Yes. She has always been a trouble."

"It is a surmise. Remember the grotesque birds she drew?" He punched the code again, calling Celeste's goose back on the screen. "That occurred during the cycle of our twice-annual check of radiation. Comps went out into the dome. I discovered that Celeste had been in the dome as well. I quietly decontaminated her, because I didn't want her to get into any more trouble. She admitted she had been there, but communicated no more. This is what I surmise. Celeste saw the birds from the dome window. She assumed that since they flew over, they must have come from somewhere and gone to somewhere, and that somewhere was clean of radiation, since they existed. Thus we are in only an island of radiation. I suspect that she has left the dome, probably at least six cycles ago."

A short silence followed. "Well, Thornton," said Royal, "they certainly picked the right person to garner the knowledge of the ancients. I always thought you had an imagination, but—"

"Principals, this is Comp 3. An emergency."

Royal touched the code. "Yes, Comp 3, what is it?"

"Zeller is dead. He has fallen on the stairway."

They all stood and rushed out into the hallway, then to the stairwell that connected the levels. All the way, Dexter was shouting, "Wait, wait," fighting his way through them, finally blocking the stair panel. "Look, this is too odd. Let me go down alone with a pulser. I think they have done something to him. Three is one of Butto's pet comps. Eolyn, you follow, armed, in about seventy counts."

"You are crazy."

"Yes, but let's just do it my way." He turned and slipped through the panel. He had his pulser with him. Eolyn went for hers. Ruthan looked anxiously down the stairs, and soon heard the thunk and saw the flash of pulsers firing. She screamed and ran for her hand weapon.

Dexter had come down cautiously but rapidly. He saw the shadow on level four as Comp 3 stepped out through the panel to get him on the way down. But the comp was as wobbly as the two had been getting Celeste's panel open. Dexter ducked flat, the pulser shattering the wall surface over his head. Then he rolled sideways and pumped a pulse into the comp, shattering his head. Dexter turned to the door panel below as another pulse flashed out, nicking his shoulder. He threw two more pulses through the opening, splattering another comp. Then he dashed through the open panel and into the first right chamber. A comp room; it was empty.

A quick glance out into the hallways showed seven comps standing idly, staring like dolls, but one appeared to have four legs. Dexter saw a pulser come over the comp's shoulder in time to duck back into the room as the pulse shattered the hinge, leaving the door canting out into the hallway. From a side room came the sudden whine of an ultrasonic pointer, cutting the comp in two. Dexter again stepped out into the hallway, moving from comp to comp there, patting them down for weapons. All of them stood staring with dilated eyes. He peered quickly into the room from which the ultrasonic pulse had come. Comp 14, Thornton's friend, sat idly there, the pointer in his hands, pretending to be as vacant as the others. Dexter immediately saw his alertness, winked, and continued his inspection, as Eolyn came through the end panel.

They found Zeller's body at the far end of the hall, a hole burned through his chest. Dexter directed two comps to strip Zeller's corpse, drag it to the recycle chute on that floor, and lift it through. It was too large to fit in. They would have to dismember it. Eolyn left, but Dexter stayed to command the process, his jaw set. The dead comps were also recycled, and even the blood vacuumed, the pinkish water from the recovery device pumped into organic short-processing. Dexter drew a brain sample from each dead comp.

Now twenty-seven comps were left. Royal and Dexter rounded up all they could find and led them to level four, each one silent as a disconnected circuit. Comps 23, 24, and 25 were missing. Dexter put in a call for them and found them to be on level seven. They claimed to be looking for Celeste. He commanded their presence on level four, decontamination room.

Royal mixed a new chemical preparation and injected each man, then got him to lie down on the floor. Soon each fell into a deep sleep. Finally the other three arrived, looking sweaty and excited. They resisted, but Dexter's pulser convinced them to submit to Royal's injection. Ruthan had dressed Dexter's shoulder, where the comp's pulser had grooved it. Her hands smoothed the dried spray dressing gently and solicitously, then rested around his neck.

As the comps lay comatose, Thornton arrived. The old man was shocked to see the small men, including his friend, 14, lying in rows. Zeller's death had sobered him further.

"How long will they be unconscious?" he finally asked.

"Another 800, at least."

"We need to go to control to discuss this."

"Action has been taken. What need is there to discuss it further? We are back on course now," said Royal.

"Except for the disappearance of Celeste, the difficulties that will arise from the death of Zeller, the loss of the oil, and the question as to whether there is a course."

Dexter interrupted, "All well and good, but we still ought to take care of our meditative friend first."

"You mean . . ."

"Yes. The same. Haven't his private influences and general gloom gone too far already?"

"Take care?"

"Confine him until his condition has been studied. Surely he has changed. He wasn't always this way. I remember his games, his laugh, his long recitations of poetry, endurance tests, and beautiful control of the comps."

"It takes a balanced person to study the ancients," Thornton said.

"Old, too," said Dexter, laughing. "His problems may have begun there, but the change in him may have led there, too. His study of that ancient poet—what was his name?"

"Jeffers. Robinson Jeffers."

"Yes. That one. That didn't help, nor did all that Oriental philosophy, whatever that is."

Royal sighed and threw up his hands. "Well, Dexter, suppose you and Eolyn take care of the matter. I will prepare an injection. We will see about talking afterward."

"Eolyn? Will you come?"

"Be careful, Dex," said Ruthan.

Dexter laughed and pinched her cheek. "Ruthan Tromtrager, don't worry. In the words of an ancient general, 'I shall return.' "

"Or of an ancient philosopher," Thornton added, " 'We have met the enemy, and he is us.' "

"Ours?"

"Us."

"Yes. Well, let's go then, Eolyn, and meet ourselves. I have the pulser set on stun. Have we a heat sensor? I think we should try the seventh level. He thinks he has been secretly hiding out there, but I guess everyone knows it."

The two set out, down the worn concrete stairs, slipping

quickly by the landings, past the pulser damage, down to the lowest level, devoted to storage after the dome people lessened their population and activities to conserve resourcs. They moved silently, in their fabric slippers, through the dark level, casting the heat sensor around, finally detecting a response in a far corner. Coming closer, they heard Butto's voice in a chant, slow and alone:

> Twisting purple, swelling vines,
> rising plants where tendril twines,
> hummingbirds on flashing wings,
> reddest skies where green wind sings,
> soon the snake will slide his scales
> across the streams and through the swales,
> alert, awake, his lovely head
> gracing meadows with its red.
> But now the sky has rushed with fire,
> the land is seared, the trees a pyre.
> Better man should die, should end
> than—"

At that point Dexter's stun pulse hit him in the spine, and he sagged over with a grunt, staring at the floor. Dexter stooped and shut his eyelids.

"Good rodents," he said, "these levels have produced some of the worst poetry imaginable."

"Maybe he made it up himself. Do you need help?"

Without answering, Dexter turned the naked Butto over, sat him up, and lifted him, straining, over his shoulders. Then he said, "Sorry about the display, Eo."

"It means nothing. Nothing but organic matter. I am well suppressed. Even my revulsion. Royal's compound. He's good at that."

"Let's get him to his chamber. Royal should be waiting."

After Butto was laid out on his sleep pad, tranquilized for the time being, the two went to control. Royal was deep in thought, tapping his long fingers on the table. "The death of Zeller makes this whole business very serious," he said. "We will need to ascertain what Butto's connection with that was."

"I think it was the comps' doing," said Dexter. "Zeller and Butto were rivals for the approval of the comps in a sense. I can't think that Butto would have set out to kill Zeller. Susan might know. I'll ask her."

"Susan? That old crone again?"

"She knew Butto better than anyone else. He used to visit her in her chamber. They would talk, and she would sing with that wooden thing of hers."

"The dulcimer."

"Yes. That. Eo, come on. Let's drop in on Susan and inquire. The comps will be out for a while. Thor, you come, too. For comfortableness. After all, we want her to open up."

Thornton stood up and sighed, dusting his hands on his thighs. "Well, I suppose if I can't be anything more auspicious, I shall be comfortable."

Susan's chamber was tucked into the farthest corner of the level. As the three neared it, they heard strummed music, and a thin, quavering voice.

Dexter sounded the tone. The reply tone hummed. The panel slid and they all entered. Susan sat curled on her sleep pad, her gray hair combed back and knotted as much as its intense curliness would allow.

"What is it?" she asked quietly. "Is it come at last? Have you voted to recycle me?"

"Sue," said Eolyn. "Don't be foolish. This is a serious thing. Did you know Zeller had been killed by the comps?"

Susan gave a little cry, putting her hand to her mouth. "Killed," she whispered.

"Yes. We found Butto later, down on the seventh level, chanting, heavily drugged. Would he be behind it? You know him better than anyone else. What do you think? Do we have a paranoid on our hands?"

Susan considered this, touching her fingertips to the dulcimer box. "I don't know that, of course," she said. "But here is something to think about. Obviously there was a rivalry between the two, but it wasn't only for control of the comps, or their loyalty. It wasn't only in their shared work. They were both somehow in love with Eolyn."

Eolyn snorted, but Susan slid off the sleep pad and moved to her panel commands. One by one she flicked a series of images up on the screen, mostly group stills of the present principals in various activities. Going through the series was a common theme. Both men looked at, stayed close to, or even stood almost touching Eolyn.

"They had followed the standard suppressant procedures, I think," said Susan. "But Eolyn would have been an absolute dream of a woman in the ancient world. Almost every normal, unsuppressed male would have felt his pulse rise as she passed, I think."

Here Susan put on the screen a series of pictures of models from ancient times, including recorded images of *Vogue* and *The New Yorker,* and a series from the slickest ancient porno journals, riffling through the pictures rapidly, concentrating on resemblances to Eolyn. The echoes she had found were striking.

"My record is incomplete, of course, including only material in the company library at the time of the blast. Anyhow, I got interested in the subject, especially knowing Butto so well, and seeing him growing gloomier and more despairing, even concluding that he himself didn't know why. He sank deeper into drug use. I have gone over the records—the known ones—of his experiments on himself. Now look at these and see if you see what I do."

Again Susan used her light screen, putting up a series of formulas. Thornton squinted, and Dexter whistled lightly.

"Now," said Susan, "let's do some combinations, knowing residual times for some of these." The screen showed further formulas, including those for some of the most primitive hallucinogens.

"The comps will be rousing soon," said Dexter. "Poor Butto. And poor Zeller. You never gave them a chance, Eo." He laughed nervously.

"The comps were clearly for Butto and saw Zeller as a threat. I was simply studying something I found curious. I had no idea it would lead to anything like this. Perhaps they did away with Celeste, too. I think at least I have shown you one thing—we don't really pay sincere attention to one another."

"Yes. Well, let's get back out to the comps," said Dexter. Eolyn preceded him out the panel. As they left, Thornton stayed back, smiling at Susan. Then he leaned down and kissed her.

She laughed. "Better take some suppressant, old Thorn."

"I think you made a point. I really do."

"It is odd, but I have ceased caring. I have only one wish left before I die."

"But I am too old to love. You nearly said so."

"Quiet. I would like to leave the dome and walk free on the earth, even though it is radioactive, even though it is empty and blasted. I haven't long to live. I would like to be the first of the dome people to leave. I would not care if I died in only two or three hundred units."

"You may have heard that I think Celeste has left the dome. But I have to go and save 14 from further machinations."

"Celeste has left? You can't go. No. I think she is recycled. By Butto's comps. Come now, Thorn." As he hurried down the corridor, she called after him, "I haven't told you the worst thing."

Thornton paused, then called back, "Thorn, indeed. We will exchange stories later. It will give us something to live for." He laughed over his shoulder. Susan stood in her panelway regarding him, but she made no attempt to traverse the levels to the decontam room.

Meanwhile, the leaking oil had begun to pool under the levels, lying on a clay subsoil and limestone outcrop. At one point it began to wick up a dry timber, forgotten in the building over eleven hundred years before, and protected from rot by pressurized chemical treatment. The tip of the old beam just penetrated the one section below the seventh level—the low-pressure reserve-oxygen storage room. It was a slow process, but it had begun.

 V

TOR sat on a promontory south of Pelbarigan, watching the sun move west, watching ants legging in a line across the rock, a wren flitting into the thicket below, then out, then in again. He took apart an iris flower, petal by petal, laying the petals out in a row on his knee, examining their shapes idly. He longed to be gone west to find his men.

Blu would be axeman this summer. Blu stood as tall as Tor himself, and was as wiry. Blu moved nearly as fast, too, as their games of Na, na showed, and he could draw the heaviest of bows and put an arrow dead where he wanted it. So Blu would take over. No. Tor knew something was missing. Was it his own extremism, the wild love of the prairie wind that so infused him the men could feel it and respond? Tor didn't know. He did know they would follow him anywhere. He had that peculiar thing all the best Shumai leaders had. What it was puzzled even him. It came as a full giving of himself to any situation, that instant reading of emergencies, that knowing precisely what to do.

Blu had some of that, too. But it was a gift, this just knowing. Tor wanted to go, but Celeste would not get well. She lay in Pelbarigan below, sick with a succession of sicknesses, and when she seemed to get over one, another would come. She called out for him as she tossed with fever, or lay listless, and he dared not fail to be there, though he did nothing for her but be there, and pray quietly for her in a halting way. The grave-faced old woman, the Haframa did everything, treating Tor like an inconvenient drug, which had to be administered now and then, in a gulp, when Celeste needed it.

But he could not stand the city itself for long, with its old stairways, its mustiness and dark corridors, so he stayed high on the bluffs, roaming the woods, watching the small horse herd the Pelbar had brought from Northwall, doing nothing, or seeing how his nephew was coming on. He had begun carving drinking noggins, with the elaborate interlaced patterns that the old Shumai imparted to their crafts when they grew slack and past the time of running. He felt old. Good Sertine, could a mere wisp of a strange girl so change his life? Yes. For Celeste, the poor waif, he would stay. And more, for what Celeste meant. She was from the dome, though she refused to admit it. She was, in fact, too sick to say much of anything half the time. Tor vaguely feared the dome.

The afternoon was waning, and far out over the river the herons flew in small groups from their feeding places in the shallows on the west shore toward the islands with tall trees. From far below, Tor could see Dailith, the guardsman, coming up the path. So Celeste must have wanted him again. Tor brushed off the iris petals and met Dailith on the path.

"Celeste?" he asked.

"Yes. It looks like chicken pox this time. She is all sores and very frightened."

"She has neglected her childhood diseases. They must have none in that dome."

"Or whatever. Come, anyhow. I will see some supper is brought to you. Everything she gets is very bad. She has enough spots for four children."

Tor trotted down the path, Dailith behind, fearing to try the pace of the axeman on the loose rock. The guardsmen at the gate watched him come up to them as they leaned on the great blocks of wall stone. Ahroe stood there and reached out an arm to him. They grasped wrists as he passed. Garet squatted near her, building an elaborate structure of short twigs.

When Tor entered the room where Celeste lay, so silently he startled the Haframa, who jerked her head, Celeste barely turned. Then she reached her hand to him and he took it.

"I am going to die, am I not?"

"Die? No. You are getting your sicknesses all at once. I have told you that. It is normal enough. All children just have to be steel, be an oak stick. You can bear up. I know you can."

"It is too awful, Tor. You will not go away, will you?"

"Not completely out of earshot, anyway. I will stay here and grow soft."

"I am sorry. And I am not a child."

"All right, chipmunk. You are not a child, though you were one just a little while ago. There is just—well, never mind."

"What is it?"

"We can talk when you are better."

"No, Tor. I am so bored I can't wait that long. Do you know there are 397 stones in this curved wall and ceiling? The angles of each stone in the curve vary between 93 and 102 degrees."

"I am the wrong man to impress with that information, chipmunk."

Celeste was silent for quite a time. Finally she said, "What were you going to say?"

"Well, it is about the dome people. I may be a wild man, looked askance at by this good woman, but I can think at least a little. I know you won't talk about them, but the problem is this—the dome will fall soon because of the erosion. They have to get out. We have to help them. Are they going to get sick like you?"

Celeste was silent, her eyes full of tears. She withdrew her hand.

"Look here, little bird. We only want to help. Something will have to be done. There is no other way. What about this? You tell me what we should do."

"Will you do it?"

"How can I say? We ought to have reasons to fear the dome, you know."

"You will have to go away now and let me be sick. Let me die."

Tor leaned over and put his forehead to hers, frowning comically from up against her. "It is something that will have to be decided, small one. We cannot just avoid a decision. I thought you would like to help us make it. Who could help more?"

"Maybe I am only a child. There are so many people here. It is all so strange. You know so little. It is like stepping back before the time of the ancients." Celeste sighed and pulled at her blanket. Tor looked at Thya the Haframa, who shook her head slightly.

"We will not talk of it anymore now."

"You will not go away, will you?"

"No. I will stay. Perhaps I could go get something to read. Haframa, would the priest of Aven lend me that roll again?"

The old woman smiled. "She is a minister," she said. "And she gave me a spare copy to keep here so you could read it." She handed it to Tor, who took it and sat by the curved stone window, frowning as he read, slowly, his lips moving, while Celeste gazed at him, her eyes finally closing in sleep.

Tor read laboriously until the light failed him, and, looking up, saw that the Haframa had gone. He was startled. He was used to noticing such things. What was happening to him? An axeman, he was supposed to feel the presence of a wild bull over a hill. It was all so peaceful, this place, and this concept of the God, Aven, kindness and love itself. He shuddered involuntarily. Was it a dream? And did it result in the Pelbar shut-in life? He wondered how it would function on the plains.

His mind, reaching out, thought of the dome, and again he felt the taste of danger. It was unknown, a mask of stone. Who knew what kind of a face it hid? Tor felt the smoke of foreboding, and suddenly wished he were out on the uplands of Kan, watching the unencumbered sky.

Steps padded on the stairs, and Tristal entered with a lamp and some steaming stew. He looked grave when he saw Celeste, and sat quietly, eating with his uncle in silence. When Celeste stirred, Tristal moved to feed her, but she wanted Tor to. The axeman caught the boy's eye with a look that told him not to mention this among the Shumai. Then he cradled the girl's head and fed her the way a father does a baby, opening his mouth in sympathy with hers. She ate, stirred, and sat up, then, seeing Tristal, drew the rough blanket up to her neck. He turned his head.

"Tor," she said abruptly. "If you will get the Protector, then I will talk about it. I am afraid. But I will tell you some things about the dome and levels. Perhaps Tristal will get her."

"She is one of those persons one goes to. One does not summon her."

"Then I suppose we will have to wait until I can go."

"I will try to get her," said Tristal, leaving. And so the Jestana, eating alone in her chambers, suddenly looked up and saw the Shumai boy, who had come unannounced and unperceived, thin and pale, standing before her.

She paused. "What? . . ." she began. Then she added, "The strange girl. Did she die, then?"

"No. The girl said she will talk about the dome and to get you. I am sorry. Tor said you didn't go to people, but they came to you. But she is too sick to come."

"Yes. Well, sit down. Can you eat some of that pudding? There is far too much for me. What is your name again, young man?"

"Tristal."

"Yes. Tristal. Let me finish here. You may sit with me if you will. Then you may summon the guardsman and we will go to her together."

Then Tristal, in a rough tunic, still dirty from his day's work with Stel, sat with the Protector of Pelbarigan as she ate, while the guardsman stood unknowing by the door outside, dreaming, counting the wall stones, humming, reviewing the long-sword drill.

The Protector's sentry was startled when three guardsmen ran down the hallway, rushed by her and through the Protector's anteroom, where old Druk sat musing at the wall, and burst into the sitting room where the Protector and Tristal were eating. Tristal started, his spoon halfway to his mouth.

The guardsmen drew up sharply, breathing hard. "We beg your pardon, Protector, but . . . the young Shumai was seen to jump the wall and swing . . . down to your balcony from the orchard side. We feared for you."

The Jestana smiled. "You may stand at ease. Thank you for your solicitude. This is Tristal." She turned to the Shumai. "I think perhaps you had better explain to us all why you didn't come through the door. These things are important, you know."

Tristal sat straight and put down his pudding. "I—I was coming from Celeste's room, and I knew that I would have to walk way around, down two levels, then pass through all those corridors to get here. It seemed much simpler and shorter. I am truly sorry. I didn't know I did something wrong."

The guardcaptain looked at him hard-mouthed. "Are you not aware that this is the Protector of Pelbarigan and that she must be accorded more respect?"

Tristal looked pinched and frightened, then dropped his eyes. "But she is the mother of Jestak," he murmured.

The Protector shot the guardcaptain an enigmatic look. "Yes," she said. "The mother of Jestak. Perhaps, Ras, you will leave two guardsmen. When we finish eating, I am going to visit the strange girl in her room." She raised her hand. "No. You mustn't object. I am sure the girl is truly too ill to come to the councilroom. She may have decided to tell us something we need to know. Now, Tristal, you must promise me and the guardsmen not to come down through the balconies again, but only the regular way if you wish to see me. If you missed that jump, you would fall all the way to the orchard. Besides, it is not proper. Do you understand?"

Tristal said he did, almost in a whisper. Then he looked out the window and said, "It is an easy jump. Even I would never miss it. But I will not do it again."

The guardcaptain shot him another look, and she and her two guardsmen withdrew.

"You like Celeste, don't you, Tristal."

He looked at her. "Yes. I don't understand it. She has no use for me."

"You may be fortunate. We know nothing of her. No. Don't disagree. All things may not be decided by the heart. Even though you aren't an old politician like me, you are involved in politics. We all are. Don't worry. There is plenty of time to find friends. When my son was your age, he hadn't even begun to think of such things. But boys come in all kinds, and I can see you are one of the lonelier kinds. I am in my lonelier period now, too. I am a widow and my son lives at Northwall. I have a grandson and two granddaughters, but I seldom see them. I am glad you came by, and I hope you will come again."

Tristal looked at her doubtfully.

"I mean it, Tristal. I know quite a bit about boys, you know. You won't hesitate to come and see me, will you? I may well be too busy much of the time, but I am sure to have some time. Now we must not keep everyone waiting." She stood and held out her arm so she could lean on Tristal as they went to the anteroom where the guardsmen waited.

Light entered the room with the Protector, for both guardsmen carried flaring lamps that sent orange flickerings around the room until they were set down and burned steadily. Tor stood for the Jestana and bowed slightly.

A guardsman moved a chair close to the bed, and, leaning on Tristal, the Jestana lowered herself into it heavily. "Now, Tristal, would you mind waiting outside with the guardsmen? I wish to have a word with you later."

Tor, who had said nothing, flicked his eyes to his nephew, to the guardsmen, then back to the Protector. "Protector, this is Celeste. Celeste, are you awake enough? This is the Protector of Pelbarigan, Adai the Jestana. You should be honored because she came all the way up here to see you."

"Yes," said Celeste.

"Tristal has told me that you wish to say some things to me."

"Yes. I—I am sorry. I am confused. There is too much

newness. Everything is different, even this sickness. I understand it, of course, but it is not pleasant."

"What do you understand, Celeste?"

"I admit that I come from the dome. We call it the dome and levels. We have an environment free of dangerous microorganisms. I have been inoculated for some diseases, but most of our antitoxin was destroyed in an accident, so we have carefully preserved the rest, and it was not available to me. Besides, we had become careless because, I suppose, we never felt we would leave the dome in our lifetimes. I am the first."

"Yes. I don't understand much of what you said, Celeste. Perhaps you could put the first part in plain words."

"The microorganisms?"

"Yes. It sounded as if you said that you could take some drugs to prevent your ever getting certain diseases."

"Not drugs. Inoculations. You know nothing of microorganisms?"

"Surprising as it may seem, my friend, no."

Celeste explained, at length, from her substantial knowledge of microscopic life and its effects on humans, as Tor increasingly frowned. The Protector sat impassive. Finally, she raised her hand and said, "But you did not want me to come up here to tell me this, did you."

"You don't believe me."

"It is all new to me. I fear you are right, but it is very different to think of myself as a sort of rabbit warren for such crowds of hostile things; however, I doubt that you could have made all that up. Again, though, since these tiny creatures have been feeding off me all these years, I will let them continue for the present. We must get on to other concerns. You say there are others in the dome, as Stel suspected, and Tor?"

"Yes."

"How many?"

"I must know that you will not harm them."

"Celeste, we seldom harm anyone. Look at us. We are as meek as mice. As I see it, there are four things that must immediately concern us. First, the dome is in danger of collapse. Next, there are people in it to be saved. Next, those people must be integrated into some society when they leave the dome—somewhat less precipitously than you did, I hope. And last, which is extremely important, not only to us but to all the Heart River peoples, and those beyond, to all the people of Urstadge—the dome people have all kinds of knowledge that has been lost ever since the time of fire. We need to reintroduce that knowledge to humankind. This is desperately important."

Celeste lay silent for a time. "Yes, they do have a great many things to teach you, but you have some to teach them, too. And I am not sure that they will want to learn them. They will want to manage everything. They will want to take over this city and do things their way. They are my people. But they aren't the way you are to each other. They have been in there too long. I am that way, too. I can see it. I feel a great emptiness."

"It is only your illness, my friend."

"No. It is more. It is a numbness. We hardly feel. My real friends are the machines and computation systems. Look. You and Tor are really strangers to each other, but I sense feelings flowing between you. I have been lying here a long time thinking about this. It is true."

"Fifteen years ago, if Tor had seen me outside the city, he would have killed me."

"That long? He was only a boy."

"What matter?"

"Yes, he told me of that. But he would have felt a certain way about you. He would not have calculated it all out."

"No. He would not have bothered," said the Protector, chuckling.

"We seldom touch each other, you know."

"What do you see in that?"

"I see that everyone here touches. Tristal comes, and Tor puts his arm around him. Tor kisses me, and I feel something like a shock flow from him. Tristal would touch me, but I won't let him. They sleep in a heap with Raran, the big dog. Stel and Ahroe come here. They touch. Garet touches them. He reaches for me."

"That is a habit. It can be learned."

"Can it? I see it, but I don't understand it. Still, I remember Tor carrying me, all muddy, to the fire. I was swept up in something. It had great power. I turned myself over to him."

"Yes, Celeste. Are you afraid, then, that your friends in the dome will not touch? That they will not feel our togetherness, that reaches from Shumai to Pelbar, and even beyond to the animals? Are you afraid that with all their knowledge, they will therefore act in ways not in our interest?"

"Yes."

"But you do love them. You can't let us leave them there to die when the dome collapses."

"Love them? I am not sure I know what you mean. I don't think so. Perhaps Thornton, but he is an old man. He is kind, though, often. I am now afraid of them."

"You love Tor. I can see that. No, don't cover your face. We all see it and accept it as normal. He obviously loves you, behind that fierce beard of his. See? He doesn't deny it. If you learned so quickly, then—"

"But you don't understand. You haven't met Eolyn, or Zeller, or Dexter. You haven't seen the comps. You haven't seen Butto trying to make babies and failing."

"Make babies?"

"Yes. In the lab. It is to control the genetics—that is, the way the child will turn out. Yes, we can do that. No, we can't. We once did, but we have forgotten how. Do you know that all our food, everything we use—oh, I am so ashamed by all this."

"But you did what you had to do. And you are changing. They will adjust."

"Will they? I am not sure. I am not sure. I don't even think I can, really."

"Then, dear child, you are worried about us more than about them. What happened in there that so drove you out that you have traded away a whole world, all you knew, for strangers?"

"They were strangers. They were. More strangers than you. I know. You have to get them out. But I am so afraid. They have great power. You are safer with less."

All three were silent in the dim room. Finally, the Protector said, "Well, Celeste, I thank you for your friendship and your openness. I will call a council to discuss this. Tor, please ask the guardsmen to come in. Now if you will rest, my friend, I am sure you will get well. After all, there are only so many diseases, and you are running through this list quite rapidly. I will not kiss you as Tor does, because I suddenly see myself as a teeming city of tiny beetles—what were they? Microorganisms. I would like to see one someday. Now good night." She patted the bedclothes and leaned on the guardsmen, slowly leaving the room.

As Tristal and the Protector slowly descended the stairs to the level of her apartments, she on the arm of a guardsman, far off at the dome the sun had set. The old structure lost the sunlight that had bathed it, and now gave up its residual outer heat to the air and the insects, alone, out in the edge of the empty place.

In her chamber, once again Eolyn looked at the pictures of beautiful women from ancient times. It was true. As Susan had said, she herself was as beautiful as they. She took one thin blond woman on a beach in the sun, holding a peculiar bottle with a long tap. She dilated the face and neck on the screen, punched a code, bringing her own face into superimposition. Yes. The bone structure was the same. Look, the slightly slanted eyes of the model made a flaw. She herself stood perfect in contrast.

She moved to the hand and spread her own to match. Again it was nearly identical, except for the ridiculously long fingernails on the model.

Perhaps then she was in the master plan of the founders, somehow. If they were to leave the dome in her lifetime, she would be the new Eve, the one perfect source, the mother of all living. No. She would not want to be that, swelling with babies. She would flow through time unchanged, a goddess of beauty. Somehow she would have to research aging and find a way to stop it. Surely that too was in the genes. Surely she could remake herself. They would have to recover and perpetuate out-of-mother systems for the life outside. They had worked well in the past.

But she knew this to be madness, to be vanity. No. She could not alter every cell in her body. She too would age, and the perfect flower of humanity would either drop its petals or pass them on to some other perfect flower. What a tragedy. How would she stand seeing her own child, grown and beautiful, move through the earth as she faded? Well, that was the method of things, or at least the human coordinates in which she must work. There was a logic, but it was evolutionary, not designed to satisfy individuals. A flaw in the system, Eolyn thought.

But when they left the dome, if they did, who would be the father for her, if she must be a mother? Could she take some of the ancient store of fluid so she would need no father? No. She shuddered. Some man would have to be involved. Still, that might not be so bad. She had been infected by the magazines. The life of the ancients, as depicted by *The New Yorker*, by *Vogue*—how satisfying it must have been to give all those gifts to oneself, the riches of the earth, knowing it was pure vanity, and childish, but having no other motive, no humanitarian ideal, and so pursuing hedonism. It was a way of becoming what one was not, to enjoy the pleasure of the fantasy, all brought about by surrounding oneself, one's pitiful body, with objects—approved objects difficult to obtain and denied others. It was like stroking oneself to hear oneself murmur with satisfaction.

What of Dexter? Yes, he was the only possible consort. He too was an excellent specimen—a bit cold, perhaps, but symmetrical, and detached enough to keep from getting sloppy. They could produce a new generation, now that Butto's failures were so evident. Dexter. Susan had shown how the men moved close to her. Not Dexter, of course—yet. But she was a magnet, despite the depressants. She smiled to herself.

At that moment, Dexter and Ruthan, in his chamber, had put in the code to prevent entry. She looked weary and spent, puzzled and frightened.

"I don't know, Dex. It is wrong somehow, isn't it? You have no bond of loyalty to me."

"I do, Ruthy. And our love will be our further bond. What bond could there be? In ancient times that was the only one that really worked. The ancient ceremony of marriage? We are all that is left on a barren and ravaged planet, and its only hope of regeneration. That itself is marriage, is it not?"

"Oh, Dex. I am not sure. It is so secret. Royal would disapprove."

"Royal? I suppose he would. Come, Ruthy. I know you love me. He took her in his arms and kissed her whole face, systematically, missing no spot. She slowly relaxed, and he deftly turned her and laid her back on his sleep pad, moving to her. The light field dimmed, and the pattern board of lights describing conditions in the rodentry stood steady, then moved and repositioned, unwatched. In the left quadrant, it recorded a birth—five new rat lives dropped gently into the corner, their tiny hearts tick-

ing, their tiny mouths opening and closing like the puls-
ings of hydra. The blip of the mother turned, indifferent.
The record of one small heart stopped. The others continued to monitor, certain and even, in that section of the
screen.

After a time, Ruthan, her arms still around Dexter,
sighed and squeezed her eyes shut, tears in their corners.
Dexter grinned down at her. Reaching over, he touched a
button. A panel in his wall slid back. Three white rats sat
bewildered in a row of three cages. A tiny signal light
went on, and all three sat up and clapped their pink
hands silently several times, then sank back down again.
Dexter slyly touched the signal again. Again they obedi-
ently sat up and clapped. Then the panel shut. Dexter
stifled his laughter.

Leaning down, he murmured in Ruthan's ear, "Well,
my love, who had no mother, you and I, who also had no
mother, may really become a mother and a father. Isn't it
all strange?" Ruthan put her face into his shoulder and
held it there.

When the Protector reentered her chambers, she motioned to Tristal to resume his seat at the eating table,
while she sat across from him in her own large chair.

The Protector seemed distracted and restless, and
Tristal sat quietly, looking around the rather stark room.
On the wall a pellute hung on a cord made of woven
sweet grasses. It had been the Jestana's late husband's, he
a quiet man, compliant in the Pelbar manner, who lived
his dreams in music and in a fierce loyalty to his only
son, Jestak, who had changed the history of the Heart
River fourteen years ago by uniting its peoples.

"Tristal," she began, "I have two things to say to you
—perhaps three. All are different, yet all are related.

"This matter of procedure. When you are out on the
prairies, and you approach a Shumai camp, what do you
do?"

"Blow the horn of greeting, or else yell, if we don't
have one."

"What will happen if you don't?"

"Perhaps nothing. Perhaps, too, a fight, if the others
think we are enemies."

"So you always do send a signal?"

"Yes. It is such a habit that we don't notice not to."

"Exactly, Tristal. Now we have such procedures as well. One is the means of approaching the Protector. I am, after all, the most important personage in Pelbarigan —or at least one holding this office is. Don't worry. I don't feel it as a source of pride, but rather as a weight. I would rather be with my son at Northwall. Now I would like you to make me a promise, and I hope you will."

"A promise?"

"Yes. I would like you to follow all Pelbar procedures while you are with us. That includes addressing me as Protector when you are with others. Will you do that?"

"Why?"

The Protector shifted in her chair. She moved her finger on the table between them. "Because that will be the only possible way I can see much of you and do much for you."

"Why would you do that?"

"What happened to your family?"

A look of pain flitted through Tristal's eyes. "They died in a fire on the prairie."

"Were you with them?"

Tristal swallowed hard and looked down, then nodded.

"You don't need to tell me. I am glad you have Tor. But he is—well, a man in motion, is he not? Pelbarigan doesn't move."

Tristal looked up. "I have Stel and Ahroe here. And Hagen."

"Yes. Well, then that is all I wanted. You may go."

"I thought there were three things."

"It does not matter. You may go now."

Tristal sat utterly still, and the Protector grew irritated at his disobedience. He dropped his head. "I meant no discourtesy," he said. "I see it was, though. You must think of it as the behavior of the mice on the great rock."

"What is that?"

"It is not a great rock to them. They treat it like any other place because they don't know better. I suppose I don't understand, either. But I am willing to try to be of use to you if you would like that. I mean it. You must understand. I know I am an ignorant boy, and my one good point is that my uncle cares for me. I will do something because of that someday."

"Your uncle? Would you be an axeman, then? That, you must realize, is a fading way of life. Even now the

Shumai are gathering at Northwall as farmers and herdsmen. I hear they are establishing farms along the Isso
River."

"But, Protector, a good axeman is something you don't
understand. And Tor is the best. The Shumai—we don't
organize into cities like you. We are free. But Tor can
organize them. They are wild and restless, but he disci-
plines them. He has a way of knowing, and they feel it."

"Knowing what?"

"It is hard to say. He seems to know where the cattle
are, where danger is, how to find water in summer in the
western plains. He knows when one of his men is angry,
or when I am so lonely he must put his arm around me;
and when he does, the loneliness vanishes. I don't know
how he knows. He just knows."

"I see. Are you good at that?"

"No. Not at all. I am not much good at anything."
Tristal said that with an openness that made it a statement of fact without any regret or lament in it. The Protector touched her fingertips together.

"You could do something for me now that no one else
is in a position to do."

"I will do it, but I am not at all sure I will do it right."

"Do you know where Northwall is?"

"Of course. Up the Heart."

"Could you take a message for me to Jestak? No one
must know. I don't want to use normal channels. It will
take you some time."

"Of course. I will start now if you would like."

"Before morning will be fine. But you must not tell anyone even where you are going. You must start off in another direction. There is too much opposition to Celeste
and the dome here."

"Tor will know."

"Tor will . . . Yes, of course. I will tell him."

Tristal got up. Then he said, "Oh, yes. There was another thing."

"Yes. Sit down. I am worried about you. You look at
Celeste the way boys look at girls, but also almost as one
would at Aven—or Sertine—if you could see Her. Are
you aware that she is a potential danger to you, to us?"

"Of course. She has, behind her words, the knowledge
that will change everything. We don't know how she will
change it, though."

The Jestana jerked her head upright and squinted at him a little. "You see that clearly then? You are an intelligent young man. Then why are you so completely in love with her? You are also only a boy, you know."

Tristal looked at her with puzzled despair, then shook his head. "I know and I don't know. Is that the kind of thing you can explain? It has just happened. I think it is because I can feel what she is feeling. Her whole world has been simply snuffed out, the way you would blow out a lamp. Her loneliness is worse than mine was. We were running, my parents and I, out on the long-grass prairie. The grass was taller than our heads. The fire came on a high wind, and it came faster than we could run, sending sparks out in front of us. There was no break in the grass and no water. Finally it was clear it was on us. My parents threw me on the ground, tore up the clods, and lay on me, covering me. I could feel them writhe as the fire took them, but they never cried out, and when it passed they were dead, and I wasn't even burnt, though my chest was so full of smoke that I have had trouble with it ever since."

The Protector stared at the table. When she finally looked up, she saw Tristal's eyes shining full. "One other thing," he said. "She was running from something in the dome. I know it. The dome is all she knows, but she fears it. That makes me fear it, too. Even more, because I don't know it. Protector, I didn't really know my parents loved me like that. They weren't that good to me. I have been beaten for very little, and that is rare among the Shumai. I have been cursed and neglected. But when it came to our deaths, they gave me my life as freely and willingly as the noblest Shumai. It cost them the most terrible agony. I know they didn't cry out because they didn't want the echoes of those cries to ring in my head forever. But you know what?"

"You hear the cries anyhow. The cries that were never uttered."

"Yes," he whispered.

"Don't worry about that. Every parent cries those cries somehow. You will yourself when you have children. It is a part of being human. You mustn't suffer anguish because at last they achieved a greatness, you know. What? What is it? There is more?"

"The other side of it. Now that I am a little older, I

don't think we should have been out there in the first place. It was a careless and reckless thing to do. They simply did not have the knowing Tor has—or even the good sense to know that the grass was tall and dry, the wind blew hard, there was no water."

"Tristal, I didn't know your parents. But I do know this—and it is not different from the problem we are in with Celeste now. It may be, you know, that the best thing we could do for the Heart River peoples is to kill her."

Tristal stood suddenly, horrified, but the Protector simply held up her hand and motioned him to sit down again. "No. We won't. She is a child to be cherished, so we will care for her and hope to bring her health back. Then what? And what of the rest in the dome? Will they rip the life of the Heart River open the way the Tantal almost did? Do you know why we will cherish Celeste? It is normal. We are launching out across a dry area, with tall grass, and no water anywhere. Don't condemn your parents. It is part of the weave of human life to do such things. Now. Do you see why you must go to Jestak? Do you see why it must be unofficial and unknown? At least he must come and see Celeste. He has traveled widely. We have Celeste. It is the others we must decide about. From what I hear, unless we do something, they will likely die. If we do attempt to help them, then what?"

"Why are you telling all this to a boy like me?"

"I am surprised at that. You practically told me the same thing before I started. Didn't you? You have the right combination of unobtrusiveness, discernment, and ability. Besides, I know what Jestak could do when he was your age."

"I am not Jestak."

"No. But you are Tristal. I will send the message to you before morning, then. Is it agreed?"

"Of course, Protector." The Jestana stood, walked around the table, and embraced Tristal, patting his back with both hands. She smelled like age and dried mint. After a long moment, Tristal embraced her in return. Then they exchanged one last glance in the lamplight, and Tristal left the room.

The Protector sat a long time, then reached for paper and a quill pen. She wrote slowly, an old woman alone in the night, small moths circling her lamp. Lines etched her face, which sagged slightly beneath the weight of years, but the set of her jaw stayed firm, and her eyes pooled with the depth and reserve of the ancient quarry ponds. Twice she smiled slightly. Finally she stood and walked to the doorway, where a braided cord hung, which she pulled. She resumed her seat.

After a time she heard a guardsman greet the hall guard, and a tall man with a fierce shock of dark hair entered, smoothing down his tunic. He came to attention.

"Dailith. Get Ahroe for me, please."

"Ahroe, Protector? She comes on duty at high night."

"If necessary we will get a substitute. Please tell no one."

"It is about Celeste, Aunty Jes?" The Protector didn't reply. "I only said that to show you that it will be plain, Protector. I am sorry."

"How is Lantin?"

"He is much better, thank you."

"Tell Ahroe to come alone. It would be better if she could stand her watch. This is not a riverside picnic."

"Yes, Protector." Dailith bowed and left. The Protector rose, got a message tube, rolled her letter, and put it in. Then she wrote another small note and sat, waiting.

Finally Ahroe appeared, her eyes still puffed with sleep. Her sturdy face showed its guardsman's hardness through a still youthful beauty, like a dusting of powder. She stood at attention. The Protector motioned her to sit at the table across from her. Ahroe was nonplussed. Guardsmen never did such things. But she sat.

"Lean over so we may talk softly. May I trust you?"

"Of course, Protector."

"Say, Jestana."

"Of course, Jestana. I am indebted to you. When Stel and I returned, you helped us start our new family name. We are grateful."

"Thank you. This is not for you, however, or for me, though some will think it is. This is for the whole Heart River."

"It has to do with Celeste?"

The Protector sighed. "Does all Pelbarigan talk of nothing else, then?"

"The city is deeply worried."

"Should we put a guardsman at her door?"

"Yes, Protector. Not tonight, though. Tor is there with her."

"I will tell Oet. Now, by tomorrow Tristal must be gone, supposedly to look in on the reed-gathering. But he will really go to Northwall to take this to Jestak. Have him tie it in his quiver. He has agreed. This other note is for Tor. Stel may know, but no others. If asked, Tristal has grown restless with building and was given this other message to allow him to roam the prairies. Is that understood? Is that acceptable?"

"Yes, Protector. Of course. Tristal?"

"He is not an old rope, Ahroe. He will hold. Now, will you go? I am sorry to have awakened you. Can you stand your duty at high night?"

"Of course, Protector."

"Good-bye, then, Ahroe Westrun. Don't worry about the hall guard. She is ours. Kiss Garet for me."

"Good-bye, Protector. Thank you." Ahroe melted through the door.

High up in the room Celeste occupied, the young girl was restive. The room lay almost completely black, but she seemed to see a shadow move. "Tor, are you there? Tor?"

"I am here, girl."

"Are you asleep?"

"No. How can anyone sleep in such a shut-in place?"

"I thought I saw—"

"Nothing. The shadows of the moon."

"I did not say what it was."

"Were it a person, I would kill him before he could walk across the room. No good person comes in the dark."

"There. It moved again."

Tor laughed. "Here, I will light the lamp for you," he said. He stooped to the punk box, blew gently, and eventually drew a flame from the welling smoke. The lamp threw strange shadows on the room.

"See?" he asked. He glanced out the doorway down the hall. "If you will feel safer, I will shut and lock the door."

"Yes. Please do that. Where is Raran?"

"With Tristal."

"Could Raran be with me?"

"Not now, little one. Move over." Celeste moved close

to the stone wall, and Tor blew out the light and lay next to her. She put out her hand and curled it around his arm.

"It is like the four of us at the overhanging place again."

"Yes. Can you sleep now? You mustn't tell the Haframa. She will have it that I will give you more diseases."

"Perhaps you will, but I think I have had most of them now." Celeste said no more, and soon Tor heard the slow breathing of her sleep. He lay unmoving, staring into the dark. The shadow had been a person. Tor had felt him in the hall before he entered the room—it was a scent, a taste of smoky earth, the sense of fear. Celeste had called out when the presence was two steps into the room. Tor's hand had gone to his axe and begun to lift it from its looped sheath. So the Pelbar conservatives feared the girl that much. Well they might, really. But this would not do. Sick or not, Tor would take her from the city if necessary. Eventually he rose quietly and checked the door. Then he returned to the bed, and he too fell asleep— about the time Tristal drifted across the river on a log to the west shore, where he could travel more openly. Raran swam beside him.

☐ VI

AFTER she stood her guard, and was relieved at dawn, Ahroe went through the high halls to Celeste's room. The door resisted, so she rattled it slightly. Tor slipped the bar almost immediately, let her in, and shut the door again.

"What is this?"

Tor shook his head slightly and shifted his eyes toward the dozing girl.

"This is from— This is for you." She handed him the note. He took it to the window and read it slowly, frowning slightly. Ahroe waited by the door.

"Have you room at your house for Celeste?" he asked. "What has happened?"

The girl stirred, and Tor turned to her and said, "We'll be out in the hall. I will not go before the Haframa comes."

After they closed the door, Tor said, "Someone came into the room in the dark last night."

"I was afraid of that. What did you do?"

"I came within a dog's whisker of killing him. Celeste saw a shadow and spoke out, and I answered. Then he slipped out and I locked the door."

"The Protector has decided to put a guard on the door at all times."

"Can she be at your house? Can a guard be put there? I am sorry that Raran is gone for a time."

"Moving her is up to the Protector—and the Haframa. But I can see that we will have to have a full council meeting on her soon. It is curious. She is so young."

"In some ways. She explains about her microorganisms and her chemicals and what are they—molecules? Ions? She makes the heads of your best people swim. They don't believe her, but she dazzles them with mathematics, then goes to sleep again with a fever."

"You believe her knowledge, then."

"Yes. I don't understand it. But it has the right feel. She is so sure of it." He paused, then added, "I brought her. Perhaps I should take her away."

"To what?"

"That is it. To nothing. Nothing but safety. At least Pelbarigan has something of the same feel for her as the dome, I think—enclosure, stone, barriers."

Later that day, Celeste was removed to the small stone house that Stel and Ahroe had built on the bluffs, outside the city to the south. She was carried by guardsmen on a litter, the Haframa attending. It was for her health, it was said. Clusters of citizens watched from walls and windows as she went. The routine of her convalescence set in. Tor was free to take a run to the oxbow lakes, but he was gone only two days. Celeste seemed to look for him constantly, but she never seemed to notice that Tristal was not around.

Toward evening three days later, Tristal, astonished, stood on the west bank of the river below Northwall. He knew that the Shumai had begun to gather there, but the flat land on the west side of the river stretched far with cultivated fields. Stone houses stood in streets, and across the river, other houses climbed the low bluffs and stretched east behind the city. Flatboats and log rafts lay in the river. Smoke rose from numerous fires, and people moved in the fields and streets. Cattle and horses grazed in pastures. Horse-drawn carts were visible. Following the Protector's instructions, he picked out what he thought must be Jestak's house in a cluster of dwellings on the hills north of the city.

It was dusk when he reached the area. In front of a nearby house he saw a bald man, somewhat stooped, sitting alone. He gave the man the Shumai greeting, then put his finger on the man's lips, quickly and lightly.

"You must be Stantu. I am Tristal. I must see Jestak."

"He is inside there, Tristal, if you can get by his daughter."

Tristal smiled, but Stantu's look maintained his deep sadness. The young Shumai left Raran with Stantu and went to the entryway of Jestak's house, then rapped on the heavy door.

It was opened by a girl slightly younger than he— Jestak's daughter, Fahna. She was just catching the bloom of young womanhood, at an early age. Her mother's dark beauty had been poured out on her, so that even this young she turned heads when she passed. She was used to it and enjoyed it. She was Jestak's daughter. It was a proper homage to pay her. And her mother, Tia, was also both beautiful and prominent, as the special friend of the former Protector, the famous Sima Pall, who had helped Jestak transform Northwall.

Fahna saw the Shumai boy, so fair he seemed wholly a bundle of dry wheat. She was prepared for the shock, confusion, and pleasure in his eyes, but he seemed to look through her.

"I am Tristal. I have come to see Jestak," he said.

"You? You must know he is too busy to see boys. Come back later—perhaps tomorrow." She went to shut the door, but his foot held it. She frowned.

"What is your business? Get out of here."

"I have told you my business," he said simply. "I am Tristal. I must see Jestak."

She stamped at his foot, but he moved it, holding the

door with his shoulder. A woman came, saying, "What is it, Thistle? Oh, who are you?"

"Tristal. I must see Jestak."

"Come in." Tia smiled and opened the door, much to Fahna's dismay.

Tristal entered, and when the door was shut, and Tia waited, he said, "I have a message."

Tia went to an inner door and opened it halfway. Light angled out from inside a rear chamber. Tristal could see heads behind Tia's. "A young man with a message for Jestak," she said.

He was ushered into the back room, and the door shut Fahna out. Her eyes narrowed. It was unfair. Strangers always came in to her own house, and she was kept away from them. And this wretched boy, all knock-kneed and high-voiced—he had not even noticed her. She went outside, where Stantu smiled slightly at her, his hand on Raran's head. She turned and went back inside.

Inside the room, Tristal unlaced his quiver and handed Jestak the tight roll from his mother. Two of those inside were Shumai, both men. A Sentani man and woman also sat at the table, and Tag, Stantu's Pelbar wife, stood leaning over it, still studying the map spread out on its surface. It showed a series of streets, and a perimeter, but Tristal only glanced at it. He watched Jestak—the great Jestak—reading the message he himself had brought, his eyes flicking across the lines.

Jestak sat down. He tapped the message on the table edge a few times.

"What is it, Jes?" said Waldura, an older Shumai dressed like an axeman.

"I don't know. Maybe nothing. Maybe everything. I may have to go to Pelbarigan. But I must have a reason. My mother says this girl we have heard of—Celeste—is indeed from the dome the Shumai watch at equinox. This young one and his uncle found her."

"His uncle?"

"Tor."

"Tor, then. The southern axeman. This must be a story. You—what is your name?"

"Tristal."

"Have you eaten? Can we get him some food? We will have to hear it all." A stew was brought, and all listened to Tristal—even Fahna, who had come in with the food—as Tristal recounted the events relating to Celeste, accenting the need for secrecy. As he spoke, Fahna frowned quizzically. He was in love with the girl. She could see that. The wretch. Even though he described her as weak and spindly, he loved her. Anyone could see that—except these stupid adults. Well, then, forget him. But still, he was earnest and modest, and even if he were a boy yet, he had a fine profile, with that true Shumai verticality of facial planes, as her father loved to call it.

Finally, when Tristal finished, they fell to musing.

"What does your mother say, Jes?" Waldura asked.

"Here, I will read you the part about the dome people —which is most of it," he replied, holding the paper quite far away:

"Beyond what you have heard about the child, Celeste, and the dome, there are some larger considerations. I have talked to her enough, and heard enough more, to know she is a chink through which the knowledge of the ancients pours, but increased. Our conservatives are afraid of this. If the ancients destroyed all once, they hold, does it seem right to reintroduce the new knowledge? What we know of the time of fire, from our tradition, from your travels, and from such other sources as the journey of Stel and Ahroe, indicates a destruction of almost unbelievable scope.

"Our conservatives say we must grow in wisdom before we can risk knowing so much again. I fear some would go so far as to harm the girl and destroy the dome. Most are merely worried, seeing the coming events as a real forking of possible futures for the Pelbar. But you would be surprised at how wide the concern is. Some, like Stel, want to go to the dome and make immediate contact with the people inside. Tristal thinks the girl is afraid of what is inside, though she will not talk about it. I am inclined to think he may be right, though it is only surmise.

"Would Northwall want to take a hand in this? Can you come and see the mood here? Can you talk to Stel and Ahroe, and to Tor, the Shumai? He is a remarkable man, though developed in only one direction.

"If you come, it should be on some pretext. The conservatives would resent my throwing your weight behind my views—and that is the way they would see it. Tristal must come separately in time and direction. Please read this letter to the Protector in confidence. We will not act independently of her, or Northwall, but I would much appreciate it if the Lauryna could empower you, on her advice, to convey her views to me. Perhaps Waldura could give the opinion of the Shumai, through you. In such a matter, your small Sentani community must be consulted as well.

"I believe we may in the end send a very small group to try to make contact, but this may be the last of my important official acts if we do. That is all right with me, because I wish to retire to Northwall to be near you. However, the transfer of power must not be to the Dahmena, who is, as you must imagine, the chief opponent.

"I look forward to news also of these rumors of a movement of the Peshtak. Are you safe with your outlying settlements? If you cannot come, please send a message by Tristal. Feed him well, and that smelly dog of his. Give my love to . . ."

Jestak sat back again and looked around. Waldura sighed. "If I come, then it will be obvious that we have been asked. That would not sit well."

"No. Pelbarigan is already upset that we have out-grown them, and that we are more than half outside tribesmen now. They would tend to choose what we do not want."

"We would want, I assume, to make the contact," said Rayag, the Sentani woman. "I can see no way to avoid it, really, and be true to Atou."

"Perhaps Mother already sees the direction of compromise—a very small group may go, so small it may not succeed. There will be a full council, no doubt."

"What concerns me more right now are the rumors of the Peshtak," said Tag.

"They are more than rumors," said Rayag. "But it seems not to be a general movement."

"Let Tor speak for me," said Waldura. "But be sure he assumes the position of a Shumai settler."

"Is that possible? I had heard he is the quintessential axeman."

"If he is, then one of his main assets is a vivid insight and imagination," Rayag returned.

"Well," said Haeol, the other Sentani, "I can see no other way than to try to make contact. Here are the issues. If there are people in the dome—and that is now obvious—they are in trouble if they stay there. We all, as honorable people, are bound to try to help them. Then, if they have knowledge, we could not only benefit from it, but we had better make them a part of us rather than against us if they get out. And with the land so empty as it is, it would be a long time before any time of fire were again needed by anyone, for any purpose. In that time, we could perhaps learn the skills of interaction that the Pelbarigan conservatives are worried about. Furthermore, we seem to be capable of immense destruction without any devices they might bring us. The fight for Northwall showed that. That was disruptive and murderous enough, was it not?

"Then there is this other aspect, which I admit is only speculation. Let's assume that the Peshtak are moving westward. What would push them? Not the Coo, with whom they are occasionally rumored to be allied. Not the Lake Sentani. The Peshtak have raided in the territory of the Tall Grass Sentani, so our reports say. That leaves only the eastern cities, exerting pressure westward. If Celeste's people have any knowledge that would help bring our power into a balance with the cities of the east, then the people in the dome will be an asset to us."

Jestak sighed. "You seem to have worked it all out, Haeol. I still can't ignore the fact that we are clearly all one people, from the eastern cities to the western mountains and beyond. I would hope to end our power struggles and see our unity."

"With the Peshtak?"

"That would be hard, I admit. But think of the dome people. Assumedly, they have been inside that structure ever since the time of fire. How pathetic that is. Some of them must be descended from blood relatives of some of us. They are surely of our culture—or what it was. We must rescue them as we would snatch somebody from a fire. What is the matter, Tristal?"

"Nothing. Just chilly, sir."

"There is another thing, too."

"What, Jes?"

"If they are people of great knowledge, perhaps they will know how to heal Stantu of his affliction from crossing the empty place."

Tag gave a light, fluttering, and bitter laugh. "Then I will go and dig them out with my bare hands."

"The dome is in an empty place," said Tristal. "Stel hoped to build a rock causeway out across it from the edge to the dome. It is near the edge, and the barren part is shrinking."

Jestak rose and crossed the room. He was limping very slightly, as he had ever since the battle at Northwall. He put his hand on Fahna's head. "Quiet, then, little one?"

A flare of annoyance crossed her face. "Of course," she said. "If that boy could bring the message, I can surely be quiet about it." Tristal blushed, and Tia moved her eyes from the boy to Fahna, amused.

"Tag," said Jestak. "Perhaps you and Stantu could put Tristal up tonight." His arm went across the boy's shoulders and squeezed him sideways. "Tristal, you are already in Heart River history. The man who found the first of the dome people." Tristal blushed again. "Now," Jestak added, "I will seek an evening audience with the Protector." He left abruptly, and Tag slowly rolled up the map as the others rose and began to leave.

Tristal and Tag were alone, with Fahna in the doorway, when Tag finished tying a string around the map cylinder. "How old are you, Tris?" she asked.

"Fourteen. Just fourteen."

Tag shook her head. "Had Stantu not had his affliction, we might have had a son almost as old. See Fahna? She is Tia's first, and Tia and Jestak were married less than a year before we were. Here, let me look at you." She took Tristal by the shoulders and looked at him straight-on. "You even resemble Stantu a little bit."

"I see no likeness whatsoever," said Fahna in the doorway.

"Ah, Thistle. I am glad to see you like him, too. Watch out, Tristal, or she will thread you on her necklace of admirers. Well, how good it would be to have a child like you." She suddenly clasped him against her. His ear squeezed tight against her breast, he could hear the even thumping of her heart. Then she quickly let him go, and said, "Come, you will need to wash and sleep. It may be a good idea for you to leave before light." Turning again, she rumpled his hair. "But you can come back and stay when secrecy is not important. Really. You could be our son."

"But Tor—"

"Yes, your uncle. Remember, though."

They passed into the front room, where Tia sat with two children smaller than Fahna. She was reading to them from a book with large pages.

"Did you have enough to eat, Tristal?" she asked.

"Yes, thank you. It was very good. Raran and I have been living on rabbits and fish on the way, and neither of us likes fish."

"Raran?"

"My dog. She is with Stantu."

"Stantu has always been natural with animals. All of them love him right off."

"Hold me once more, Dexter. I don't want to leave. Why can't we tell the others? Let me stay with you. Surely they will see that their genetic methods have not worked."

"Not yet, my love. We will have to be careful. They may separate us, or drug us. Then we will feel nothing for one another. Now. You must really go before 2920. I am due to make a routine check of the rodentry, by instrument from here, and that is something they could monitor."

"Oh, Dexter. What are we to do?"

"Do? Don't worry, Ruthan. It will all work out all right. Now, please go. The hallway is clear."

Ruthan kissed him and slipped out the panel. Dexter turned, shook his head, and suddenly grinned to himself. He ran his rodentry check. Nearly all was in order. But on row 27B, another mother had unaccountably killed two newborn offspring. He would have to go over that. This tendency seemed on the increase. He touched a control, and a panel slid back, revealing an enormous, and fat, white rat. Dexter took an algae biscuit in his lips and held it up to the animal, which put its pink paws against his cheeks and reached out to nip the biscuit from his mouth. He dug her in the fat belly with a forefinger as she retreated into the cage to eat it.

"Ha. My love, very good. You do tricks almost as well as Ruthan, and you are much easier to satisfy. You get your reward and go." He shook his head. "It is a different sort of game, Ariadne. Rodents seem to think much more clearly than humans. You are so marvelously objective. Don't you think so?" He held up three fingers. Ariadne nodded her head three times and went back to her chewing. "Ah. I'm glad you agree." Dexter chuckled, commanding the front panel to shut. Then he set out for the rodentry to harvest the mother rat on row 27B and reassign the remaining tiny newborns to mechanical feederwarmers.

Raran still sat by Stantu, panting lightly. She stood as Tristal and Tag came, then turned and rooted her nose under Stantu's hand. Stantu rubbed her nose, then, with effort, stood.

"Look, Stan. Tristal could be a member of your family. See how he looks like you," Tag said.

"I saw. The south Shumai often look like that. It is a small group. Well, did you settle your business? I saw Jes go to the city."

"We are settling it. Tristal will stay with us tonight. I think he will probably leave before sunup, to separate his coming from whatever has to be done. Tris, will you be rested enough?"

The boy shrugged, arms out. "I'm all right. I will run a while, probably, then rest tomorrow afternoon. I am in no hurry."

They went inside and prepared Tristal a basin of water and a place to sleep on a small, raised dais in the front room, under the west window. They gave him two fresh-smelling quilts and a feather pillow, then went back outside to the bench there. Tristal heard them conversing in low tones as he prepared for bed. He was not sleepy and watched the moonlight move slowly across the wall. He heard Jestak return, and further low talk. After a time, Tag came in and went toward the inner room, then paused, looked at Tristal, and came and sat by him in the semidarkness. He didn't move. He breathed evenly, and guardedly squinted at Tag, who gazed dimly down at him. After a time Stantu came in.

"Stan," she whispered.

He paused and turned. Then he came over and sat on the other side of Tristal, the only room left on the dais. They sat silently a long time.

"You mustn't bring these feelings up in yourself, Tag," Stantu whispered.

"It is not sad. Look at him. Isn't he beautiful?"

"Beautiful? He is a boy, Tag. But he is a handsome one, yes."

"Do you think he might stay with us?"

"Tor is really his father now."

"But this Tor has had to give up his band and his hunting. Would he not want to resume it?"

"I don't know, Tag, my love. We have to face it. I will not be with you long. My helplessness increases. I don't know how you stand me now as I am, doddering and useless, ugly and sagging."

Tristal could hear Tag sobbing very quietly.

Finally she said, "You—you have changed some. It would be idle to deny it. But you still have the same spirit. And you still radiate calm loyalty. Look. Didn't the dog still feel it? She accepted you instantly. Those things are what you are to me, and they will always be there."

Stantu sat silently a long time, then whispered, "You still have never experienced the wild free life Tristal has known, with the wind in your face, the open skies of the plains, the joy of running, the sharp points of the stars when you are sleeping out uncovered, alone at night—the whole sky alive with them, each in its place, and you thinking, Here I am, alone, alone with Sertine and all the lovely earth, and hard enough to bear it, to love it, to feel it run through my backbone. That is what he has known, my love. He has no Tag to draw him from it, and he has Tor to lead him to it. Let him sleep. If it would please you, we can talk to Tor about it. Let's not trouble the boy. He has his own life. Ours has been rich, but it is full of trouble. Let's not pull him into more trouble."

"Kiss me."

The two leaned across Tristal and slowly kissed each other. Then they quietly went into the inner room and shut the curtain. Raran, who had been sitting by the door, came over to Tristal and clumped down by him, stretching her neck out and sighing.

Tristal lay thinking. He almost felt like crying out, "Yes, yes. I will stay with you. It doesn't matter, Stantu. When you die, Tag and I will—" No. Tag was still young enough. Her wound would close. Someone would fill Stantu's place, though that would seem unthinkable to her now. She would have her peace. Tristal realized that he was the embodiment of a lost hope, lost as part of the continuing price of the time of fire, and feeling that, he felt more alone than ever. But he also felt the hard strength of Tor's loyalty—and his own unaccountable attraction to Celeste. Raran edged closer to him. At last he slept, sinking into it like a deep pool, deeper and deeper, as if forever. Then he felt a hand reach down into the well of his slumber and gently draw him out of it.

It was Stantu. "I have fixed you some breakfast," he said, giving Tristal a pouch. "Eat it after you have crossed the river. Go upriver first. You will find a path to the bank. Look for three cottonwoods. A boat lies fast to one of them. Take it. We will return it. Draw it up on the west bank and tie it to one of the silver maples by the shore near the stone wharf. Good-bye now."

Tristal sat up, still drenched in sleep, but shaking it off. When he stood, Stantu embraced him, and Tristal felt the residual strength in his back and shoulders.

"Good-bye, Stantu," he said. "Tell the others good-bye. May Sertine bless you all." He returned Stantu's embrace, then turned and left the house, Raran at his heels. He felt the shock of cool night air and came suddenly awake. The first hint of light grew in the east. He stirred into a silent jog, which he maintained until he found the path to the bank.

He was on the river, watching the west bank beyond Raran's upright ears, before he really felt alone and wary again, as if the circle of thought from the hills above Northwall radiated outward, and he had just broken through it. It was like a dream. Were Tag and Stantu real? What had he heard in the night? Did Tag really think to assuage her own agony with a boy like him? What a mistake she would make there. Tristal cinched the boat line fast and trotted westward along a clear path upriver from the Shumai farms. Lights glowed from some of the houses. Tristal stirred his sleepy legs to be beyond them when the dawn finally rose.

VII

ONCE again Eolyn was worried. She had rechecked *The New Yorker* tapes. Clearly those slender shapes from ancient times, mouths pursed in hauteur, resembled her. She had even shaken out her hair and redone it, clasping it with the finest polyethylene lab clips, in pale yellow, and Dexter still didn't notice. But he seemed also to stay aloof from Ruthan. That was new. On her part, Ruthan maintained her usual demure bearing, as well as apparently being wholly fascinated by some new genetic studies she was conducting on her beans and tomatoes, but also, to Eolyn's awakened eye, she seemed to glow in a quiet radiation of satisfaction. That itself was a clue. Something was going on. Eolyn determined that she would find out.

Late that time cycle, she prepared a tiny electronic tracer for each, as small as the moon on her forefingernail, and as they stood chatting before seating themselves for a meeting of principals, she managed to affix one to each of their neckbands. The minuscule, flat, adhesive buttons were designed to transmit only when in proximity.

Then Royal called the meeting to order to discuss the disposition of Butto and the comps. The aberrant principal had now recovered from his drug-induced confusion and seemed calm and sensible. For the moment, though, they kept him confined. The comps also remained partially sedated, though otherwise apparently drug-free. The one exception was Bill, for whom Cohen-Davies had spoken, then Dexter. As a result, he was made an official principal, replacing the dead Zeller. Whether that would work, with him directing his former equals, remained to be seen.

Royal began the meeting with his own report on Butto. "My examinations and tests have confirmed several things regarding Butto," he said. "The depression which caused his creation of that strange nest down on level seven was entirely drug-induced. He now shows none of those tendencies and is, in fact, amazed and uncomprehending when I explain his former behavior to him.

"Then, too, I am not wholly sure that he is free of echoes of drug behavior, because spontaneous combination of chemicals he has absorbed has created new compounds related to hallucinogens, and the components of these compounds remain, in tiny amounts, in his system. New compounds could form at any time and reinduce his former state.

"Furthermore, Butto exhibits the oddly emotional nature that seems to harbor and perpetuate such reactions. An individual like Eolyn, with her superbly logical attitudes, would be able to handle the situation well enough.

"However, Butto has a reason for depression. He has discovered that the fluids in our genetic banks have not kept well. The production of monstrosities in the Brat Shack is not wholly a matter of his lack of skill. Microscopic examination of cells chosen at random has indicated a disruption of the genetic structure. He has gone over the whole history of the storage of these materials, and as far as he can tell, there is no fault in it. He concludes that their capacity to remain in storage is limited. He has tried to induce growth from whole cells, as in the theoretical cloning process, but has not had success.

"Furthermore, Butto has found that tests on the present people of the dome and levels indicates that much sterility is present. Of course, he has not tested all. But he knows that all the comps, he himself, and probably Eolyn are incapable of producing offspring. Zeller was sterile as well. I know I am too old, as Susan is, of course. Celeste is nowhere to be found. He proposes testing the others as soon as possible, and I concur.

"I suggest allowing Butto to resume status as a principal, while monitoring his condition as closely as possible to insure that he will not revert to his depression, and, while under it, perform some disastrous action against the survival of our environment. Are there any questions?"

None was posed. By silent assent, the principals readmitted Butto to their number, and he was summoned by Bill, who freed him from his confinement. He came, thinner, rubbing his hands, sheepishly embarrassed, but also grinning, elfish, and apparently bubbling with good spirits.

He sat down without a word, then, casting his eyes

around, stopped his look at Eolyn and whistled lightly. "Well, Eo, you surely look lovely. Have I awakened in paradise? Are you an angel? Bill is your cherub, surely. We must bring in the other comps to hover about—"

"Butto," Royal interrupted. "If it is all right, we have business to conduct."

"Ah, yes. True. Sorry." He looked down abruptly but continued occasionally to gaze at Eolyn.

"Bill, have you investigated the dome, as requested, for signs of anything Celeste might have done there?"

"Yes, Royal," said the small man, "I have, and I found the seal on one lower door had been burned back, probably with an ultrasonic pointer."

"A lower door? But that leads only to earth."

"Not any longer, I believe, sir. I tested the locking levers and found they moved quite easily. I could see that the pointer had cleaned them as well. While I was moving them, the door cracked open, and light entered."

Eolyn gasped. "That would admit radiation. What was the reading?"

"Extremely low, Eolyn. Less than a ten thousandth of that emitted by our upper wand."

"Did you investigate further?"

"No, Royal. I didn't feel authorized to. I returned directly to decontam. My opinion, though, is that Celeste has left the dome by means of that door."

"Poor child," said Butto. "She has surely died of radiation by now, or is wandering lost out there if she took supplies. If you wish, I shall put on a radiation suit and try to find her."

"Impossible," said Eolyn. "She would be dead by now. The wand readings are such that no one wearing a radiation suit could long withstand them. We must regard her as terminated."

A silence followed, interrupted by Bill, who said, "There is an even more grave implication to all this."

"Yes?"

"If that door is above ground, and the slope, as viewed by our one window, descends toward the far end of the dome, then the entire dome must be suspended in midair, including the whole weight of the isotopic generator. I don't think the structure was made to withstand such stresses."

"There are pilings, all of reinforced concrete."

"I have checked the diagrams. I believe they are dangling in the air, and the generator is above them."

The principals looked at each other. Finally, Royal said, "Eolyn, can you construct a device that could tell us electronically about the slope under the dome. It would have to operate through the floor."

She pondered. "I don't know. I will try."

"Now then, Butto, please check the comps. Put them back into service as soon as possible. Bill, go over the recycling tanks and the algae. The rest, then, to our work. We will have to reconsider this. I can't conceive of leaving the dome and levels in such a storm of radiation. But it may be that the days of the dome are indeed numbered. It may be that we will have to sacrifice some to go out and reinforce the structure. I will give it some study. Let us then adjourn."

At that moment, in Pelbarigan, a full council moved quietly into the central council hall to discuss the matter of Celeste. All the quadrants of the city were represented. The guard stood fully in place, and as the sun reached the third quarter of morning, the Protector raised her staff for order and announced the proceedings.

"We are here, as you know, to determine our attitudes toward the girl from the dome—Celeste—and to discuss and decide what actions, if any, we will take to make some contact with the survivors in the dome. Since this is so important a question, I have designated speakers I know hold the three major opinions. Then additional views, if they are indeed additive, may freely be voiced. In keeping with the vital nature of these considerations, I here call for the whole assembly to begin four sunwidths of prayer in silence."

Then the Protector placed the heels of her hands against her eyes and sat perfectly still. Seeing this position, some immediately, some reluctantly, also assumed the position of prayer. The two inside guards flanking the Protector scanned the group, and soon all had at least adopted the prescribed pose. From far below, a faint sound of hammering could be heard, where workmen were erecting a scaffold to repair the wall.

Finally the clear, high *ting* of the triangle sounded, ending the prayer. The council removed their hands from their eyes, blinked, and then rubbed them. The Protector again raised her staff. "Now I request your attention to the Southcounsel, Obel the Ormana, who will speak in favor of making contact if that is possible." Turning, she extended her staff to the Southcounsel, as was the custom in formal debate.

Obel was a young woman for a family head, robust from her years as a guardcaptain. She stood and moved down to the front of her section, facing the three sides of the council chamber as she talked.

"I will try to be brief," she began. "But we feel there are several considerations in favor of aiding the dome people. First, they are human beings we know are in need of help. Our commitment to ethics and to Aven demands it. To refuse would be to turn back from the purpose that built the Pelbar cities. We are concerned not for our own safety alone, but for the restoration of the civilization we know was lost somehow. As we have gained perspective, we have seen that the loss occurred in the time of fire, when the whole land and all its people, but for small remnants, were eradicated.

"Second, it is evident from Celeste that much of the knowledge of the ancients has been preserved—at least their technology. She has already done much to teach us basic concepts of chemistry that she is amazed we didn't know. She is only a child. We must assume that adults exist in the dome. Their knowledge, and their means of conveying it, must be much greater than that of the child. We can offer them survival and help in adjusting. In return, perhaps they will render us some of the information that has now passed entirely from Urstadge, perhaps the entire earth, aiding us in restoring human greatness.

"Third, let us suppose that we don't aid them and they manage to leave the dome anyway. We would have a far greater chance of appearing their enemies, of earning only their hostility, not the gratitude that friendship brings. As Tor has told us, even Celeste carried a small box, which is some sort of weapon, we think. It affected Tristal's dog, he believes. But we know nothing about it. If such weapons exist, we would do better to be friendly with their owners than hostile.

"Fourth, let us suppose again that the dome people manage to leave the dome without our aid. Other peoples may ally with them to our detriment. If, for example, they went eastward and met the Peshtak, rendering them knowledge of their technology and weaponry, we would be in real and grave danger. Let us suppose again that the eastern cities gained that knowledge. We might once more be in some jeopardy.

"These are my chief reasons. However, the primary one is our devotion to Aven and the ethics that evolve from Her. Thank you for your indulgence." The South-counsel bowed formally and resumed her chair.

The Protector nodded to her, then pointed her staff toward the Northcounsel. "Dahmena, please give us the contrary view." The Dahmena, an old and slight woman, the mother of Ahroe, who had left the family in an old argument, stood, and with the aid of her assistant made her way to the central floor.

"Thank you, Protector," she said, bowing slightly. "We take the contrary view from that just stated. I have several points to present to you which would indicate, I believe, that it would be folly to aid these dome people and that for the good not only of our community but of all the Heart River peoples, this child, Celeste, should be kept happy but imprisoned here in Pelbarigan so that her pernicious ideas will not infect us as diseases have infected her so continually.

"First, we all know well that the Pelbar people are the real civilization of the Heart River country. While we have recently allied ourselves with the outside tribes, nonetheless we have gained nothing from them but peace. They have gained from us the central ideas of decency, the rule of women, forbearance, gentleness, justice, honesty, industry, learning, and above all a sound and organized religion.

"It is in that point, really, that the main thrust of my argument lies. What I have learned of this Celeste indicates that she has no knowledge of Aven or of this same Supreme Being called by any other name, even that of God, which our errant members have encountered in other cultures. Let us suppose that we were to rescue the people in the dome, and that they became influential members of the community. Naturally their views would be respected. They would have no knowledge of our cornerstone—our foundation—which is the worship of Aven according to the methods that our ministers have developed as correct over many centuries now. These methods have proved profitable not only for their truth but for their positive effect on the community, binding it together in the single purpose of goodness and order, as the leadership of womanhood alone will permit. I fear this would be lost. The effect on the Heart River peoples would be severe, indeed catastrophic. In fact, we might say it would set us back, far back, on the road of progress, and the truly faithful Pelbar, if they could not be left in possession of this city, would surely leave and found their own city, to perpetuate the true and just society they would be deprived of here. It would indeed be a tragic and unjust eventuality, destructive of righteous order in every way.

"In fact, I would advise, with much support, that not only should we not aid the dome people, but that we should do what is possible to see to the destruction of the dome, people and all, before its pernicious influence spreads."

A murmur of protest spread around the hall, and the Protector's guards rapped the floor with the butts of their long swords to restore silence.

"Does that complete your statement, Dahmena?" the Protector asked mildly.

"For the present, if it must. We will not give in on this issue."

"You will of course if the majority wills it so, Dahmena."

The Northcounsel did not reply, but resumed her seat in some agitation.

"Now one more view has been requested, that of Plaat, the chief of manufactures and stores. Please take the floor now, Plaat."

She was short, a wide woman who walked with something of a waddle, but with quick, businesslike motions.

Assuming the floor, she too bowed. She too began with the customary thanks to the Protector. "My view is brief, and does not involve any high-sounding philosophy," she continued. "It is simply this. Anything we do will have an impact on our supplies, our manufactures, our trade. There is more trade now. Northwall has outgrown us, largely by incorporating so many Shumai into its enterprises. They also have made greater use of power devices, both water and wind. We need technology. Celeste has already told us of methods of wood preservation, though she has seen almost no wood all her life. The potential for

us is too great to miss. Our men should be put to work involving skill, not made to labor like beasts if that is not
necessary. We need what we can gain from these people."
She abruptly took her seat.

The Protector raised her staff, but a voice interrupted.
"One more word, Protector, if it is possible."

"Yes, of course, Westcounsel, please speak—but only
if you offer new views, new material entirely."

"I believe I do, yes. Thank you, Protector." She stood,
a tall, thin woman, aged but erect. "This is also brief, but
very important. It is also a largely secular view. It has to
do with the men. Before the great truce, the old order
preserved our cities, with the proper judgment of women,
because the men had no alternative. Now conditions are
different. I understand that at Northwall Pelbar men are
often marrying Shumai women—as Jestak did. It gives
them more freedom. They are living outside the walls,
farming, trading, traveling. They no longer feel bound by
the rule of the law of Aven as we know it.

"We are feeling the early restiveness here. It is only
since last Buckmonth that Awkem, as you know, left his
wife and family, after a serious dispute, and went west.
The guardsmen found him at a Shumai farm over a hundred ayas from here, but when they tried to command his
return, they were resisted by the Shumai. There he remains.

"We must ask what effect on the men this new infusion
of technology will have. I am afraid that I agree with the
Northcounsel and disagree with Plaat. If the men are to
be kept to the order of Pell, then we had better continue
as much as possible as we have and avoid any more disruptive cultural elements. Now that we know more of
the time of fire, I think we may see in the rolls of Pell that
the rule of men, in ancient times, was largely responsible
for the great disaster that overcame the whole world.
That must not happen again."

"One contrary word, Protector?"

"Contrary? Very well, Ayfor." The Protector extended
her staff.

"The views of both the Northcounsel and the Westcounsel are serious ones, and of course, as a minister of
Aven, I deeply appreciate them. But I too have thought
long and deeply on this subject. It seems to me if the
truths of Aven depend on one physical mode of life, or

organization of society, and will be destroyed by another mode of life, equally moral, ethical, gentle, pious, then the word of Aven is weak. I do not believe it to be weak. I believe that if it is to prevail and bring order to all of Urstadge, as I hope it will someday, then it has to be flexible enough to meet the new conditions which will inevitably be coming.

"I have heard from Northwall that the effect of the presence of the Shumai and Sentani has not been to weaken the worship of Aven but to promote discussion, to include the outside peoples. Surely, then, this is a new challenge that our truth is valid enough to handle. I see no purpose in hedging in Aven as if the Governor of the Universe needed the walls of Pelbarigan to survive." Smoothing down her robe, Ayfor resumed her seat.

The Protector called for another prayer. Until high-sun recess, the debate continued in orderly and measured speech, though no substantially new views were added. At high sun the Protector called for a break of a full quarter of the afternoon, and when the group resumed much more agitation was evident. Plainly the people of similar views had been talking and saw an impasse developing. Seldom had the city been so divided. The Jestana was clearly worried, though her calm and occasional calls for silence kept the discussion in reasonable order.

As the sun was setting, the Southcounsel asked for the floor and said, "Council members, I believe we are not making much progress at the moment. Would it please you to call Tor, the Shumai? I would like to hear his views on the matter. After all, he found and brought the girl."

Protests arose as well as support. The Protector used her right of command to ask for the presence of the axeman, to glean his views both of Celeste and of the dome. "We must ascertain, without really asking," said the Protector, "what possible effect any action we take will have on the Shumai. They are now involved."

Tor arrived, his axe sheath empty, accompanied by two guardsmen, as the last red sunset streamed in the west windows and Eol lit the lamps. He stood bathed in orange light, his slim height far above anyone else in the room. He looked a little intimidated by the presence of the ranked rows of council members, all in their maroon tunics and overrobes, sitting formally, but soon his usual amusement returned.

Asked to state his views, he first held his hands out level sideways, in the Shumai gesture of unsureness. "Only two views permit themselves, I feel," he began. "Celeste is a little girl and must be protected in her innocence from any interference with her happiness. That is axiomatic. If you will not do it, then I will take her and do what I can. I brought her, perhaps troubling you overly, and I am willing to take her away. You must realize that any interference with her freedom is something I will resist. And if you take that lightly, I mean by 'I' all of the Shumai. They would regard harm done her as a matter of dishonor. I have been reading the rolls of Aven, though, and I know well that Pelbar principles, if adhered to, will not permit any such thing.

"However, there is another side. Clearly Celeste was fleeing from the dome. I know you understand this well. I am not sure we should try to make contact with, or aid, whatever it was that frightened her.

"And yet, as I am sure the right-minded among you have pointed out, if there are people in there who need help, and if we all withhold it, then we are loathsome and unworthy of consideration."

"You can say that, Axeman, because if things work out poorly, you can just leave." This interruption came from the north quadrant.

The guards rapped their sword handles, but Tor simply held up his hand. "I understand your concern. I have of course mused about all that. I am a wanderer. You are fixed in your city. Whatever happens, you are stuck with it, not I. That is the way it must look to you, but I would like to invite you to consider a contrary view, one which has prevented me in part from simply calling you a gang of hypocrites for not immediately helping the dome people. You see, I understand what it is to have one's way of life destroyed.

"I am an axeman. That may not seem much to you, but to me it does. Before the peace, we had a vital function. We followed the herds first. We constituted the main military arm of our people, an extra force to come in whenever and wherever needed. We also lived the most idyllic and adventurous life one can imagine. That is the life I know. Yet it is draining away. I have not found a new life. I could surely never accede to stay in a city ruled by women. I would find it hard to take up a farm as so many of my people have. That would mean an end of free running, of sharp danger, constant readiness, the peace of the lonely plains, leisure for contemplation and play. I am a man without a function, though I am looking to find one again.

"The opening of the dome may put you in a similar position. I see it as difficult, because I have experienced it. But adjustments must be made to new conditions. To hold to the old ways, which no longer are truly viable, is foolishness, and anyone so doing is already living in a dream.

"But I would like to stress that though you seem to feel that you have the only right to decide the fate of Celeste herself, you do not have that right. I forbid it. If you harm her in any way, I will die in her defense, and if I do, then I assure you that the peace will either end or be damaged. I am not asking anything but justice for a little girl. I am not threatening. Some voices among you are threatening. I would prefer to live, but I am not afraid to die for her. If you want that, you are of course free to choose it, but if you do, it will be the vicious among you who do, and if the vicious prevail, then the society is that much the loser. You know that as well as I.

"Why don't you accept your destiny and do the obvious good? Save the dome people if they can be saved. You may think that is a Shumai answer, and that we, the barbarians, rush in against logic, without even Sentani considerations, surely without Pelbar prudence. But we are a populous people, and we have not wholly lost out by our attitudes."

"You are also an orator," the Protector said, smiling. "However, we have to weigh many things in deciding this matter."

"Yet one thing you are not free to weigh, and that is the safety of Celeste."

"Will you allow a barbarian to threaten us in our own council chamber?" This voice came as a shout from the northern quadrant. "Take him. Take him and either eject him or shackle him!" Most of the council stood. Shouting was general, but over it and behind it the steady and loud pounding of the sword handles of the guardsmen slowly restored order. Neither Tor nor the Protector had moved.

The Shumai stood, hands clasped in front of him, looking at the floor.

When silence had been restored, he turned, and said, "Good evening, Protector," and walked to the door behind her. The guardsmen stood aside, after hesitating just a moment. Tor didn't even glance at them.

"Well, you certainly have covered yourselves with honor tonight," said the Protector. "This meeting stands adjourned from business. We will convene again in the morning at the end of the first quarter. I will give my decision at that time. I will not put it to a vote. We are divided enough."

"I warn you," said the Dahmena, "we will withdraw. We will start our own community free of this sinful revision."

The Protector sighed. "Were you addressing me?"

"Yes. You and all the other degradations of this place."

"Yes, what?"

The Dahmena dropped her eyes. "Yes, Protector," she muttered.

"I didn't hear you."

"Yes, Protector."

"You begin to overreach yourself, Dahmena. It perhaps would be best for Pelbarigan if you and your type did withdraw. However, we will not exclude you at this time. Now, under the circumstances, I feel it is necessary for us to end with a prayer, so we may all go with the peace of the Protector. Uld, set the sand timer."

The Protector set her palms over her eyes again and sat in perfect stillness. Again, the others followed suit, the north quadrant the last. The sand slowly filtered down from the upper glass, and at last Uld touched the triangle signal. After its light ring, the assembly rose and filed out in silence. The Protector remained, staring at the empty room, scarcely moving, her two guardsmen remaining behind her.

After a time, a guardcaptain entered and said, "Protector, Jestak is here to see you."

"Jestak? How fortuitous. Send him in, please."

"Yes, Protector."

Jestak slipped in, saw his mother's concern, and drew a chair near hers. "Hello, Protector. I brought a new pair of horses. And I came to inquire of this new person, Celeste.

Stantu is failing. Is it possible that she might know how to nullify the poisons of the empty place and save him?"

Adai turned and put her hand on her son's shoulder. "I don't know. You have come at a strange time. We have just had the most tumultuous council meeting I can remember. We insulted a guest, the Shumai Tor. The Protector was treated with discourtesy, and yet I practically let it pass. Perhaps it is near time I retired. Come. Come to my chambers so Uld can put out the lamps. I need some tea." She looked more closely at him. "The gray hair is moving up your temples," she said, reaching out to touch it. They stood and embraced, then she preceded him from the chamber.

Outside the cottage of Stel and Ahroe, shadows moved. Two guardsmen stood by the door, and the old Shumai, Hagen, sat outside, leaning on the wall.

"Guardsmen, are the windows barred?" the old man asked.

"Yes, we have checked them. Why do you ask?"

"Here come some skulking river rats after the child."

One guardsman lifted his horn to blow it, but a shrouded figure rushed from the corner of the house and took him off his feet. Another tied him, as three more took down the other guard. Hagen rose and shouted, rushing toward them. A sword flashed, striking him down. Torches flared up on the wall, and shouts called across. The shrouded figures returned the yells with guardsmen's answers, and three more ducked into the cottage. It was empty. They flung through the rooms, turning over furniture, looking in clothes alcoves, then, as torches approached from the city, ran out the door and away, leaving the guards struggling, gagged and bound, on the ground.

The lead guardsmen, short-swords drawn, panted up the slope. Reaching the guards on the ground, they drew off the gags and sliced the cords, as the two said, "They went inside. Look inside. Take care of the old Shumai." Turning, they found Hagen face down, bleeding profusely from the neck.

Soon a guardsman emerged from the house. "No one is in there," he said. "Did they get them all?"

"No. I think not. I saw them leave alone, six I think. They went up the slope. Call to the city. Have them shut the entrances. We must check the northern quadrant and guard the walls."

A light flared in the house, and Stel emerged. "You," said a guardsman. "I don't understand."

"We provided a hiding place. Hagen. Good Aven, Hagen."

Ahroe came out behind him and, with a light cry, ran to the old man. He was conscious and tried to smile up at her, though his face winced and twisted.

"Aven, Hagen," she said. "Why did you insist on staying outside?" Turning to the guardsmen, she added, "Help me bring him inside." They expertly lifted him and carried him on a rough litter into the front room. One guardsman ran for the Haframa.

"Celeste. They were after Celeste. Where is she?"

"Is she not here?" Ahroe asked, looking around. "Then she must be gone."

"Where were you hidden?"

"Hidden? They must have missed us."

"Come now, Ahroe. You must cooperate. We are trying to help."

"You must know," said Stel, "that there are all quadrants in the guard."

"You don't trust us, then?"

"You have been a great help, surely," said Ahroe. "You know we appreciate that. You also know that if Celeste had been here, she would be dead now. We thank you for all your help, and for saving Hagen."

"Come now, we couldn't help——"

"Shut up. Look at him bleeding. Who is following the intruders?"

"No one. It is pitch night. We would have no chance. We have set a watch around the city."

On the high bluff south of the city, far beyond the cottage, a figure running slowly in the dark stopped to catch his breath. He heard a sound, slight but close. "What? Who is there? Is it you, Begge?" Suddenly he was lifted, spun, and flung out and down, beyond the outcrop, turning in the black air, shrieking, striking the rough talus slope, sliding and bouncing down it until a small tree caught and stopped him. He moved a little, then lay still.

At the cottage, a guardsman caught the shriek. "Captain," he said, entering the house, "a scream from the south bluffs."

"A scream?"

"Yes. Far away."

"Sound for a triple squad, with torches. We will have to search the whole area."

The Protector and Jestak had no more than reached the Jestana's chambers when a guardcaptain came running, her boots clicking down the hallway.

She entered, breathless. "Protector, forgive me. There has been some sort of attack on the cottage of Stel and Ahroe. They hid. Celeste had already vanished. The two guards were tied and gagged, and the old Shumai, Hagen, took a deep sword cut on the neck."

"Is he alive?"

"Yes, but in poor shape, we fear. We have thrown a guard around the city. We are checking the northern quadrant as much as is lawful."

"Is anyone in pursuit?"

"Not at this time, Protector, in the night."

"Yes," said Jestak from the far room with the high window. "I see torches moving on the slope now."

"Then they have changed their minds for some reason," said the Protector.

"Protector, what of Celeste? Where has she gone?"

"Sit down," said the Protector. "Catch your breath." The guardcaptain complied, looking at the Protector, who rubbed her chin in silence. "I don't know. But I strongly suspect that Tor found a way to get her away secretly. He left the council meeting abruptly. He knew there would be trouble. I should have, too. But aside from Hagen, we have not done badly. And yet . . ."

"Yes, Protector?"

"This is the first such crime of Pelbar against Pelbar I can recall—discounting family troubles. This dome has certainly brought us trouble. How nice not to have any politics. To live alone in a walled city, the only people in a world without tensions. But that isn't the way the world is, is it?"

"No, Protector."

"Well, at least it isn't dull. Thank you for your report. If there are any more developments, come, or tell the next duty captain—at any time of the night, please."

"Yes, Protector." The guardcaptain bowed and withdrew.

Adai turned and faced her son. "You see how it is," she said.

"Yes. Good old Pelbarigan. Would you like me to go see Hagen, the old one? What if he dies? That will be very bad."

"No. You came with horses, and to find out if Celeste could help Stantu. Remember? And because I wish to talk to you about all this. What do you think?"

The two talked into the night. Jestak was far more willing to seize the saving of the dome people as a new opportunity, but his mother perceived that Pelbarigan, with its conservative strain, would not simply open its hearts to the new. Pelbarigan had to be cherished and gently led. And yet the city was tearing apart. She had to find a compromise answer. Northwall could not take this over. Nor could Threerivers, which was even more conservative than Pelbarigan.

Meanwhile, to the south and away from the bluffs, Celeste said, "Tor, how much farther?" She sat on his shoulders as he walked quietly.

"Less than two ayas. Not far."

"Two what? Oh, yes. Ayas. Each one is about one-point-three-five kilometers, I believe. But I don't know what that really is, either. We seldom traveled. I am afraid. But not with you."

"I have prepared a place for you, little one. I feared this day might come. After this, who knows? Your proper place is with the Pelbar, though. Perhaps we can go to Northwall."

The triple squad of guardsmen moved along the bluff edge slowly with their line of torches flaring the late spring woods, startling the roosting and nesting birds. Finally one guardsman sounded a horn. They had found a figure near the base of the bluff, dressed in black. The torches converged on the long, dark body splayed out on the lower slope.

"Is he alive?"

"There is a pulse. He is a mess, I fear."

"Turn him over very carefully."

"Who is it?"

"I don't know."

"I do. It is Cyklo. He is a blacksmith. Cyklo Dahmen, a Dahmen by birth. He is unmarried."

"Make a litter. We will have to get flat boards and bind him to it. We need straps and about three blankets."

At the dome, Eolyn was eating bean soup, a new recipe devised by Ruthan, or so Dexter had told her. This was the second time he had brought it. So unlike the standard food cubes, it was very tasty, but somewhat lumpy. Dexter had called it "unblended bean," left that way to bring out the texture, and to try the teeth a bit. She was alone in her room, studying a field diagram on her lightboard. She had been disappointed not to have caught the pair together. Her tracing transmitters had never yet sounded to indicate a proximity of under twenty centimeters. Perhaps she had made an error. She drank in the last of the soup. *There!* It sounded, and the winking light went on. She moved quickly over and fine-tuned it. That close? Amazing. Now she had them.

Commanding the panel, she slid out into the hall and jogged down it and around the corner to Dexter's room, quickly giving the override command on his door panel. It slid back. In a flash the hall was alive with running rats, white bodies skidding, sliding on the smooth surface. Eolyn screamed. Dexter put his head out the panel.

"Good galloping algae, Eo, what are you doing? Now I have to catch them all. I am training them, you know. Come. You must help."

Eolyn thrust her head into the room and looked around. The sounder continued its laconic beeping.

"What are you looking for? Come on and help." Dexter handed her a net and started off after the rats, commanding the far doors to close. Rodents scuttled around, squealing, as he deftly scooped them up, filling his net as Eolyn managed to snare only two. At last they had them all. Eolyn's sounder still sent out its thin notes.

"What's that I hear?" Dexter asked. "One of your electronic devices? That's unpleasant—like a mechanical rat. Shut it off."

Eolyn shut off the monitor. "What are you doing with all these rats anyhow?"

"Training them. I told you. I hope to get them to perform useful tasks someday. So far they are capable only of a few tricks. There. That's all of them safe." He hefted the bulging netful of startled rats. "Thank you. Now I have duties below at the rodentry, so excuse me. My class probably would like a rest after this chase. Shut the panel when you leave, please."

Dexter strode down the hallway with his rats, slid down the steel bannisters, and gleefully trotted along the lower hall. Entering the rodentry, he raised the light on the glow panels and returned all the rats to their cages. Then he commanded all the rats in the upper row to clap, as he himself walked back and forth on his hands in front of them, laughing. Then he sat on the floor. Tears streamed down his face as he continued to laugh. All the rats stood silent, watching him with round, black eyes. He lay full length on the floor, grinning up at them. "My friends," he said, "alas, how I wish you could have enjoyed that."

Eolyn returned to her room. What was wrong? She flicked on the monitor again. The sound began once more, high and annoying. Eolyn frowned. She pondered, then attached a directional indicator to the monitor. With her modules, that was the work of only a few moments. The needle pointed at her. She moved. It followed her. She moved again, and again the needle pointed its arrow directly at her. She turned it vertically. The needle indicated her midsection. She moved it close, raising and lowering it. So. It indicated her stomach. She felt through the waist section of her suit, removing the belt. That didn't affect the indication. Eolyn sat down. What could it mean? Oh, no. She had ingested the tracers—surely it was that soup. Dexter's lumpy bean soup. Damn him. Damn, damn, damn him. Dexter had outsmarted himself. Eolyn would set another trap.

As she turned, her door slid open and Dexter leaned in. He was serious. "Next time you want to know something, ask."

Eolyn trembled with anger and threw the monitor at him. He caught it and turned it up to full volume. Then he shut it off and entered the rcom, striding up to her and shoving her back on the sleep pad. She looked up, astonished. "You listen," he began. "If you interfere with me, so much as a finger's breadth, you'll regret it. That is a promise. You may be a domeleader, but I do my duties well enough. I will not be traced. I am not an experiment." His hand darted out and lifted her quickly to her feet by the hair. Then he slapped her face, fast, back and forth, twice, shoved her back, and left the room.

Eolyn lay on the pad, sobbing, angry, and helpless. After a time the door opened again and Ruthan came in. Eolyn sat up, red-faced. "Eo, what's the matter?" Ruthan asked, crossing to her and kneeling down.

"Get out, get out, damn you."

Ruthan didn't. She took Eolyn's hands, then put her arms around her and held her. "I told you to get out," Eolyn said against her shoulder.

"Why? What have I done? Tell me. I'm sorry." Ruthan leaned back, smoothed Eolyn's hair away from her face, and looked at her. Eolyn could see that she clearly knew nothing of what happened.

"I'm sorry. I was upset. Forgive me," she said. "Please let me alone now." Ruthan leaned down and kissed her forehead. "Please. Let's leave off the archaic behavior. I am upset."

"Of course. If I can help you, please let me, though." Ruthan commanded a wet washsquare from Eolyn's supply and wiped the older woman's cheeks and mouth, then handed it to her, patted her shoulders again, and left.

Eolyn sat staring. What did it all mean? Ruthan had just showed her more affection than she had felt in a long time. Eolyn decided that she liked it. But that itself was another clue. Perhaps Dexter had managed the trick with the tracers alone, but Ruthan had just shown her awakened affections. She even kissed readily. Yes, clearly something was going on between the two. What would she do about it? Now she feared Dexter. Perhaps it was a good idea not to hurt Ruthan, who was a potential ally. But the whole dome could not do what it pleased. Behavior must be planned. That was absolutely necessary.

Below the dome, the oil continued to seep and pool. The subsoil resisted its penetration, and the oil tended to gather behind a clay dam that had been formed beneath the levels. The old timber continued to wick oil upward to the oxygen-storage room, and the dark soak moved slowly through the soil from the cracked tank, downhill at a glacial pace.

VIII

JESTAK and his mother were still talking when the guardcaptain again knocked and entered. "Forgive me again, Protector, but one of the people at Ahroe's house tonight has been taken. It is Cyklo, a Dahmen. He was dressed all in black and had a sword. The sword had blood on it. He apparently fell from the bluff. He is still alive but in very poor shape."

"And the Shumai, Hagen?"

"The Haframa says he will recover unless things take an unexpected turn."

"Has the Dahmena been informed?"

"Yes. She is with Cyklo now. She openly condemns him for his actions in the most vituperative terms. She speaks of exclusion from Pelbarigan."

"Very clever."

"What?"

"Bring her to me here, please. You must come with her, Ithring, and stay with us. I am not as agile as I used to be."

"There is Jestak, Protector."

"He will not be here."

"Yes, Protector." The guardcaptain withdrew.

"You see how it is, Jes."

"Yes." He shook his head. "It is serious."

"Perhaps. But perhaps the Dahmena suggested the solution today in council. She threatened to withdraw, either to a new city or to Threerivers."

"Threerivers is all Dahmen, for all purposes."

"Perhaps. But to be conservative is one thing. To be violent is another. They have reached the point of breaking law, if indeed they have not really been doing it for some time. Threerivers is perhaps a proper environment for them. I am quite sure that Ales, the Protector, will not

104

permit their sort of tactics. Now you must go. Are you sleepy?"

Jestak laughed. "No, Mother. I have traveled since before daybreak and entered a rebellion. I am tired, but this is too interesting."

"I have changed my mind. Go to Ahroe's cottage. See Hagen if you can. If he is awake, send him my comfort and thanks. See to the others also."

"Of course." The two embraced, and Jestak abruptly left. The Jestana sat down again, thinking. Then she stood, moved the table, put her hair up for the night, changed to her night robe, removed all the chairs but one, and sat in it, turning the lamp to throw its light away from her.

The guardcaptain knocked, and the Jestana sounded her small bell of admittance. Ithring entered with the Dahmena, who was pale and tight-mouthed. The Protector looked up at her and sighed.

"I trust that your relative, this Cyklo, will recover in good time, and I hope that he has not been hurt badly."

The Dahmena said nothing.

"Guardcaptain, please search the Northcounsel and remove any weapons she may have with her."

"But—"

"Do it."

"Protector, I protest," said the Dahmena. "I will bring this up to the full council."

"Stand, Dahmena. I intend to carry out the orders of the Protector."

"I will requite you this dishonor."

"You have already. I assume you were addressing me."

"Yes . . . Protector."

"Thank you. Now, for once, you will listen and I will talk."

Ithring removed a small knife from the sleeve of the Dahmena's robe and a thin folding knife from her waistband. She handed them to the Protector, who hefted them in her hand. "Is it usual with you to carry weapons, Northcounsel? That seems an odd procedure for a council member."

"This is an odd council, Protector, and these are odd times. You see I have violent people in my own family. We see the whole Pelbar system undermined before our eyes. A strong Protector could halt this change. Not you.

I am afraid now. I feel the need to protect myself. We lived over a thousand years with closed walls. We could do it again and preserve our way of life."

"Not over a thousand years, Northcounsel. It was hundreds of years after the time of fire before Pelbarigan was built, as you must know. But that is not the point. You must realize that it is the duty of every social leader to help the society to survive. If we are to survive, we must meet the world on its own terms. Before the world began opening up again, the old Pelbar way served admirably. It no longer does. If we shut out the Shumai and Sentani, while Northwall has admitted them, quite successfully, and to its own enrichment, then we are dividing the peoples. You must see that."

"Why must I?"

"It is so obvious. You would otherwise be stupid."

"You seem to allow for no breadth of opinion, Protector."

"I do not? It is a marvel you should say that. Your family has had that reputation as long as I can remember. But I do not propose to argue the obvious with you, merely to offer you the options. First, continuing as things are is not one of them. You have gone too far. You will realize that our investigations will be full, and they will disclose what now lies hidden. I am absolutely sure that you will not retain your seat on the council. You may, as you proposed, take your party and construct a new settlement. We will even help you do it. You may, with the permission of Threerivers, join them. You may request a council vote on the matter."

"If we leave the city, the heart goes out of it. We have always been the backbone of Pelbarigan."

"You are its appendix, Dahmena. And infected. Now go." The Protector rose to leave the room.

"A curse on you," the Dahmena hissed after her.

"Are you addressing me?" the Protector asked, turning.

"A curse on you, Protector."

"That is better. As you leave, you might explain to yourself how the backbone of Pelbarigan curses when Aven does not curse and we are all worshipers of Aven. Now, Ithring, remove her."

The guardcaptain took the arm of the Northcounsel, not gently, and steered her toward the door.

As Jestak approached the cottage of Stel and Ahroe, he

heard a slight sound in the shadow. "Who is it?" he asked.

"Tor."

"Tor. Good. I am Jestak."

"Come and talk a moment."

Unhesitatingly, Jestak moved into the shadow, and the two palmed hands in greeting. Tor stood a full head above Jestak, who was not short for a Pelbar.

"Celeste, Tor? Is she safe?"

"Yes. She is snug and hidden. Where is Tristal?"

"He is on his way here, I assume. He is a fine young man. If you want Celeste to go to Northwall, she will be safe there, and we will welcome her."

"That may be best. We will see. She is only a child. It is foolish to treat her as she has been."

"She is a child, but also a charge of explosive. She stands to transform Heart River society, and some of us can't stand it."

"So I have seen. By the way, I took Celeste out the back—Stel's special provision—when we heard them coming. We were downriver on the bluffs when I heard one nearby. Celeste moved, so I had to pitch him off the bluff."

"Ah. That explains it. He is in the city now. He had blood on his sword, so they assume him to be the one who slashed Hagen."

"Hagen? Is he dead, then?"

"I don't think so. I have come to see to him in part. We should go to the house."

As they entered, they found Hagen lying, weak and pale, in the front room. His eyes shone when Tor entered and leaned to embrace him. Ahroe sat by him, her face wet. Tor introduced Jestak, whom Hagen had never seen, and the old man felt a certain awe in the presence of the man who had so changed the Heart River peoples.

Jestak knelt by him and took his hand. "Again the Pelbar have much reason to thank you. I'm afraid we have been much trouble to you."

"No trouble. I am glad everyone is safe."

"Safe? And how is the waif?" Stel asked Tor.

"Safe, too. Let's leave the rest to the guardsmen and go to bed," said Jestak. Tor waved to them and glided out into the darkness.

Deep in the north quadrant, a small meeting of women from several families heard the Dahmena say, "I have never been so humiliated. I seem to have lost control even of my own quadrant. Who authorized the attack on the girl? They all think I did."

"But, Dahmena, if you didn't, you surely indicated that you wished her out of the way."

"This time we have been so undercut that we may never regain position. We must have some reserve. Increasingly we are in the minority. Some drastic change is coming. This old city has been our home for so many centuries. How can we give it up?"

"Give it up? You mean you want us to leave Pelbarigan?"

"How else can we live?"

"We can perhaps adjust, you know, Dahmena."

"Adjust? Do what they say? They are destroying all that is precious. Never!" The Dahmena punctuated her statement by stabbing her palm with her forefinger. As she spoke, her voice rose, and for a moment she seemed to generate such an aura of anger that the whole room seemed to tremble with white light.

"Dahmena, you must realize that although we stand together as a quadrant when we can, I am not a Dahmen. I can't follow you in all things. Cyklo's action is hardly one of the whole quadrant."

"Nor of the Dahmens. I never authorized anything like that."

"But you made it clear that you wished it. I feel you have so weakened yourself that you must accede."

"I must do nothing not in our interest."

"Ah. You have already. Or it has been done. I know four families will not stand with you."

"I will repudiate Cyklo. I mean it."

"You have sharpened the knive and will not take it back now that it is bloody?"

"I will not accept that description."

"Moder is right, Dahmena," said the Judgema, head of the second largest of the north-quadrant families. "I'm afraid that you must listen. I have a proposal that has the backing of six families."

"Six? What is it?"

"Send for Ahroe. Ask her to come here and talk frankly. We must draw together and heal the wounds."

"Never."

"Then we will meet with her without you. We will explain our feelings. We join with you in deploring the presence of the girl. We do not wish to pursue contact with the dome. But we see the necessity of being civilized. If we lose our case, then we have lost, but as Pelbar. If we are afraid of renewed savagery, then we must not illustrate it ourselves."

"You would do that without me?" Again the Dahmena's anger took her. "I am still Northcounsel."

"At the moment." The Judgema went to the Dahmena and put her arms around her. "Please? We beg it of you. I think we have lost, yes. But we must act decently. We must recover our honor."

The Dahmena freed herself. "This shame is more than I can bear." She turned and left the room.

Moder turned and asked, "Well, should we ask Ahroe to meet with us?"

"I don't know. It is of little use now. Let us see what lead the Dahmena will take when she has thought further. We will have to play the numbers on the dice as they were cast."

Not long after, the Dahmena let herself out the small south door. A guardsman stood outside it. "It is late, Northcounsel," he said.

"Too late, I am afraid, guardsman. Do you object to my leaving by this door?"

"No, Dahmena. Some of those who attacked Ahroe's cottage are still outside, we believe. We are simply noting who is coming in."

"Yes. Very prudent. Good night."

"It is past midnight. Good morning, Dahmena."

She did not reply, but walked out into the dark and disappeared. He could hear her footsteps crunch the gravel path leading toward the river. Apprehension crept into him. She had violated no rule. But what she was doing was odd. Well, he would report it at guardchange. Shortly after, the door opened again, and Moder stepped out.

"Guardsman, I wish to speak with Ahroe. Is that possible?"

"I believe she is asleep, ma'am. Is that where the Dahmena went?—No. She went toward the river."

"The Dahmena? Toward the river? When?"

"Just now. Two sunwidths. Something is amiss, isn't

it?" He put his horn to his mouth and blew four short notes. "Wait here, please," he said to Moder.

The guardcaptain soon trotted up, panting. "Yes?"

"Moder wishes to talk with Ahroe. But the Dahmena just a while ago left the city here and walked toward the river. I fear something is wrong."

"The Dahmena? That way? Good Aven, what now? Stand your post. Blow six." As the guardsman blew, the guardcaptain ran down the path toward the city front, where, in response to the six blasts, torches flared on the corner post and south on the bluffs near Ahroe and Stel's. The guardcaptain appeared, running by the four guardsmen at the city corner, calling and waving.

"Bring your torches. To the river. We will see what is up now." They ran down along the bank, holding the torches high so as not to flare in their eyes. The flickering orange glow caught a figure downstream, waist deep, wading out.

"Halt," the guardcaptain called, panting, plunging into the water after the figure, which leaned forward, wading faster. The guardcaptain surged out into the dark river and caught the Dahmena at shoulder depth. She struggled, grim and silent. He twisted her arm back and gripped her across the chest, backing up as a second guardsman took her feet.

"Let me go," she screamed. "I have committed no crime. You have no right. I insist."

"Perhaps. Now, quiet. If you are correct, we will apologize. Come now. We have you. Relax. This is no place for an old woman."

"Old woman! What strange curse is on me? I can do nothing. I am thwarted even in my own personal wishes."

"Yes. Later. Look, here is Ahroe come down to the shore. Come now."

"Get her away. Let me go." The Dahmena struggled.

"Bring her up to my house," said Ahroe, grim-faced.

"Never. No."

"Please, guardcaptain. Mother. Please, Mother. Please come to me." Ahroe reached out to her as the guardsmen set her down, and held her mother against her. The old woman seemed to sag, panting, nearly limp. Ahroe supported her tightly. The Dahmena began to sob, uncontrollably. Ahroe said nothing, but waited for the older woman to recover her composure.

"You can't call me Mother. You repudiated the family when you returned from the west. I want nothing to do with you."

"For once in your life, Mother, can't you shut up? Come up to the house. You are all wet. Please? See? You are shivering. Look. Here is Stel. The guardsmen have a litter. We will carry you."

"Never," said the Dahmena, but when the litter was laid out, she sighed and lay down on it. Stel and Ahroe picked it up and carried her to the cottage on the bluffs. One guardsman carried a torch alongside.

The guardcaptain and the others stood on the shore looking after them. "I'll be a limp-eared, fish-gutted son of an everlovin' muck heap," he said. One of the other men laughed. The guardcaptain glared at him, then began to laugh himself. "Come on. I'm soaked. What stinking mud. Let's go and clean up. Urch. You go and get Sorge to replace me, and get Spon to come for Hayl. I can't believe it. Look where she is going, the old dried apple."

Stel and Ahroe laid the Dahmena down on the mats on the front-room floor. Stel got a towel and dry robe, then left the room as Ahroe helped the old woman out of her wet clothes and into dry ones. Nothing was said. Stel reappeared with a cup of hot tea and handed it to the Dahmena, who took it and sat down in a soft chair. Ahroe put a cushion behind her and kissed her. The Dahmena looked grim.

Finally she said, "I never sent those men up here. I would not do that."

"All I know is that they came," said Ahroe. "Hagen is badly hurt in the other room. I don't know why everything the Dahmens touch turns to misery. Surely you must feel it, Mother. Does it need to be that way?"

"Everyone laid the debt at my door. I tried to pay for it. I was prevented."

"No one wishes your death, Mother. Can't we just let all this go? Can't we say that the old Dahmena kept walking into the river and I have my mother back? Can't you just let politics take its course and calm down and live?"

"So much is wrong. It is just wrong."

"Please, Mother. Let all this wrong, wrong, wrong go

its own way. Relax. It is a big world. There is room for everyone."

"My world is Pelbarigan. I have lived here over seventy years, most of it shut away in fear of the tribesmen. It was a good world. It had order, discipline. Now that is all broken and sliding away."

"If clinging to it is such bitterness, why cling?"

"I am weary to death. Do you have anywhere I can sleep?"

"In our room is best. Hagen is there. There will be a little light because I am sitting up with him. He is asleep, though. I will be nearby."

"With Hagen? Well, that will have to do. I cannot go back home now." The Dahmena rose slowly, put down the teacup, and walked, with her hand on Ahroe's arm, into the back room. The doorway seemed to recede before her in her weariness.

Once in bed, she looked up at Ahroe, sitting in a chair, and at the old Shumai sleeping across the room. She was panting. Then she drifted off to sleep, and when she awoke again, it was broad daylight, and she looked up at Tor. He took no notice of her. He was frowning down at Hagen; then he reached down and adjusted the blankets. The old man stirred. Celeste stood behind him, thin and tired, looking at the old woman with fear. The Dahmena shut her eyes again. She was weary of all this. Fear, worry, hurt. Perhaps Ahroe was right. How had she let herself be brought here? She heard Tor talk softly in the front room, then heard Jestak's voice.

He was talking to Celeste. Would she know how to cure Stantu? No, she feared she would not. It was radiation sickness, Celeste thought. Royal would know. Who was Royal? The child had never mentioned anyone in the dome before, and when questioned, she didn't reply. The girl was frightened. See? Didn't that prove the Dahmena right? But strangely, at the moment the old woman was little interested in being proved right. She was still tired, so deeply tired she felt she would melt and seep into the mattress. She breathed hard. Her feet were cold.

Toward high sun a low, moaning cry startled her to wakefulness. Ahroe rushed into the room, looking haggard, followed by others, including the Haframa.

"Hagen. What is it, Hagen?"

"I can't move my legs. They—they lie there like wood."

The Haframa undid the bindings on Hagen's neck, while he winced. The wound was angry and swollen. Celeste looked over the Haframa's shoulder, grimacing with sympathetic pain.

"I don't understand," said the Haframa.

"Have you no antibiotics, then?" Celeste asked.

The Haframa turned and looked at her, puzzled. "No. It is infected. We tried to clean it as you described. No. We have nothing."

"It is the swelling. It has pressed the nerves in the neck or something. Unless they were damaged by the blow itself. It is serious."

"I can see that. It is beyond my skill now, except to dull the pain."

"If Royal were here . . ."

"Royal? From the dome?"

Celeste frowned. "He would be no good without his materials, though. Could we take him to the dome?"

"No, child. I do know that."

Celeste began to cry. Garet moved next to the old man and put his small arm around him. Ahroe drew her son away. They covered the wound and stood back, unable to lift him to drink because of his pain. Tor stood silent in the middle of the room, his mouth tight, through the whole procedure. Hagen looked up at him, and they exchanged a long, silent communication.

Ahroe looked from one to the other, eyes filled. "No. It is not so. You are wrong, Tor." She put her arms around Hagen, weeping.

Vague and sleepy, the Dahmena regarded this from across the room. What was all this fuss over a man, an old man, a Shumai, scruffy and ignorant? Her daughter, wrenched with sorrow, and the child Garet. Well, the child had known the old man all his life, as an infant had traipsed the dry plains with him in search of that wretch, Stel. Where was Stel?—there, in the doorway. His jaws were tight, too. This sort of sentiment was unnatural, unbelievable. She had never felt it, never. It belonged to Aven only. She had not felt it for her own husband, dutiful though he was, and meticulously obedient. Still, she missed him. She had hated his humming in the room, and forbade him to do it. He would, however, when she wasn't there. She would hear him as she came down the hall, but he had always stopped when she reached the room.

How silent the room had been when he died. He had
loved her. She knew it only when she had lost him. But
he was a man, and without judgment. Hume. She saw him
now, in her mind's eye, sad it seemed, and attentive.
A little frightened. She had sat with him while he lay
ill. She had even held his hand when he had requested
it. That was foolish, yet people seemed to want it. Look,
Garet held the old man's hand even now.

Why was she so cold, so tired? Perhaps she would try
to change when she recovered. She would try to rees-
tablish a relationship with Ahroe, whose concerned glances
she caught now and then.

The day wore on, turning gray and rainy. Stel propped
her up and fed her some soup, even blotting her mouth so
she wouldn't have to raise her hands. Late in the day, Hagen stirred and sat up.

He seemed to address Tor, who had never left the
room. In a low voice, he said, "The tall grass bends in
the wind. The dark bull has mounted the hill. Lashing his
tail, he scoops away all the stray light from the sky. He
flings it back as stars. One by one they blink out, Iox
and Til, Ruk, Mir, and Tosh, all gone. He is rolling, crush-
ing the earth. Ah, Sertine, it is I, Hagen. I am here. The
bull has lowered his head, his horns pointed like iron
stakes. He makes no sound, rushing at me. I see his
whole humped back looming over. Lift me up, Sertine,
lift me over." He sank back. Tor stood unmoving.

"What? What is that?" said Ahroe, her hands open and
fluttering toward Hagen.

"Leave him alone now."

"Why? No. No. What can we do?"

"Nothing. It is his death statement. He is willing to go
now."

"Death?" Ahroe whispered. She turned. Hagen was
looking at her.

"Ahroe, you have been better than any daughter,"
he said, his chest heaving. "Put me up by Fitzhugh."

"No, Hagen, no."

He did not reply, but closed his eyes.

Tor took Garet from the room. It remained soundless
except for the heavy breathing of the two old people.
Ahroe sat with her eyes closed, praying. Then, slowly,
she became aware that she heard only one breath coming
heavily—her mother's. She started up. Already Tor had

her arm and took her from the room, insistent, inexorable. In the front room he gave her to Stel, then left the house.

The Dahmena watched the three guardsmen take Hagen. He was to have a funeral, a service in Pelbarigan. It was wrong, wrong. Nothing was suitable anymore. She shut her eyes to it. Eventually, when she opened them, it was dusk, and the Haframa was looking down at her gravely. Again she shut her eyes. Soon she heard a sound and looked again. It was Garet, who took her hand.

"You are my other grandmother. I have never talked to you," he said.

"No. Not really, child. I—"

"Why is your hand so cold? Are you all right?" He set his palm on her forehead.

It seemed to her almost fiery. Had the boy a fever? She saw alarm in his eyes, already red with his crying over the barbarian. A thought glided past her as soundlessly as an owl's flight. No. No, that was not possible.

Garet turned abruptly and ran out the door, calling, "Haframa, Haframa."

She could hear the hushed voices of the boy and the old doctor in the front room. She dozed, waking to find a lamp burning by the bed. Moder's face was looking down at her, but then it faded away. In the dark, the boy eventually returned to her, slowly, like a lazy leaf in the wind, like a single snowflake, the first flurry of winter.

It wasn't winter. Why was she so cold? Lacking an overcoat, she seemed to feel herself hugging her winter tunic over her. Standing on the tower at Pelbarigan, she watched the snow out over the river, coming from the west, drifting in large flakes, graying and obscuring the dark trees. Her young husband, Hume, tiny and clustered with the others down on the river, cut ice. She could see, far below, the vague figures moving against the white. Again the snow increased, and she strained her eyes after him, Hume, down on the river, small and dark, entirely blotted out now by the cold and snow, falling, falling around her, mounding on the walls of the tower, heaping over all. What was it she was looking at? She forgot. Snow fell. The whole world was snow and cold, vanishing and vanishing.

IX

THE Protector, who had postponed the council because of the Dahmena's illness, postponed it again after her death and Hagen's. Then, she issued another controversial order. She commanded that the two funerals be held together in the chapel of Pelbarigan. The north quadrant, which normally would have bridled and protested, acquiesced in their shame, and as the service developed, in the tall, dim stone room, it seemed to acquire a strange logic.

The two coffins lay side by side on trestles, one the neat, plain boards of a Shumai hunter, the other the curved and polished, cloth-draped casket of the most adamant of Pelbar traditionalists. Here they came together in their passing. Hagen had become a local folk hero, through his western adventure with Ahroe, and was beloved by a large portion of the old city, especially by the men and boys. In their deaths, another striking story had been added to the city's aura, a contemporary legend commensurate with the flight of the two lovers, Ornay and Lynd, or of the courage of the guardsman Murdon, some eighty years earlier, when the Sentani had come upon the wood gatherers unexpectedly in winter.

The Protector chose not to speak, but to let the whole meaning of the event sink in through the singing of the Pelbar choir, fully massed, occupying the fore end of the chapel on raised steps.

Tor and Celeste stood on the side balcony, and as the songs rose, the sounds melding into one another, forming a swelling blend of sadness and exaltation, the girl took the axeman's hand, tears flowing freely down her face for the first time she could remember. She cried partly for Hagen, whom she had come to know, partly for the rich sadness of human drama joining this unlikely pair. An old order had struggled to maintain itself, then faded out into the new. How strange it all was, this depth of feeling, this web of relationships forming a large society, always altering and shifting—as if the commands she so familiarly keyed into the electronic networks of the dome would produce different results at different times, not the steady and reliable calculations she was used to. For the first time she caught a glimpse of the kaleidoscopic nature of humanity, its patterns changing, re-forming continually. It seemed frightening and unreliable.

In dying, Hagen had asked to be buried near his old Ozar companion, Fitzhugh. As they followed his coffin up the bluffs to Fitzhugh's high, south overlook, Celeste pondered this, still holding Tor's hand. The day was warm, and her hand sweat, but she clung to his, as Tor glanced occasionally down at her to see what was troubling her.

As Hagen was lowered into the neatly squared hole, and Ahroe sprinkled the symbolic grass on the coffin, and the shovel-loads of earth began to thud and thunder down on him, Celeste had another odd sensation. Was he gone? Would he always be here? She felt a vague unease. Recycling was neater, easier. What would they prove by this? What would Ahroe think every time her eye turned to that familiar bluff? As the grave was filled, and the earth tamped and mounded, Celeste raised her eyes and suddenly became aware of the flood of sunset light lying on the wild flatland across the river, filling the slight late-spring haze with a tinge of red. As she looked around, she saw it bathed all the serious faces in ruddy light.

Here was the eastern edge of Hagen's plains, stretching tirelessly westward. The sunset was receding across them, the light fading like his way of life, the free running of the hunter, just as the Dahmena's rigidities seemed softened by the glow of light on the stone walls of Pelbarigan.

She turned to Tor, who clasped his hands behind him, standing back. What was he thinking? He too was a runner, a hunter. She could not see him toiling in the city, digging in a field. Nor could he. She read that on his face. He caught her eye a moment, and they exchanged a full understanding. Then he winked and smiled slyly, and the moment passed.

Eolyn commanded entrance to Dexter's room. He lay idling on his couch, and looked up silently, giving her no welcome. She sighed and sat on the edge of his work-table. He still said nothing.

"Dexter," she began. "Please don't interrupt me until I am through."

"That sounds ominous. I have warned you not to interfere with me."

"It is not ominous. I am not threatening you. This is important to me. Now, will you listen?"

"Why should I?"

"For my sake? You may profit from it. I mean you no harm."

Dexter sighed, gave her a quizzical look, and sat up. "Go ahead."

"All right. Now I know, and you know I know, that you and Ruthan are—don't now. I am merely sketching in informational background—that you and Ruthan are seeing one another. I have told no one and will tell no one unless the dome and levels are threatened in some way by this. At present I perceive no threat. You are both careful and balanced people. My concern is only self-interest at this point."

"Self-interest?"

"Clearly you must see that you are the only male here of any possible interest to a woman. Butto is so unreliable and illogical that—"

"Are you—what are you saying? I can't believe this."

"Why not? Why should you not take an interest in me? We need not become emotionally involved. Life is unrewarding, isn't it? I have to have some reason for spending my time on routines, on the development of new systems, on trying to solve the problem of probing the dome floor electronically, don't I? Think of it as maintenance. I have come to the conclusion that I need maintaining."

"Good God. There are always suppressants, Eo."

"At last. At least you will discuss it. Take a logical view. Don't you maintain the rodentry? Don't we check the systems? I don't want suppressants. What happened to Butto has me worried. I want to minimize my drug use. Besides, from a purely scientific point of view, I would like to discover several things: one, if it is really possible to remain detached; two, if there is a vague chance it is possible for me to bear children to replenish our population; three, if it will affect my outlook; and four, if it is genuinely amusing. It is so long since I have been genuinely amused."

Dexter stood suddenly, and paced the small chamber, then stopped. "One," he said, "it is possible to remain detached, but that is not the point. The point is to become involved. Two, you can test whether or not it is possible for you to bear by more scientific means; three, it will indeed affect your outlook, but we need you the way you are—clear and logical; four . . . I forget what four was. Eolyn, you have taken the wrong approach to the whole thing. You have to give yourself emotionally."

"I have watched your behavior in meetings. You have not given yourself. Ruthan has, but you have not."

Dexter sat down. "No, I haven't. I have discovered that I don't know how. But she has, and that has saved the whole thing. You would hate it. It would be nothing but emptiness."

"You are really an archaic moralist, just giving me excuses. Are we not friends? Are we not obligated to help our friends? I find I am in need of help. I am a calculator in need of adjustment. My circuits are eroding. Can't you treat me as just a piece of equipment?" Her face twisted in an anguish of confessed loneliness. Then she covered it with her hands and shook with dry sobbing.

Dexter stood up, nonplussed. He opened his mouth, then shut it. Then he reached out and drew her down on the sleep pad beside him. He saw her shapely ear, the wisps of hair around it. No—it was too grotesque. He would have to find a way to suppress her. Still, that would be dangerous. He dared not make an enemy of her. This was a confined world. The dome and levels needed her, especially now that Zeller was dead. Dexter felt no moral compunctions, except for what he understood as the aura of Ruthan's feelings.

"You will not tell Ruthan?" Eolyn shook her head, still buried in her hands. The array of lights on Dexter's rodentry monitor shifted and marched, flicking dimly as a new feeding period took place. After a time, a flashing dot on the second level indicated a new birth, then another, a third, a fourth. One by one, three of them blinked out. Dexter wasn't looking. Nor did he command Ariadne to clap. Eventually Eolyn rose to leave, then stopped.

"Are you readjusted?"

"No. No. It amounts to nothing after all. I am sorry. I forced you into it. It was a mistake. I don't understand. The pictures."

"The pictures? What? You may change your mind. I hope for your sake you do."

"And for yours?"

"My God, Eolyn. What was your point one? Detachment? You and I are the most detached creatures in this whole meager and miserable bunch, but I cannot remain that detached."

"It is guilt, then. What an archaic value."

"Perhaps. If all values are archaic, then where . . ." Dexter looked up at his lightboard. "Oh, no! Cassiopeia has just killed her new litter. I've got to get down there." He rushed by Eolyn and down to the rodentry.

Eolyn stood in the hall. She pointed her toe and traced an arc on the floor wondering if something subtle had been omitted from her makeup, wondering if that too was planned, if she was the ultimate man of the geneticists, designed to resist the boredom of the levels by failure to feel. Consciously she began to force the issue behind her. She would persist with what she was. Slowly she began to hate Dexter, even though she recognized that this emotion was irrational. If Ruthan had supplied what he lacked, then he should have supplied what she lacked. It was his duty as a friend. He had not done it. Well, that was foolish. And yet it was there.

On the morning following the funeral at Pelbarigan, the full council finally gathered again. Still looking drained, Ahroe was present as a witness, should she be needed.

The Protector commanded silence, then, after the prayer, made a formal opening statement. "Counselors, much has happened since we last gathered here. However, the original question has not been settled. It has simply exploded in our faces like an unwatched pot. We have two courses this morning. The first would be to resume discussion, not of Celeste, because I have given her the Protector's safety, but of the question of the dome itself. The second option, as I see it, would be for me to decide the matter myself, subject to your veto. I would prefer that second option, and in fact am willing to weigh my continuance in office on it. If anyone is unwilling to accede to that, please speak now."

The council had surmised that this would be the Protector's course, and, because they had prepared themselves, no one was shocked or spoke against it. The north quadrant saw this as perhaps their only possible way of regaining any influence—that is, if the Protector's choice went wrong. It was a perilous choice. But they felt helpless.

"I thank you for your confidence. Now, weighing the evidence, here is what I propose: that a small expedition be sent to build a causeway across the empty place to the dome. Stel shall be in charge of it. Dailith, from the Protector's guard, will accompany him. A mason or guardsman from each quadrant may go if the quadrant wishes it. This will not be a major expedition or effort. Ahroe will remain here. If this expedition meets with disaster, we will not mount a large effort to save it, unless the whole council agrees to without debate. Is this agreeable?"

The room remained silent. Ahroe's face fell. Was she, then, to be separated from Stel? Perhaps for the summer? Putting him in danger? And yet she saw the Protector's reasoning, and let the anxiety show on her face, sure that some in the north quadrant would bask in her confusion. The Protector had managed to give something to each faction after all. But why had she so often to bear such difficulties?

With the matter decided so quickly, the council was restless, but the Protector insisted on a short silence, of two sunwidths, before she dismissed them. She sat, as the sun clock moved, in perfect repose, her old body sagging but still erect, eyes closed, face strangely rapt. Then she raised her hand, and the guardsmen tapped for adjournment.

Later, Druk led Ahroe to the Jestana's quarters. The Protector faced away from the door, looking out a balcony window, hands behind her.

"Protector?" said Ahroe. "I am here."

"Yes, Ahroe. Thank you. Only a word at this troublesome time for you. I am sorry for what I had to do. I know you will understand. Be sure to tell Stel to be careful, to do nothing rash. If anything goes wrong, you may of course go. I am sure you appreciate the need for your presence here."

"Yes, Protector. It is hard for me, but I understand."

The Protector still had not turned, even as she continued to speak: "Ahroe, I have had this office longer than I would have liked to. It is not an easy one. My old bones wish to retire. If anything goes wrong, even slightly, I will retire. It is my feeling that the next Protector will not have a very easy time of it. I can see, with the removal of the outside threat, that our old system of government needs modification. My decree this morning had the old ring to it—the authority of the Protector. Eventually that authority will be eroded. New systems will come in to replace it. Its virtue is neatness, quickness. Its great flaw is that the Protector might make a great mistake. I may have just made one. I am, like everyone, a person of limited insight. I have had to rely on ethics, on the values of Aven, and stick close to them. They have never failed me, but sometimes the going has been hard."

"Yes, Protector," said Ahroe, a bit nonplussed.

"I am arranging for you to become a guardcaptain soon, Ahroe. And Oet is near retirement. It may not be long before you command the entire guard."

"But why—I don't understand."

"You received your mother, who had disowned you, Ahroe. You held her in your arms and gave her comfort in her last hours. Do not think that will be lost on the north quadrant. You have traveled farther than any Pelbar woman in our known history. You have returned, proved loyal, stuck when sticking was the thing to do. You relate easily to the Shumai and Sentani. Now, do you see?"

"No, Protector. All this feels like a weight, as you put it."

"Being Protector is a much greater weight. I have borne it for some years now. I feel it slipping. Do you realize that the Dahmena spent her very first night outside the city at your house? Do you realize that I have visited Northwall once, many years ago, and save for that one trip, I too have remained in this city all the nights of my life? How am I to make decisions for the new world opening up?"

A distant lamp flared in Ahroe's mind. No. Could the Protector mean that? It was too much. Could she bear the weight?

Eventually the Protector said, "You are quiet. It may

well be, you know, that you will indeed be a Protector in the future. I am glad you feel it to be a burden. If you were proud, then you would do it badly. Of course, you can refuse. Or the council may never elect you. But I feel it. You need to think about it. You must remember, we are still Pelbar. We are still servants to Aven. When there is right to be done, we must do it, despite the cost to ourselves. Now, Ahroe, you must go and help Stel prepare his expedition."

"Yes, Protector. Thank you. This is all bewildering. I will need to sort it out."

"One more thing. This worries me about you. You will need to know more of Aven than you believe possible. I have not observed you among the devout. You will need to become so. I don't mean empty piety. I mean a probing of the rolls of Pell, of the fragments of ancient scripture, such as we have. I see your friend Tor looks into them. You will not make clear decisions without that underpinning. Decisions are not made by the head only. If they are, they are often bad and stupid. Now, you may go."

Ahroe bowed at the Protector's back, for she had never turned. "Yes. Thank you, Protector," she said, and left. After a time, the Protector did turn. Her face remained grave and tense as she walked from the window to summon Druk for some tea.

Ahroe found Stel in the front room, arranging small piles of things to take along. He seemed more pensive than eager and shot her a look that showed her he would miss her. He was tossing something lightly in his hand.

"What is that?"

"It is the box that Tristal found. It was Celeste's. We never gave it back. He thought it was some kind of weapon that hurt his dog, but I don't see it. Look. If you press here, a small rod protrudes from the end."

Ahroe seemed uninterested. Stel set it down on a small table, looked at it, and touched another square cut in the surface. Then he turned to his piles, moving them from the center of the room. He felt odd. His head suddenly hurt. He turned to Ahroe, who fell, clutching her ears. Suddenly, the sound grew, and a small hole was blasted through the stone wall of the cottage, as if it had been struck with a great hammer. Stel leaped at the box and slammed the button. The rod withdrew.

Ahroe ran into the other room retching, and Stel stood sheepishly until she came back. She was wiping sweat from her forehead. She looked angry, but then she began to laugh and cry at the same time as they came together and held each other.

"I guess it *was* a weapon. Some kind of weapon."

"Awful. I will put it away. Too bad we didn't have it when Cyklo came."

"Just as well, Ahroe. It all worked out. Unless Hagen had it."

Once more Ahroe sobbed against his shoulder. "Be careful. I have a terrible feeling about this. Be careful down there."

Stel didn't reply. He could still feel a sharp singing in his head.

Two mornings after, Stel and Dailith departed, with three other guardsmen, Egar, Aybray, and Nuva. The north quadrant sent no one. In two large, fabric-covered canoes, the party pushed off the crowded bank in the early-morning glare, amid laughter, dipping their paddles rhythmically in the muddy water, leaning their backs into it, surging out into the channel. Ahroe watched them go, straight-mouthed. As earlier that spring, the guardsmen blew the horn notes of departure at the proper time, followed by the ascending notes of the guardsmen's salute, and the Pelbar lifted their paddles in response. Ahroe watched them out of sight, Garet with her, again still and sulking. Raran put her nose in his hand and butted him lightly with her head, wagging her tail, for Tristal had returned. Garet went to push the dog away, but stroked her broad head instead, with its short, velvet fur.

"I will take messages for you," said Tristal. "Don't worry, Ahroe. They will be all right." She said nothing but turned away from him to mount the hill to Hagen's grave, where she could see the small boats far down the river.

Dexter saw his communicator light up. "Dex," came Eolyn's voice. "I am sorry. You will need to explain some things to me. All of this is so irrational. I am afraid of what has awakened inside me."

Dexter sighed. "We have been over it all before, Eo. Meet me in central conference. We will study the life-systems reports there. But I have only until 7210."

"Ruthan?"

Dexter switched off. Before leaving, he glanced at the rodentry monitor, slammed his hand against the outside wall, and left the room rubbing his palm.

 X

It was a hard summer, both inside and outside the dome. In the heat and the repeated thunderstorms, Stel and the guardsmen toiled to break and trim rock, dragging it from the outcrop they now called Tor's Ledge through the woods and up to the rim of the empty place. Slowly the stone causeway grew down the hill toward the dome. But it had to be built without touching the poison soil the stones were set into. Thick, glassy surfaces had to be pounded and broken. As much as possible, they kept the dust of the place off them, bathing twice a day in the stream below the ledge. When the wind blew, they masked their faces with cloth, sweating in the sun.

Dailith proved an able worker, willing and supremely dutiful. Egar and Nuva worked more and more unwillingly. Being far from Pelbarigan weighed on them. Nights under the ledge frightened them, and the preparing of food, often wild food killed by Stel or Aybray, seemed irregular and uncivilized to them. Eventually it was clear they longed to return to the city, though they manfully tried to continue. Stel grew peremptory with them, seeing that they were used to taking orders. They did, gritting their teeth.

The problem with Aybray was the opposite. Freedom from the city gave a new world to him, and he was so overwhelmed that he took on the job of most of the hunting and fishing needed to support the work. But often he simply wandered the woods, or pushed out through the tall prairie grass drinking in the size and silence of his surroundings. "He has a Shumai soul," Stel remarked to Dailith one evening.

Nonetheless, the causeway slowly progressed down the hill. Tristal came from Pelbarigan, carrying messages and supplies, and staying three days to haul rock. He was rapidly maturing, his whole body deepening and hardening. Already he stood taller than Stel. A new confidence seemed to radiate from him, though a shadow of trouble as well.

One evening he told Stel of it. "Am I as wholly uncivilized as Celeste seems to think?" he asked.

"Of course not. You mustn't mind her. She knows very little about people. She is happiest with her mathematics. What is she doing now?"

"Working out a system of lenses so the Pelbar can see the tiny things she talks of—the microorganisms. She calls it a microscope."

"Is she progressing?"

"She seems to be. She works at it long hours, with two helpers to grind and polish glass. She is trying to find ways of measuring the things. That seems very important and difficult."

"Well, I'm glad she is happy."

"Stel."

"Yes?"

"It is all very strange. I think I love her. I want to be with her. What do you think? Am I old enough to love somebody?"

Stel squinted up at him. "It's hard to say. Sometimes these things pass like mist from the river. Other times they stand like stone. That's the way it was with Ahroe and me, though we had our troubles." He chuckled.

"She looks through me as if I wasn't there. She even loves Raran, but she seems to discount me entirely. I'm glad to be here. It is hard for me to stand it when I'm there. She looks at Tor as if he were Sertine himself—but even him she is beginning to forget with all this glass grinding."

Stel quietly stirred the fire. "I can't help you, Tris. No man can. These things are never easy. It goes with being a person. Who can say what she will notice? She is strange. This may well be just a phase of your life. Keep it all in perspective. In the long run, you will have to be true to your own best self and let everything else go. You will have to stand whatever comes along."

"Is that what you did?"

Stel laughed. "I tried to. I failed miserably, then learned slowly. I think I did learn, though we all fail now and then, and I often. What I did discover, though, was that you should be the best Tristal you know how to be, and if this leads Celeste to you, good. If not, you will have to bear it."

"I can't bear it. I can't get her out of my head, even here."

"Will you be able to give up Tor, and the free running out on the plains?"

"I think Tor himself is worrying about that, Stel. There are fewer running bands all the time. Everyone is settling down."

"Yes. They find life is easier that way. But Tor never will settle."

"He can't see himself doing it. Right now he is trying to wean Celeste away from him. He feels the need to look in on her."

"He would have made a good Pelbar. He is a mother."

Tristal looked annoyed at this, but then saw Stel was serious, and so thought it over. He rose and dusted himself off.

"One thing more," Stel said. "Don't expect it to be easy. Loving is the chief source of most of our personal anguish. You must see that by now. Pray. And try to be your best self. Say to yourself that if you are to attract what you love, and to you, you yourself, then you have to be a wholehearted self. I know that sounds stupid, but that is what character involves."

Tristal didn't look convinced. Stel watched him walk away, wishing he could have said what he meant, or known what he meant—thinking that Celeste was not Ahroe, that so much of a man's happiness depended on being close to a woman who had somewhere in the river of her life a deep channel of outflowing love, still and slow. Even though Ahroe was in Pelbarigan, he felt that union of endeavors, that strong line of connected hopes. He felt the resilience of her loyalty, which would not snap, and knew, to himself, that the meagerness of Celeste's machine-companioned childhood would never encourage any such development.

Not far away, inside the dome, Dexter and Eolyn again were together in the conference room, ostensibly discussing modifications to the rodentry cages to prevent further killing of the young. It seemed to happen so quickly. The mothers were now turning on their newborns in the first moments of their lives. The problem was not an easy one. Already the meat component of the protein supply had decreased.

Partly they were discussing this. But Eolyn was miserable. Her theory of being a mechanism in need of adjustment had not worked, as Dexter had predicted. She had insisted they try again, but again she felt shriveled by the whole event. After that he had refused. Begging him, she had threatened, even threatened to tell Ruthan, but she never would, and he knew it. Dexter tried to steer her toward Butto, who still bubbled with his newfound normality and overflowed with emotion. He often gazed at Eolyn. She was revolted by him, though.

"It would seem that as the feelings die, disgust and anger are the last," said Dexter.

"Don't rub it in," she replied.

"I'm not. Merely thinking it out. If I could help, I would."

"I think you could if you really tried."

"We've been through that. Ice runs in the arteries of both of us."

"What is it like, Dex? What is it like when it is real?"

He looked at her, startled. "I'm not sure I know. If I can judge by Ruthan, it suffuses the whole being with a radiance, not so much the mere sensation but the aura of loving. All I catch of that is reflected heat, really."

The panel slid. Ruthan entered, seemed to catch a look from the other two, hesitated, and sat down. What was this? Dexter with Eolyn? Something more hovered in the air beside the diagrams on the lightboard. "Am I interrupting?" she asked.

"No, Ruthy. We are trying to determine how to modify the cages so the mothers won't kill the young. It is happening with alarming frequency. Here, look at the chart."

Dexter commanded a series of touch buttons, and brought on the screen a graph with a steeply rising line. She looked at it, almost dreamily, then leaned back.

"Do you think plants have emotions?" she said. The others looked surprised. "I am not being merely silly—I hope. I seem to sense a response from them. But the point is that the rodents must have emotions. Why would the mothers want to kill their young? They have always done some of that, I suppose, but if the rate is increasing, the place to look for a solution is not in cages, but in happy rats. Dex, do you love them?"

"Love the rats?" he shouted, screwing up his face. "They amuse me, but good God I am so sick of them sometimes. I wish we could put them back on tranquilizers."

"But the food. It was getting to us as well."

"There must be a way of processing it that will remove any residues."

"Our supplies are limited—much more so now with the loss of the oil."

"Well, Ruthan," said Eolyn. "If you were to love them, what would you do? You must know you would be faking it. You would intend to kill them eventually, wouldn't you?"

A slow smile spread on Ruthan's face. "I would play with them, and talk to them, and project my love at them. I do it to the plants, and because I really feel it. Here they are, valiantly growing, all for us. I know they can't help it, but it is a lovely thing for them to do. I tell them. Now. I know you think I'm crazy, but here are some of my graphs." Reaching out, she commanded a new set of lines on the lightboard. "The upward movement of these lines shows tomato production by my favorite plants. See? It is all calculated by weight of fruit. That other set, the dashes, is production on thirty vines tended solely by comps." The broken line wavered slightly, but remained level.

"How do you account for the sudden recent rise in production?" Eolyn asked. "Is this a new experiment?"

Ruthan smiled slowly. Dexter covertly frowned at her. "I don't know," she said. A tension entered the air, and with it, Susan Ward slid the panel back and entered the room, slowly, carrying her dulcimer, moving to sit down.

"Susan. You are out of your room. What is it? Bored?"

"Bored. Yes. Bored. But something has happened. I feel it. What is different now? I don't know that I like it."

"What has happened? Can you give us more specific information?"

"Undoubtedly there must be information somewhere, buried in my enfeebled cortexes. I have lived a long time, and I have detected a shift in the atmosphere of the dome and levels."

"The comps are not drugged now. Zeller is gone. Celeste, too. We are having trouble with the Brat Shack. The rats are killing their young. And Ruthan has increased tomato production. Other than that all is normal. Even Butto is back to himself. In fact he is more himself than he has ever been. Oh yes, and we have lost the oil."

Susan looked at Eolyn. "That is not it." She glanced around the room. "So you won't tell me. Well, I will return to my own proper cell, then."

She turned to go. Dexter felt an increase in tension. "I will go, too. Go down and love my rats. A good place to start." He gave a strange laugh as he and Susan left the room.

Ruthan looked over at Eolyn, who, unaccountably, suddenly, looked at her level and straight, seeming to transmit a pulse of hatred like a force. Ruthan reeled slightly and stood, looking puzzled. Understanding began to grow. Eolyn knew about Dexter. Ruthan started to rush out, then went to Eolyn, kneeling by her chair, putting her head against the older woman's side and crying. Eolyn remained rigid.

"I'm sorry," Ruthan said softly. "I really am."

"For what? What is the matter with you?"

Ruthan stood, brushing her hair from her face. What was this? Had she made a mistake? No, there was no mistake. Eolyn's face betrayed her knowledge. So she was choosing to ignore it. Ruthan leaned down and kissed her. Then she fled. Eolyn sat rigid, growing slowly more angry and frustrated. Finally she rubbed away the kiss furiously and left.

Susan stood in her room, musing. It was time to go, she thought. She had toyed with the idea of leaving the dome, even if it killed her. Something was wrong here. She couldn't pin it down, but it seemed to hang like an evil atmosphere. She would use Celeste's door. It would take careful planning. She would nullify the alarm system as Celeste had done. She would take supplies and a pointer. She was willing to die out there. She would even take along a euthanasia pill. She smiled to herself, thinking that Royal would not get to recycle her, nor to dissect her for information. Sitting down at her lightboard, she began to plan.

Late in Heatmonth, Stel and his crew finally lowered the last blocks of stone next to the dome. Dailith reached out and slapped the concrete surface with a boyish laugh. They stood right below Celeste's door. Sweat ran down all all their faces, and each took a turn at touching the dome, even Egar and Nuva.

"Well," said Stel. "Let's take the rest of the day off. We have to build some kind of short ladder to reach that door easily."

No one left right away, though. They had accomplished something. They could look back up the elevated path of rock as it rose toward the rim of the empty place, even and ordered. Finally, the guardsmen left, but Stel remained, still musing about the proper next steps. He was in shadow now, and cooler. Above, he seemed to hear a sound. Was it the door? Yes, it was swinging open. Stel touched his short-sword, then drew his hand away.

An old, dark-skinned woman looked out, blinking. Her face was kindly but skull-like, her arms unfleshed as sticks. She turned and looked behind, then seemed to see Stel and drew back, startled.

"Hello," Stel said, laughing lightly. "Coming out? You're just in time. We just built you this walk."

"Who are you?"

"Stel. Stel Westrun of Pelbarigan. Celeste is at Pelbarigan now. Do you know Celeste?"

Fear crossed the old woman's face. She hesitated and turned, then turned back again to look at Stel.

"Wait," said Stel. "Before you decide to come out here, you will have to know that Celeste got really sick. She had a whole succession of things. She is all right now, though. Will you be able to take it? You look old to me. I may be wrong. You are in shadow. You are stark in the dark. The light is slight."

Susan smiled vaguely. She turned again. "I am immune," she said. "Here, catch this first. Be careful with it." She tossed down a parcel made of a bodysuit with the arms and legs tied up. Then, stiffly, she leaned out and down, and launched out slowly into Stel's arms. He took her weight, which was not great, stepping back, and set her down. They looked at each other, and both laughed.

Reaching up, Stel took his smallknife and swung the heavy door shut, wedging the blade into it so he could open it later.

"Can you walk?" he asked.

"Where? Up there?" She squinted into the light uphill, shading her eyes.

"Yes. Out of this empty place into the woods and to our camp. We will take you to Pelbarigan where you will be comfortable. What is your name?"

"Woods? What? You mean trees?"

"Yes. Oaks mostly. What is your name?"

"Susan. Susan Ward. Woods? Up there?" She turned and began to walk, slowly, holding Stel's arm. When the stone path grew steep, he picked her up and carried her. She looked back, frowning as she saw the whole dome jutting out over the deep gully, then ahead again, breathing hard, to get her first glimpse of trees. She saw the grass and weeds as they drew near the rim, then the tops of oaks, vibrantly green. Her eyes streamed tears from the unaccustomed light. Then they were in the grass, walking toward the trees.

"Put me down. Put me down," Susan said in a strange, husky voice. As Stel set her slowly down, she stood, then, reaching out, knelt, feeling the rank grass and goldenrod, the drying wild carrot stems, uttering birdlike sounds, then, finally, sitting and crying inconsolably. Her hands ripped the grass as she lay full length in it. Then suddenly she sat up. "Take me to a tree," she said.

As she neared a tall black oak, steadied by Stel, she reached toward it, felt its rough bark, stretched her arms around it, again gripping. "So hard," she murmured. A beetle landed on the back of her hand, and she drew the insect toward her face, staring.

The shadows had swung a good distance before Stel brought her to Tor's Ledge, where the idling guardsmen, having washed, lay talking under the cool rock. Aybray jerked upright and looked. Then the others followed. Stel held up a hand, so they only walked toward the two, Aybray first, his hand out, grinning, saying loudly, "Welcome, welcome to the Heart River Valley."

Susan drew back both her hands and said distantly, "I believe I have lived here all my life, young man."

Aybray's smile faded. "Well, I thought . . ." He fell silent.

"Susan? Susan Ward. This is Aybray, Dailith, and Egar and Nuva. We are all from Pelbarigan. Are you hungry. Let me leave you to Dailith. I need a bath."

"So I noticed. Hello. Please show me a place I can lie down," said Susan, walking forward, taking Aybray's arm, turning to see her makeshift bag. "Take care of that," she added. "It has a dulcimer in it."

They did nothing for two days, while Susan Ward grew used to the world. They could easily see her deep grief that this world had lain just beyond her sight for all of a long lifetime shut in the dome. Sometimes this feeling welled up in such anger and frustration that her veins swelled and they feared for her. But she was exacting, did not like dirt, which she had never dealt with, and she was appalled at the first horsefly that settled on her arm and, after arranging its legs, drilled for blood.

Eventually, they made her a chair on poles, and the three younger guardsmen left to take her to Pelbarigan, her parcel in her lap. Dailith and Stel watched, and as they walked out on the prairie eastward, and disappeared, Stel said, "Now. I'm going to enter the dome."

"Be careful. I will come, too."

"No. Only one. Then the other can go if I need help."

"I will go."

Stel looked narrowly at him. Dailith had never seen the solid force of the smaller man before. No wonder he had been able to keep them at the causeway in that blinding heat. "All right," Dailith said. "You go."

"First we must pray." The two men put the heels of their hands against their eyes, and, standing, prayed silently until Stel nudged Dailith's arm, grinned, and walked once more down the causeway. After he had worked the door open, Dailith boosted him inside.

An air monitor within the dome finally registered the change of atmosphere and sent a warning to central conference and five other locations. Comp 5 monitored it and notified Dexter, who ran to decontam. Four comps met him, each rapidly slipping into a dome suit.

"It is subsiding now," said one.

"Perhaps a malfunction."

"Not likely."

"What else?"

"A door opening?"

They all laughed. Dexter looked alarmed. "We will enter the dome in perfect silence," he said.

Stel didn't see or hear them. He was picking his way slowly through the tall dome, noticing the high window, the ladder to it, the structure to raise the rod, the multitude of lines and pipes, the eerie, sourceless lights, yellow and dim, and the great, humming block in the center of the room. It sat, complex and square, radiating a slight warmth.

Stel was staring at it, hands on hips, when he heard a slight sound. Turning, he caught the stunning pulse from Dexter's weapon in the midsection. He crumpled with a fluttering cry and lay jerking on the floor.

"Be careful," said Bill. "Turn him over." Gloved hands rolled Stel onto his back. "He is a man. Where from?"

"Or he looks like one," said Dexter. "Quick. Help me get him to decontam before the stun wears off. Five, you call Eolyn and Royal. Under no circumstances are any of you to tell any of the others, comps or principals. Understood?"

"Understood, Principal Dexter."

Stel stirred and moaned slightly on the floor of decontam, but Royal, summoned, injected a small, clear vial into his arm, and soon he went limp again.

"He reacts like a man, Dex," said Royal.

"Anyone who could stand that radiation is no man. A mutant of some sort. Look at those primitive fibers in his clothes. Look. That thick belt substance. Here is a knife. They must come from some vast shelter and have other life substances with them."

"Don't touch him until we radiation-test him."

Eolyn entered, put on a radiation suit, and watched the test. A very slight response showed from Stel's clothes and legs. "So. A mutant from outside? There is some life left out there, it would seem. Somehow he is able to reject radiation. Look. It is clearly not in him but only dusted on him from his surroundings. I will take a blood sample." She drew blood from his arm and made a slide for Royal. He took it and departed for his lab.

Eolyn ran her glove across Stel's arms and chest. "Primitive," she said. "Feel that heavy muscle pack. Think what he must be able to lift. A reversion to early man."

Dexter shot a look at her. She glared back. "Well, we will have plenty of time to study him," Dexter said. "He isn't going anywhere. Think of it. Somewhere out there is a small band of primitive mutants, surviving all these centuries, probably undergoing untold sufferings. Somehow they have developed organs for purging themselves of radiation. Now they are trying to get into the dome. See? He has another long knife. Look how worn it is. They are plainly dangerous. We will have to revamp all our security. I will rebuild and activate the helmet weapons. Comp 7, did you dog down that door?"

"Yes, Principal."

"Good. Now, no word to the rest. They will make trouble—especially the humanists. Double the sensors. And determine why that door did not warn us when he opened it."

"Principal? What if he has friends outside?"

Dexter paused and sucked in his breath. "That is what the helmet pulsers will counter. They will handle anything."

Royal returned with his blood slide. "It is not abnormal at all—type O. But it is loaded with all sorts of creatures. He is a walking zoo in an uncontrolled environment of microorganisms. Be sure everyone has a shot of panimmune. Give him a double. Can he talk?"

Dexter laughed. "He made a sound when I stunned him. I doubt he can. Look. He is almost an animal. Look at the calluses on his hands. Here. Help me put him on the table. We will have to study him in detail. Perhaps vivisection will tell us the most about him."

"Vivisection?" said Eolyn. "What if he is indeed human? There is that chance."

"We certainly go over all our own dead carefully enough if they are complete. Before recycling. Look what we will learn. If the dome is eroding out, and the oil gone, we may have to leave the dome ourselves, somehow."

"Not with all that radiation."

"Exactly. He has stood it. We may have to modify our bodies to make the same adjustment he has. We may even need his organs."

"It may not be that easy."

"So. Do you see the point, then, of vivisection? Look. We have already learned that he has not absorbed the radiation his environment has offered him. It is on his clothes and skin. It is not in him."

"Perhaps you are right. But we must go slowly."

They put Stel on the table, strapping him down after stripping him.

"Don't stare, Eo," said Dexter.

"Shut up. He is of purely scientific interest. Look at his scars. He has healed well in a hostile environment. Before we vivisect him, we must keep him intact and study him. Cover him with a cloth so he remains warm for now."

Comp 7 reentered the decontamination room. "Yes, Comp?" said Dexter.

"The door did not indicate its opening because the alarm system was nullified, Principal."

"How?"

"It would appear the Principal Ward nullified it."

"Of all the twisted genetic mistakes," Dexter spat. "Bring her here."

"She appears to have left the dome and levels by means of the door," said Comp 7. "She left a message." He touched it up on the wall panel. They all read her words:

> Alas, poor Dex, I know you well,
> and all you who'd recycle me
> if I died in our citadel,
> so I'm our second absentee.
> At last, in age, I've cracked my shell.
> I may die soon—but outside, free.
> And you, old Royal, who'd compel
> my body's yielding to your knife,
> your last embraces I'll repel
> by leaving now while I have life.

"Is doggerel a sign of maladjustment in this place?" Dexter asked, waving his hands.

Royal reached over and erased the image, shaking his head. "What a waste. She would have been the best opportunity to study the effects of aging I would have had in my entire life."

"At least this one will recycle just as well or better. He is a gain in protein over Susan," said Dexter.

"Dex, you can't talk of that now. Look. He is a young and healthy being."

"Besides," Royal added, "we can't just recycle him

willy-nilly without knowing what he would do to our protein mix. Analysis must always precede action."

The team worked on Stel for a full 3500 units, then left decontam, promising silence about the primitive's presence. The lights dimmed. Stel lay still on the table, strapped down, covered in his drape. After a time, Eolyn returned alone. She flipped back the drape and raised the lights, then stood gazing at him for a time. Reaching out, she touched the heavy muscles of his upper arm, his deltoids and pectorals. Then she covered him again and stood still, frowning. Finally she shook her head and left.

In the middle of the rest cycle, Dexter and Royal moved Stel to Susan Ward's room, as a place less likely to reveal his presence. They did not want to be interrupted in their analysis by the irrationalities of Butto and Cohen-Davies.

Two more work cycles spent on Stel revealed that his clothing was made of mixed plant fibers and animal hair, his belt and shoes of animal skin of some unknown type. Antibodies in his system protected him from what Royal called his "internal zoo." He appeared to be a creature of some intelligence, judging from his brain action. This eventually made them decide to lessen the sedative injections. In addition, Stel's body began to show signs of acute distress.

Down on level three, Bill, encountering Butto, told him the whole situation, as the heavy principal frowned down at him. "They are going to recycle him? Have they talked to him?"

"No, Principal. They have made no attempt. They assume he is a mutant because of his ability to withstand the radiation. And I think they are afraid of his strength."

"Don't worry. I will take care of it." Butto put a hand on Bill's shoulder. "And I won't tell. I'll simply be looking in on Susan." The former comp smiled wryly.

Not long after, as Dexter and Royal watched Stel begin to stir and mumble, the panel slid and Butto walked in saying, "Susan, I haven't seen— What is this? Who is he?"

"None of your affair, Butto. Get out."

"Here, what have you done to him? What is he saying?"

"You are disturbing our investigation. Please remove yourself."

"Why? Going to stun me again, Dex? Look. He's trying to say something. Have you fed him? Look at his lips. He must be thirsty." Butto turned to Susan's water tap, drew a cup, and reached toward Stel. Dexter stood between. Butto pulsed him with a slight stun, and Dexter collapsed in a heap. Butto stepped over him. "Want that, too, Royal?" he asked.

"You unutterable organic slop."

"Ah. So you do." He raised the pulser.

"No, no. Get away from him."

"You've starved him. How long has he been here? Look at his cracking lips." Butto cradled Stel's head and moistened his lips with a finger, then put the cup to them. Stel blinked and exchanged a look with Butto. "Here, can you drink?"

Stel grunted in reply, then drank slowly. Dexter began to move on the floor, so Butto turned and gave him another low stun. "I've been wanting to pay you back," he said. "Royal, put him over on the table. Here. I will help you."

Butto lifted Dexter onto Susan's worktable, dumping him awkwardly. Then he touched the command panel, summoning Ruthan.

"You slurry brain," Royal said. "Now you've spoiled everything."

"What?" said Stel, stirring. "What have you done to me? My head is cracking open."

"Ah, the beast speaks," said Butto. "Royal, get something to deaden the headache. If it deadens anything else, I will deaden you." Turning to Stel, he said, "Hello. My name is Butto. How are you?"

"Awful. My name is Stel. Stel Westrun of Pelbarigan." Stel passed out again.

"What has the poor man done that you should treat him this way?"

"You go too far, Butto. You have destroyed our analysis, which was progressive, as his system changed."

"What have you learned? That you could starve him?" Butto turned to command some warm food cubes, steaming from the server.

"None of your affair."

"Did you learn that his name was Stel? I bet not. Stel

something of somewhere. Come on, now, Stel, wake up."

Eolyn and Ruthan entered, Ruthan staring. She quickly covered Stel with a bedcloth.

"See what the technocrats have been hiding, Ruthy? A poor man named Stel. They've been deliberately torturing him."

"He invaded the dome. You've no right. We are trying to determine his makeup, and how he has withstood the radiation."

"Why didn't you ask him? Here, he is awakening again. Come on, Stel, eat some of this."

"Water," Stel said faintly. "More water, please."

Butto gave him a drink, then fed him, cube after cube of rations.

"Is this what you eat?" Stel asked. "Good Aven, is it ever dreadful. A fudge of sludge. What is it?" Then, as if suddenly realizing something, he asked, "How long have I been in here?"

"I don't know," said Butto. "How long, Royal?"

"Royal? Then you are Royal."

"You know of Royal?"

"Celeste told me about him. Royal, do you have some means of curing what Celeste calls radiation sickness?"

Royal looked bewildered, but he still frowned. "That depends on how bad it is. Where is Celeste?"

"At Pelbarigan. How long have I been here?"

No one had been watching Dexter. He had reawakened, slid off the table, grasped Susan's hand pulser, and moved around Butto. Now he said, "About five cycles of 100,000." Butto turned, and Dexter gave him a full stun, then stunned Stel.

Ruthan cried out, bending over the crumpled Butto.

"Why? Why have you done all this?" she screamed. "You are all staring crazy. Nothing was wrong."

"Nothing wrong, Ruthy? That big blob of meat has just barged in and disrupted our investigation. This creature invaded the dome. This is—"

"He is not a creature. He was talking to us. He knows Celeste. Royal, you tell him."

Royal had moved to Stel and was examining him. He turned, shaking his head. "That was quite a stun, Dexter. I wish you had not done that, with his weakened system. Butto, unfortunately, was right. Why did it not occur to us to talk with him? I am amazed now. But he seemed so . . . different."

"We still don't know anything about him," Eolyn said. "Dexter may be right. We know nothing of his motives. Look. He was armed. He did invade the dome. We don't know if he is telling the truth. There are so few of us. We must be extremely careful."

"He sounded friendly," said Ruthan. "How long has he been here? Has it really been five full cycles? What if he has friends outside? They will be worried about him. What then?"

Outside, at the moment, Dailith was beating on the door. He had chipped away the concrete and peeled back a lead shield, but a heavy plastic layer had proved very difficult, and now a thick steel core entirely defied him. It had been nearly six days that Stel had been gone. Dailith sweat profusely. Looking up, he saw a thundercloud boiling up in the west again, tall and rolling, dark at the core, leaning out over the landscape, sun streaming around its edges. He wiped the sweat away from his forehead and cheeks. That would be a heavy storm, but at least it might bring relief from the heat.

He heard a call from the hill, and, turning, he saw Tor and Ahroe, and another guardsman, a young woman he didn't know. He turned and trotted up the hill.

"Stel? Where is Stel?" said Ahroe.

"In there. He has been in there almost six days."

"You can't get in, then?"

"No. I've been trying. I've made progress, but there is a heavy metal plate I am unable even to dent."

"Six days?"

"Almost. I didn't know you could come."

"Tor convinced me something was wrong. On the way we met the old woman on the river. She has led the guardsmen a merry time."

"What do you mean?"

"The outside world is almost too much for her to bear. She was sleeping when they got her to the river. They were well out on it before she woke up, and when she finally saw it, she stared for a time, then screamed at them to take her back. Finally, they did, but when they touched the bank, she screamed at them to take her out on the river again. She is so flabbergasted with the ordinary earth, and so angry, that she is near dying."

"Could we get on top?" Tor asked, speaking for the first time. "Look. The rod is rising again. Could we get a rope over it?"

"Look at that cloud," said Dailith. "The rod will draw lightning. We have had some wild and grim storms around here lately."

"We've got to get Stel out of there," said Ahroe.

"A rope thrown from your ladder by the dome might snag it," said Tor. The wind rose, and the first drops skittered on the ground. Tor turned to the guardsman. "Get that rope we saw at the ledge." She turned and ran. "Dailith, we will have to use your ladder."

Inside the dome, Comp 9, having raised the rod, said into his communicator, "Still no mistake, Principal Dexter. The radiation readings hold. I can see out the window. It is darkening, and water is falling."

"Very well, Comp. Come to decontam. That is called rain. Take another look before you come."

"Lights are flashing out there, Principal."

"Lights? Are you sure?"

"Yes. They are lighting up the whole landscape."

"Surely you mistake."

"No, Principal."

"Well, return now. Follow all procedures."

"Yes, Principal." As Comp 9 turned to lower the rod, a blast of lightning crashed down it, flaring the whole interior of the dome, blowing the small man off the high ladder to the floor, where he lay smoking. The lightning had also run down the side of the dome, on its wet surface, exploding into the earth at its foot. Tor was on the ladder with the rope, and felt a flash of electricity spring up his legs and hands.

"Come down," Ahroe shouted up at him.

"No. Stay by the door. I will be all right." He whirled the weighted rope and swung it out at the rod high above, missing.

"Tor, there is fire underneath," Dailith yelled. Black smoke welled up from the great pool of oil ignited by the lightning. Tor didn't answer, but coiled the rope and swung it out again, catching the rod.

"Stay by the door," he shouted down at Ahroe, already swinging and skidding up the rope. He reached the rod, feeling his hair rise with the electricity, slipping on the surface in the pouring rain, but running on all fours to the dome end. There he leaned out over the curve and looked down, discovering the window. He could see nothing inside. Taking his axe, he swung hard at the glass, cracking it slightly. Swinging again and again, he eventually cracked and broke through the thick glass. Hanging on hard with his knees, he cleared the shards away, sheathed his axe, and swung over the edge, slipping, swaying there, hanging by his arms, and finally reaching in the window, cutting his hand on some glass, but gripping the inner edge of the concrete frame and sliding in.

Ahead stood a ladder. He climbed down it rapidly, blinking in the dimness. Stooping, he felt the body of the comp, noting its smallness with a strange fear. Crossing the dome, he located the door, solved its locking dogs, and swung it back. Black smoke billowed in.

"Ahroe, Ahroe," he yelled, reaching out, as she caught his hand and leaped up into the opening. She saw a movement and dodged through the smoke behind the square structure that occupied the center of the room. Tor stood and turned, as Dexter stunned him with a pulser. The big Shumai collapsed by the door. Dexter ran across with a hand pulser, and behind him Ruthan and Eolyn with helmet weapons fitted to their heads looked on, the firing tweezers held between their lips. Heavy energy packs rode on their shoulders.

"Stay back," Dexter called, arriving at Tor, who rolled slowly over as he got there, looking vaguely up at a figure aiming something at him, then whipping his legs around, knocking Dexter down, grappling with him, the two standing and struggling. Ruthan screamed and aimed as well as she could, firing a pulse at half-power at the giant man holding Dexter by the throat.

Tor felt a blinding shock as the pulse tore off his right forearm. A draining blow and sudden disbelief struck him. In the next instant, Dexter, falling toward him, was caught and blown apart by another pulse. Tor groaned and sank, as Ruthan, screaming and tearing off her helmet, ran across the dome to Dexter, who lay half under Tor.

Eolyn stood by the door to decontam, shouting, "Ruthan, get out of the way. That primitive is still alive. Get out of the way!" She didn't see Ahroe move around the pile, rush her, slam her helmet off with the side of her short-sword, and dash into the levels, yelling, "Stel! Stel!"

At the dome entrance, Ruthan shrieked inconsolably, screaming and beating her knees with her arms. Beside her, Tor rolled over, got to his knees, and, taking the belt from his tunic, looped it over the stump of his right arm, cinched it tight, and at last cried out in pain. Ruthan turned to him, looked, and screamed again.

"You," Tor said, vaguely. "You've got to get out of here. The whole dome is on fire. Lightning has started it."

"No," she screeched. "No. Get away. Look what you did!"

"I just—just came to get Stel. Now, come." He rose, staggering, took Ruthan under his left arm, kicked the door open, and, turning, plunged down the ladder through the smoke.

Dailith met him at the bottom, hardly able to see. "Go inside and help," Tor yelled, turning and scrabbling his way out of the smoke and up the causeway in the driving rain, still holding Ruthan like a sack, running and falling, slowing, stumbling, feeling the supporting hand of the other guardsman as he got to the steep part, with Ruthan still screaming in terror, finally reaching the rim and the weeds and grass, as the world began to rush and tilt, dropping Ruthan, then sitting himself and slumping over. Skahie, the guardsman, supported him, then first noticed his arm and went weak, uttering a strange cry.

"Tor, Tor. What has happened? My Aven, Tor." Ruthan seemed to awaken, sat up, and looked around. She was sitting in plants, tangled and wild. Water poured down. A giant, bearded man, his right arm all blood, leaned weakly against a woman, who looked levelly at her.

"What did you do to him?" Skahie asked.

Ruthan crawled toward them. "Lay him down," she said. "Loosen his clothes. He will go into shock."

As Dailith plunged through the smoke into the dome, he saw a figure by the open door across the room. She was putting on a strange helmetlike device. She stood thin and utterly lovely in a bodysuit. He ran toward her as she turned, her strange, masking helmet on.

"Stand back, go back, or I'll kill you."

"You've got to get out. You all do. The whole dome is on fire from underneath."

"I mean it. Get away. Get back out."

"Where is Stel? Where are all the others of you? You've got to get out. Look at the smoke. I mean it. I wish you no harm."

She hesitated. Dailith, who had been edging sideways, ran through the door beyond her, finding another door and a long hall. He met a tiny man at the head of the stairs.

"You," he said. "The whole dome is burning underneath. You've got to get out, you and the others." Beyond him, down the long hall, Ahroe came out from a panel, with Stel, weak, leaning on her.

"Butto," Stel said. "Get Butto. A man named Butto."

Ahroe yelled out, "Butto, Butto." The comp with Dailith ran down the hall and pressed a panel command. The door slid open, and he darted through, soon reappearing with Butto, stripping binding cords off him. Butto seemed bewildered, startled.

"Help me," said Ahroe. "Get all your people. The dome is on fire. You've got to get out."

"You," he said. "You have—"

"Later," she yelled. "Outside. I am Ahroe, Stel's wife. Now. Get the other short ones." She froze, looking ahead. Eolyn stood confronting them all, her pulser helmet on. "You must be Eolyn," Ahroe said. "Celeste told me about you. You'd kill us all, wouldn't you—yourself included. Please. We have to get out."

"No. This has gone far enough," said Eolyn. "Butto, get away." A comp came behind her and, running, caved her knees forward. Ahroe stepped to her, lifted her, and propelled her down the hall.

"Thanks, small man," she said.

"Thirteen," he returned.

"Ahroe. Are there others?"

"The comps are coming. There is Principal Thornton. Ah, here he comes." Turning, they saw a rumpled and bewildered Cohen-Davies lurching down the hall. Dailith grabbed his arm and urged him on toward the door, where Eolyn was again standing. They all poured by her, shoving, then raced across the cluttered dome floor toward the gout of smoke coming in the canted door. Royal came behind, led by a comp. Dailith helped them down through the smoke, and they emerged, amazed, into heavy rain and lightning, on the causeway. Several comps hesitated and turned, but when they saw the black smoke from the pool of oil under the dome, and the rising flames now, they turned again, in wild fear, and ran on up the stone path.

"Stay on the stones," Ahroe called, as she and Butto led Stel up the hill.

At the top they found Tor lying, eyes open, breathing in shallow, quick inhalations. Skahie bent over him, and Ruthan, looking vaguely around, cried, "Dexter, oh Dexter."

Ahroe gave Stel to Dailith. "Never mind Dexter," she said. "Help us bring Tor to the ledge. At least we will get him out of the rain."

"No," Tor murmured, in a strange, light voice. "It is all right here. Look. The dog of darkness has come. He is shy as a fawn. He has laid his head on my knee. He looks gently up. His head is growing. The eyes glow, burning now, flames in the night. The weight of his head presses . . ."

Ahroe suddenly rushed over, pushed him down, put her fist in his mouth, yelling, "No, no, Tor. Don't give up now. Where is the steel in your backbone? Stop, stop. Stop. Stop." She took her hand back from his face.

He looked vaguely up at her, sitting astride him. "At least, at least," he said, "let me die in peace. Stop shaking me."

"Die? Hasn't anyone ever lost an arm before? Stop it now. If we ever needed you, it is now."

"Now?" He trembled a slight laugh. "A bloodless axeman without a right arm?"

Ruthan had been staring down at him. She took his head in her lap. Her face was gray, but she said, "You will be all right. Royal will help. Won't you, Royal?" She looked up. He had on a pulser helmet, as did Eolyn.

"Get away from them, Ruthan," she said, muffled by the helmet. "We cannot be at their mercy. We have lost almost everything, but not quite all."

"Are you crazy?"

"We will wait out the fire here, then return to the dome. Then we will emerge, as it is clear we must, in our own time with our own equipment and protections."

"The whole dome will be destroyed," said Tor in a husky whisper.

"Ruthan, get away from that savage," said Eolyn.

"No. Never."

"I will stun you." Ruthan shut her eyes against it. Then from far to the east, the faint sound of dogs barking came through the rain. Ahroe raised her horn and sounded a long blast, cut off when Eolyn turned and blew the end off her cow horn with a quick pulse.

"You, there. What is that?"

"The Shumai. You had better join us and stop this nonsense. We have to take Tor to the ledge and bind his arm. They won't take your interference kindly."

"I mean what I say. Look, now." Eolyn turned and sent a full pulse out at a tall oak tree, exploding the whole top of it in a shower of fire.

"Thank you," said Ahroe, calmly, as the others had scattered, running back.

"What?"

"For warning the Shumai."

"It is Blu and the men," said Tor, absently. "Someone is with them. Jestak, I imagine."

"How do you know?"

As if in answer, a semicircle of horns sounded when the Shumai had spread out in the woods.

"Eolyn, take that helmet off. Someone will be killed," said Ruthan.

"Please, Eo," Butto added. "Look at what you've done to Stel—and that man. Let's settle this thing. Now. Come on."

Jestak came up the hill, running and slipping in the rain, a big dog next to him. It was Raran, who turned and loped over to Tor, whining, bristling as she saw Ruthan, who drew back with a shriek. Raran cowered down and put her head on Tor as Jestak stopped in the middle of the two groups.

"Which is Royal?" said Jestak abruptly.

"I."

"I need help for Stantu, my friend. I see the dome is burning. Tell me how to get in and get the medicine for his radiation poisoning. Celeste says you can help."

"It isn't that easy," said Royal. "It could be many things. A whole shelf of chemicals will be needed, and many tests."

"Tell me, quick. Where? I will bring it all."

"Don't let him go," said Tor from the ground. "He will die if he goes."

Jestak turned angrily. "I have to go. If I don't, Stan will die."

"Blu," Tor called out with sudden strength. "Don't let Jestak go."

Seven men seemed to appear from nowhere. Jestak turned, touched his short-sword, then ran toward the causeway. Two men caught him and wrestled him down. Blu came over to Tor.

"Good Sertine, Tor. What happened?"

"I did it," said Ruthan.

Blu flashed her a look of pure hatred, then, seeing her in abject misery, found it melting away.

"And I killed Dexter," said Ruthan, dissolving wholly into tears.

"No. No you didn't," Tor murmured. "That other one did. She killed the other man."

"What? She?" Ruthan looked up at Eolyn, still standing in her pulser helmet, back off, in a knot of dome people, aloof now and watchful.

Jestak was still wrestling, as they brought him over to Tor. He drew in his breath as he saw the axeman's arm, but he was blind with anger. "You may be hurt, you fat piece of bull dung. But let me go. I have come all this way to save Stantu. Damn you, fish guts, let me—"

"You would be killed," said Tor, absently, in a deep voice.

"I'd be in there by now, and out before—" The whole hill seemed to buck and heave as a great balloon of fire gushed upward from the dome and levels, the immense structure seeming to rise, float high, rest in the air, fragment, and then settle, in a terrific roaring, orange sphere. The two men dropped Jestak's arms. He turned and ran to the hill rim, stood staring, then slumped to the ground, crying.

Blu went to him and squatted down. "Come," he said. "We have to get Tor out of the rain. Come. See? Tor has a way of knowing. You would be dead now, and that wouldn't help Stantu." Jestak didn't move, and Blu waved at the others, all of whom, dome people, Shumai, and Pelbar, left the hill, carrying Tor down toward the ledge, leaving Jestak and Blu sitting in the rain.

XI

THE rain slowed, and Jestak sat up, then looked at Blu as if seeing him for the first time. "I met Stantu in the eastern city of Innanigan," he said. "We were both young. Our friendship has grown to be the friendship of all our people. There must be a way to save him."

"I have seen him, Jestak. Will saving him restore his hair, his running, his laugh, the free movement of his limbs? I can't think it. Now there are people down there to be organized, and Tor's arm—Tor's arm must be cared for. Come on down."

"You go."

"Jestak, you are the merger of peoples. I am only a substitute axeman. That savage woman and her gnomes may kill us all. You have to come."

Jestak stood up. "Look at us," he said. "We are soaking." Blu laughed and wiped his hands on his thighs.

Below, the two groups still remained mostly separate, but Ruthan had convinced Royal to help Tor, and a small group bent over him in a rough shelter under the rocks. Stel had erected it for privacy early in the summer. Skahie held Tor's head. Royal, frustrated at the dirt and the crude tools, gave orders to Bill, who shuttled out to a pot of boiling water, bringing whatever the old physician required. Ruthan held Tor's arm and watched his expression.

"We have nothing to deaden the pain," she said.

"I have myself," Tor said, his eyes glazed over.

Farther down, under the overhang, Eolyn, still in her pulser helmet, said, "Look at them down there fussing over that walking anachronism. Look at these people. We are past the year 3000. Bows and axes. Good God, what has everything come to? People survived, but they have regressed. Devolved to the primitive."

No one replied. Butto and Cohen-Davies were too surprised and shaken, and too much in awe of the new world to listen. Each smell, each bird call, a cloud of gnats, astonished them. Finally, Butto said, "I wonder if there are snakes."

After a time, Blu and Jestak came down the hill. Jestak took off his tunic and wrung it out as he walked, then hung it on a rack near a fire the Shumai had built. In his wet pants only, he walked over to the dome group. "Who's in charge here?"

"I am," said Eolyn. "I and Royal. And that's close enough."

"Don't be silly. I am Jestak. I am Chief Outside Planner of the City of Northwall. Look here. I will draw you a map and show you where you are."

"We know where we are—in southeastern Missouri not all that far from St. Louis."

"What? Saint what? You may know what this once was, I suppose. Now you are in the middle of Urstadge, about forty-four ayas west of the Heart." Taking a stick, Jestak cut a rough map in the dirt. Cohen-Davies squatted down and watched closely.

"St. Louis must be about there," he said, "if that is north."

"Nothing is there. Nothing even grows. An empty place. And it is really there."

"But the river."

"It has moved. You can see when you are there. It flows as I have shown. I think you had better come to Pelbarigan—provided that you agree not to use those incredible weapons of yours."

"And if we don't agree?" said Eolyn.

"Then we will have to leave you here. We must agree in friendship."

"Suppose we force you? As you said, we have the incredible weapons."

Jestak stood and looked at her eyes through the helmet windows. "You wouldn't get us all," he said. "Soon the whole countryside would be aroused. You mustn't exaggerate your power. Besides, what would you eat?"

"Look at all this." She waved her hands at the woods. "If we have eaten and recycled for over a thousand years, we can surely manage here."

Jestak turned to Butto. "I don't understand," he said. "Perhaps you can explain. I see no reason for hostility.

All Stel did was to get into the dome to save you from its collapse. It was hanging out over the gully. There are so few of us left in the world, even now. We need to pool our knowledge. Clearly you have things to teach us. Already Celeste is building what she calls a microscope, and she has regular classes in chemistry and mathematics."

Eolyn snorted. "Her?"

"She is a good little girl," Stel said. He was propped against the rock wall. Ahroe was with him, holding water so he could sip it. He couldn't seem to get enough.

"If a little girl can teach you, then why should we do what you say? We should obviously be directing things."

"Your technological understanding is extensive. That's clear enough. But your social development is decidedly primitive."

Eolyn snorted again. "Having the technology, we have all that's important."

"Anybody who would make those men tiny is not fit to direct an outhouse," said Blu, who had been standing silently by.

"We are just fine. We don't need any help," said Comp 13.

"Well, you are going to be better," said Blu, reaching out and ruffling the small man's hair. Comp 13 frowned.

Cohen-Davies stood up and dusted himself off. "You, Jestak? Eolyn may do what she wants, but I am going with you. I suspect Bill will as well. I would like to see Celeste again and watch her teach her classes. I am the former resident expert on the ancient times. I would be pleased to pool my knowledge with yours. If this Pelbarigan is the only city remaining, clearly that is where we must start. All this is very strange to me, and I must confess I'm too old to sit around while water falls on me, then have all these creatures land on me and crawl around. It is too unnatural. Or perhaps it is too natural. So lead on, Jestak. I'll follow. Butto—are you coming?"

"I would like to. Come on, Eo."

She said nothing. Jestak waited, hands clasped behind him.

Then she said, "Royal and I will talk when he is through with that genetic throwback over there."

"Good," said Jestak, and held out his hand.

"What is that?" she asked.

"You are supposed to clasp his hand," said Cohen-Davies. "It is an ancient custom that signifies agreement."

Eolyn sighed and shook Jestak's hand. Then she took off her pulser helmet and smoothed her hair. She saw Jestak and Blu staring at her. "What? What's the matter now?" she asked.

"Nothing," said Jestak, grinning. "Nothing at all. I had no idea so formidable a person would be so incredibly beautiful."

Shortly after, Tristal arrived, carrying a heavy pack of food. He was astonished at what had happened and unable to speak when he saw his uncle's arm. Royal had finished suturing the wound, and Tor lay back. Ruthan still sat by him.

Blu sent two men to Pelbarigan to bring more boats. Jestak and Butto viewed the dome from the hilltop, still burning, and wholly shattered, and decided that nothing worth saving remained. One white rat, its side singed naked, wandered on the empty ground in the mud. As they watched, a large gray hawk stooped and took it, flying heavily across the gully, banking north toward the trees. The Shumai brought a black yearling calf, butchered it, and roasted large chunks over a long fire. Stel eventually took out his flute, and as the sun set in broad red bands under the clouds, he played a slow series of Pelbar hymns, haunting and calming. The mixed group of people ate meat and twists of quickbread from Tristal's new supplies, largely in silence. After a late-summer darkness fell, they slowly settled down to a strange and troubled night.

As the darkness deepened, Eolyn finally went to the shelter where Tor lay and stood over him. "Ruthan, I would like to speak to this man alone," she said.

Tor looked at them both, and at Tristal, who sat in a corner sewing a running shoe, almost by feel in the darkness. Raran began a throaty growl, but Tor held out his left hand to the dog, and she stopped. "All right," he said. "Tris, take Raran."

When they were alone, Tor said, "Well?"

"I wanted to express our regrets that we have done this to you," said Eolyn.

"You didn't do it. The other one, Ruthan, did. You

killed the man—Dexter. I was luckier than he." He laughed ruefully, holding up his arm stump.

Eolyn ignored that remark. "Will you be at this city of Pelbarigan long?" she asked.

"I don't know. I don't want to. We will see."

"I feel responsible. We will devise a prosthetic attachment so you can use your arm again. Of course you will have to live a more settled life."

"I don't know what you mean, but I don't think I will do that," said Tor, quietly.

"You could learn a great deal. You look like a person of intelligence. You could master the technology we will bring this society."

"Technology? I have no need of it. What I need is my arm, and I see I will have to learn to live without it. But look, Eolyn—is that your name? You didn't come in here to say these things. What is it? I feel some unspoken thought in you fighting to get out. What is it?"

"I don't understand how you know things. You knew the dome would explode, you knew who was coming, you know . . ." She fell silent and sat still a long time.

At last Tor said, "It doesn't matter. Tris was right. You are extremely beautiful. I wish— something is missing in you, though, isn't it? You don't feel bad about that man, Dexter, and wonder why. And yet you do. It was too bad that you had to live all that time shut up in that artificial cave."

She stood, angry. "You needn't pity me. We did very nicely." She turned to go.

"Wait," said Tor. "Please come back." She did come, but remained standing. Tor reached out with his left hand and took hold of her ankle. "I sense a great regret. I think it is my regret more than yours. You think of me as a savage, don't you? That's all right, I suppose. The country is vast and open, and there is room enough for both of us in it. But still . . .".

"I don't know what you are talking about. Now, please let go of my ankle."

Tor held it nearly a full sunspan longer, Eolyn waiting impatiently. Then he released it. "I wonder if you would ask Stel and Ahroe to come in here when you go, please." Eolyn left, without a further word, but soon Stel and Ahroe did enter the small enclosure.

Ahroe knelt down by Tor and put her arms around

him, pushing her face down into his shoulder. "I have you to thank for getting Stel back," she said, her voice muffled against him. "And now this. This. What can we say?"

Tor sighed. "It is more than that, isn't it. Lean up now. You are embarrassing me. It is more than that. We all had to do this. If we didn't, and they were lost, that would have been wrong. The time of the running hunters is drawing to an end, anyway. Even Blu feels it. I sense it in him. He'll try to keep it up for a while. Then we will all quit. This stretching land, these lovely plains and hills, all stitched together for the Shumai by the passing and repassing of the young hunters. Soon it will be empty of them, and they will be plodding along, carrying burdens and messages, or following a horse in a furrow. It won't be the same. But that's not what I wanted to see you about. It's that woman, Eolyn."

"Eolyn?"

"I really fear her. It isn't that she is independent in thought. That's surely all right. She has no morality."

"Tor, give her a chance. You've barely met her."

"I feel it. Watch her. It isn't that she's wicked. There isn't that much purpose in her. But she has a potential for wickedness. It radiates from her. She is groping, without boundaries to her possibilities. Stel, tell her. You must feel it."

"It's true, my love. She did treat me like a piece of raw meat. But even so I gathered that she had more regard for me as a human being than did the dead one, Dexter. He wanted to vivisect me."

"Vivisect?"

"I think it meant cut me up while I was still alive to see how I worked."

Tor shuddered, wincing as his arm pulled. "Ahroe, deal with them on wholly logical grounds if you can. They seem to understand only that—except Ruthan."

"And the old one, Cohen-Davies. And the fat one, Butto."

"They don't count."

"I think they do," said Stel. "Not in their own group. But they are the ones we'll get the most from eventually."

"Don't be too sure. They seem to have divided up their responsibilities. Each has something to offer. Now please give my impressions to Jestak. And let him do the negotiating, Ahroe, even if he is a man. Please? And thank you for shaking me out of my shock. I think I might have died."

"It was Hagen over again. I couldn't stand it."

"Ahroe, I'm not sure yet I can stand it. What am I to do?"

"Aven will tell you," said Stel. "All things and people have a function if they give themselves to it. That may sound like nonsense, but I learned it."

"It's my impression, Tor, that all along it's been your mind that your men followed, not your right arm," said Ahroe.

"Without the right arm, out on the plains, the mind has no tool."

"There is the left," said Stel. "I am left-handed myself. Now you are, too."

Ahroe embraced him again, and the couple stooped out of the shelter. Ruthan was standing with Blu, and the two joined them. "Blu, I am worried. He is concerned with us, surely, but profoundly depressed. I think someone should be with him all the time, especially tonight," Stel said.

"I will be with him," Ruthan returned. "I did it. I will be with him."

Blu shot her a look. "He will need physical care," he said.

"I will give him any care he needs."

"That includes—"

"I know. That is nothing. We had few ceremonies, you know, in the dome and levels. We even recycled . . . everything."

"Well," said Blu. "I will come, too."

"No. I will. You just stay nearby. If he needs any special help, I will call you."

"I will—"

"Blu," said Stel. "She will be all right. Let her."

The Shumai was irritated, but saw Stel smiling at him whimsically. He seemed to catch a meaning but was not sure. He didn't much like it. What did Stel know? Ahroe looked slightly scandalized. She shook her head. Ruthan covered her face, but went into the shelter.

"I—but—all this is no way to— It—"

"I am sure that Tor won't knowingly assault her, Blu,"

said Ahroe, turning away. "He wouldn't anyway, even if he were well. Let her make her peace."

Late that night, with two fires flickering outside, and only the two Shumai guards and a comp talking in low tones, Tor felt the pressure of his loss coming on him again, weighing him down, as if he spiraled through water, a slowly settling rock, inert and helpless. It was the dog of darkness come again. He cried out in his dream, a light moan. Then something was pulling him, lifting him up. A struggle ensued, long and strange, between the weight and the lifting force, as if two arms held him, becoming bird's talons, lifting him up through the deep water, out into the night, where he could see the star-circle and the hunter group wheeling slowly above him. Strong hands bore him up, and the pulsing of wings, beating and beating, into a blinding light. He shut his eyes against it, squeezing them. The light seemed to grow and burst out from inside. Then he was soaring, still in pain, still held, still high and free, gliding, out, far away from the dog of darkness, gliding to a hilltop on the prairies, gravelly with eroded outcrop, flowers nodding in the dawn. Eventually it all faded and he was back again, in Stel's shelter, a weight on his chest. Feeling, he found it was Ruthan's head. She was sleeping. He didn't understand, but she was no burden. Her hair was as fine as brook water. He felt it with his fingers and watched the faint flickering of the firelight across the brush wall.

He grew drowsy. His dream seemed to recall one of the rolls of Pell. "Aven," he whispered to himself, "Aven, Mother of all life, protect us all, lift us over these barriers. Let us ride free on the wings of Your thought, guiding us in the trackless air over the river, with Your surety, gently and safely." The Haframa had read that one to Celeste, but the girl gave no sign of understanding it. Tor liked it, but he too had no idea what it meant. Then he slept, for the first time since his wound, gaining some sense of peace.

The morning rose clear, promising to renew the recent heat. The dome people had spent a fitful and uncomfortable night. Jestak and Blu had not gone out of their way to provide comforts, and had seen to it that the fires lay downwind from them, encouraging mosquitoes. They hoped to "use the tiny swords of insects to point out the logic of going to Pelbarigan," as Jestak had put it.

Much of the morning was taken up with formal agreement, which Royal and Eolyn insisted upon, proposing several points. They would be free to go anywhere at any time. They would receive no opposition to their departure. In exchange for supplies, protection, and direction, they would agree to teach their knowledge at a fixed rate of exchange until either side terminated the agreement. The exchange would involve real estate, supplies of various kinds, and defense. It would also include access to such information as was available from the Pelbar.

At one juncture, Jestak said, imitating Eolyn's manner wryly, "Several points ought to be made here. First, what you feel you have to bargain for the Pelbar have always freely given to anyone who asked. Hence you are incurring obligations you need not incur. Second, unlike the eastern cities, we have no medium of exchange, nothing of what you call a monetary system, and it would be too cumbersome to devise one here under this rock in the heat. Third, you are in nearly total ignorance of the nature of the world as it is today. In this regard, I might point out several things: (a) We will be giving you at least as much knowledge of the nature of things today as you will be giving us about ancient learning. That too has a value. (b) You seem to anticipate supplies and materials will be available as they used to be. That is not true. You will experience the same steep drop in abilities that the surviving ancients did because of their interdependence, their need of transportation to supply their economy, their near-complete reliance on the skills of others for basic aspects of their lives. (c) It has not really sunk in on you, I feel, that nearly everyone died. After all these years, the land is still almost empty of people. You will need to depend on those people who did survive, that is, on us, their descendants, for our mutual advancement if it is to be rapid.

"A fourth point is that we are a functioning economy. While we would be grateful for your knowledge as a contribution to our goal of reuniting the scattered societies into one again, we are progressing without it. What you offer is an aid, not an essence. Fifth, evidently your group in the dome anticipated emerging onto a blasted earth as its first men. Through our help you will be advanced many generations beyond that, and it ought to be a cause for gratitude."

"Bravo. Well outlined, Jestak," said Butto.

Eolyn looked at him narrowly. "We are not interested in gratitude but in fair exchange. We—"

"I am interested in gratitude," said Bill.

Eolyn whirled on the little man, who looked mildly up at her. So he regarded himself a free agent now. That complicated things.

"I am interested in gratitude, too," said Cohen-Davies. "I see no point in bargaining with a group of people who are willing to admit us into their community. We are not in the dome. I see no reason why our old structure of rule should still hold."

"Perhaps you can settle that among yourselves sometime," said Jestak. "But for the time being, so we can get underway, let us assume that Eolyn is correct. She is the one who seems to need an agreement."

"We are not even sure you are genuinely of our species," Eolyn returned. "That one, Stel, showed he was able to reject radiation. So has this whole biological community. We are unsure what shielding we will need to survive."

"Radiation? Celeste spoke of radiation. It makes people sick when they go to the empty places. I don't believe there is any right here."

"More likely," said Royal, "it is some sort of poisoning in these empty places, perhaps involving plutonium and radiation. We would have to run an analysis. But we are unsure of why the radiation monitor always showed heavy radiation. Always. It was no malfunction."

"You mean the rod?"

"Yes, the wand we sent up from the dome."

"Perhaps it received this radiation at the time of fire and retained it. The top looked burned and fused."

"It was installed much later, our history assures us, by people several generations into our stay there."

"Impossible," said Stel. "Just before you shot me, I looked at it from inside the dome. The whole structure had been made as a unit with the dome at the beginning. I can recall the bracing and the concrete matrix."

Eolyn and Royal looked at each other. "That isn't what our history said," she replied.

"Nonetheless, that is the fact," said Stel. "But it

doesn't matter. You are talking nonsense anyway. There is no radiation here. People live to be old. And Celeste is as human a person as I know. She lives with us. She laughs, sweats, cries, grows angry, loves. Everything is the same. Don't try to fob yourselves off as superior creatures. You are just more people. A pretty surly bunch, by and large, I might say."

"Surly? Surely, Stel, you just jest. Bunch? Please at least describe us as an organization, a group; if not a hierarchy, at least a lowarchy," said Butto.

Eolyn shook her head. "Butto at least is merely confused. But the point is that no matter how you describe us, we have knowledge. Knowledge otherwise lost, and precious."

"And some incredible ignorance, too. Celeste is slowly learning to communicate with ease, but she still works better with her growing supply of devices than with people. She—"

"She is a freak. She underwent an accident that left her speechless."

"Until she was with Tris and Tor awhile. She talks freely enough. I think you are all a bunch of freaks."

"Stel," said Ahroe. "Let Jestak talk for us. You resent their mistreatment. Bad as it was, you must forgive them."

"Forgive them? I forgive them enough, though I would probably be dead if Butto hadn't come along. I am intensely disappointed, that's all. I spent an entire sweating summer trying to warn these louts that their whole structure was going to fall apart and dump them down the gully, and they act like a gang of damned goatherders. I—"

"Stel," said Jestak. "Enough. Be generous. You haven't been shut up all your life. We can give them all they require."

"All I require is something to keep these tiny beasts off me," said Cohen-Davies. "I should be glad to get to Pelbarigan if they could be deterred."

Still Eolyn wouldn't yield any gratitude or concessions. It was clear that Royal looked to her lead and backed her. Finally the decision was made to agree to all of Eolyn's terms except anything to do with a rate of exchange. That would await discussion between Eolyn and the Protector. By noon the party was ready to leave. Six of Blu's men would go along, but Blu and the rest would remain with Tor. Ruthan insisted on remaining as well, and no arguments could dissuade her, even though her body was, like those of the other dome people, showing the distress of the food of the outside world. Blu stayed because Ruthan did, or so he said. He not only had oddly conventional proprieties, but he was genuinely worried about Tor.

The party set out, hoping to reach the slow-flowing Raimac by nightfall. Blu and Ruthan watched them go, as Dailith and Stel had watched the guardsmen take Susan on her litter earlier. Blu put his arm around Ruthan's shoulder. She looked at him, startled.

"Come to the top of the rocks," he said. "We need to talk awhile."

She felt hesitant, a little frightened. But he smiled slightly. She felt she had no real choice. As they went, climbing a path south of the overhang, she grew more and more assured. She even began to ask him about the plants, but found his knowledge to be either unsystematic or selective. He knew the habits and uses of plants he had no names for. Some he knew intimately. Eventually they reached the rim of the hill. Looking westward, they could see faint, dark smoke still rising from the ruined dome.

"Ruthan," Blu began. "Is that your only name? Ruthan?"

"I have another I never use. Ruthan Tromtrager. But I have no family. None of us does. We—we were born ... well, in a laboratory."

Blu looked at her, puzzled and shocked. "What do you mean?"

"I had no mother, quite literally. I was the product of the joining of biological materials in a special genetic laboratory."

"I don't understand. It doesn't matter. You look all right."

"What do you want with me?"

"Simply that you mustn't fall in love with Tor."

She turned. "What? What do you mean by that? I—"

"Sit down."

"I don't—"

"Just sit down. Please?" She did. "We will have to get you some decent clothes," said Blu.

"Did you bring me up here to tell me that? Just tell me what you want to. I will take care of my clothes. I may—" She stopped.

Blu looked over, quizzically. "Well, it is this. It is one thing to care for Tor in remorse for hurting him. It is another to—"

"To love him?"

Blu swallowed. "Perhaps it is futile. I don't know. Tor is a rare man. He was taken by the Tusco as a child, and sold by them to the Alats, far to the south. Somehow he survived all that, escaped, and grew to be an unusual axeman. But even before he reached his full maturity, the fight took place at Northwall—one of the Pelbar cities. And that ended the hostilities between Shumai and Pelbar. And even the Sentani. Jestak—you just met him —he was more responsible for it than anyone else. He has begun making one people out of us. All the Shumai seem to be settling down. I admit the old way of life is a hard one. But it is hard for us to give it up. Yet even this summer two of the bands have dropped out to join a cattle farm up on the Isso River. I feel the restlessness of the others. Tor didn't lead the band this summer. I did. But I am not Tor. He is pure axeman."

"Pure axeman?"

"They are married to the country, usually having nothing to do with women. They are often curiously quiet and abstracted, like Tor. They often seem idle. But they have a way of knowing things, like the tanwolves, as if by instinct. They are often orators of considerable skill. They are capable of great physical acts."

"And you are afraid I might spoil all that?"

"In a sense. But that isn't the problem. You would be brought to grief as well. Tor has been brooding about the vanishing of the running bands. You can see it. He knows he will never be a farmer or live in a settlement. Now his life will be triply hard with the loss of his arm. But I am sure he will remain an axeman at heart, no matter what. Tristal has been sick, but now that he is better, and Celeste is more on her own—"

"Celeste? What has she to do with this?"

"Tristal and Raran—his dog—found Celeste wandering on the hill. They took her to Tor, and then they all went to Pelbarigan. She grew very sick. Tor watched over her like a father. She grew dependent on him. She—"

"You mean Celeste fell in love with him?" Ruthan began to laugh.

Blu frowned at her. "It may seem funny, but Tor wouldn't simply abandon her. She had no one else. She is beginning to be a woman now, so Stel says. She is more balanced, now that she is well and in a city. Tor did it, you know. The cost, I fear, was the integrity of the band, because I am not Tor. But perhaps he is seeing ahead even now. But he has lost himself, really. He has no idea what to do. This will be redoubled now that—"

"Don't say it again."

"Oh."

"So you are asking me to let him alone, then? You fear he may waste himself on me?" Again she began to laugh in a fluttering high tone. Blu stared at her. "It is too much. New worlds coming and going. Good God, why can't I die?"

"Die? There is no need to die. You have just been released. Your life will knit together." He reached out an arm to touch her.

"How long will it continue to knit together when it keeps being torn apart?" She looked at him, mocking. "Your life will knit together," she said, imitating his voice. "You sanctimonious animal!" She stood and kicked him, hurting her foot, then pounded on him with her fists. He seemed not to notice, but finally took her wrists and held them. She bit at his hands, but he simply spread them, staring at her. Finally, she went limp, and he lowered her to the ground. She lay crying for a time, then sat up. Blu sat on his heels, watching her.

"What are you going to do now?" she asked.

He spread his hands. "What would you want me to do?"

"I don't know. How would I know? Are you crazy?"

"Perhaps. What we ought to do is wait for Tor to get better, then go to Pelbarigan. You know about plants, you say. You could teach them what you know, and they you."

"I am sorry."

"No need. I can see that you and I will be friends yet. You aren't like that Eolyn ghost. Was she made without a mother, too? No offense. But they left out her feelings."

"I have too many."

"No. You have just enough." They laughed nervously.

Blu stood, hearing a sound on the path. It was Dard, who said, "Blu, Tor is up. He wants to go to Pelbarigan."

"Up? Already? How can that be? How does he look?"

"Awful. Weak. But he wants to go."

"Are you ready?"

"The men are about packed. We have made the boots for this woman."

"Then it is time to go. Are you ready, Ruthan Tromtrager?"

"He should not be moved."

"He says so. Come on down. We will see if your running boots fit. Sark has made them. This is Dard, Sark's son."

"Yes. Hello. Running? I will have to walk."

"So will Tor, for now. Come on."

Because of Ruthan and Tor, they moved slowly, Tor almost dreamily, Ruthan constantly questioning Blu and Dard. Bill strove manfully to keep up on his short legs, but finally Sark swept him up and put him on his shoulders. At first Bill thought to object, but the ease and the new height so charmed him that he simply held on and looked. The tall late-summer prairie grass topped even Sark's head, but Bill could see out over the high, turkey-foot seed heads.

"You, Bill," said Sark.

"Yes?"

"Watch for smoke. The grass is drying again. Prairie fire. If there is one, we have to run."

"Fire? Out here? What stops it?"

"Nothing. Nothing at all sometimes, but a river or a rain."

Bill shuddered. But he would not be back in the dome for anything, though his eyes were dazzled and his white skin began to burn in the sun. Ahead, as they walked, Skall, another older man, pulled stems and wove them, finally turning and placing a crude straw hat on Bill.

Eventually Ruthan tired so she couldn't walk further. Blu set her up on his shoulders and they continued, but slowly.

Finally, Tor said, "Who wants to carry me? No one? I

suggest we stop at the stream ahead. I'm sorry. I need some rest and meat."

The other group did make it to the Raimac, though it was only at sunset, and the dome people were tired to the core. Most of the way the Shumai and Dailith carried the comps, switching off, and even Royal rode on the Pelbar guardsman for a time. Eolyn insisted on walking the whole way. Cohen-Davies showed a surprising stamina, owing to his private daily exercises, and Butto struggled along on grit.

The Shumai gave their light summercloths to the dome people, dirty as they were, for the hunters used them for towels, holders for hot objects, sun hoods, and blankets. They were not long in shooting several fish to mix in with the dried meat and herbs in the skin pot they threw rocks into, hot from the fire, for cooking. Eolyn looked on the process with enormous distaste, but she was hungry enough not to care. She relied on her panimmune to protect her.

After they ate, sitting near the firelight, Dailith sought her out. "We could rest a day. There is no hurry," he said.

"I am all right. Royal may need a rest, but we should move on. I am oppressed by all this openness. And those roads. We crossed two of them. Wide ones. They are ancient highways. It really is true. The whole land is empty. Where are the ruins?"

"There are ruins. Plenty of them. But the time of fire was a long time ago. How are your legs? The second day is usually worse if you aren't in good condition. They may be stiff and sore."

"No doubt. But they are all right. It is my feet."

Without asking, Dailith took off the running boots the Shumai had quickly sewn together for her.

"Don't," she said.

"You have no blisters. Don't wash. It softens the skin. I will get you some rabbit fur for the red places." He turned and left, and she watched his broad back with some wonder. It made no sense. What did he want?

Jestak sat by Cohen-Davies as the old man questioned Oro about wood fires. He waited in silence until they were through.

"What did Eolyn say was our location?" he asked.

"Missouri. That was a section of a country called the United States of America. What do you call it now?"

"We seldom call it anything, really, but when we do refer to it, it is Urstadge. That has no real boundaries because few travel to the ends of what we know of it. I have been to the eastern cities, by the ocean to the east."

"The Atlantic."

"The Atlantic? No one there called it anything but the Eastern Sea. There are islands in it—the Saltstream Islands. I have been to them, too. I met the Saltstream prophets there. That is the easternmost place anyone knows about."

"There are no islands in the Atlantic I know of, unless you mean Bermuda, which is quite far south, or the Azores, which are very far off."

"I think these are new. One had a smoking mountain. I have learned that they are called volcanic. Do you know about that?"

"Quite a bit. I will have to recall it."

"Don't worry about it now. We will have to question you at great length at Pelbarigan and get it all written down. We are piecing the world back together. It is an unbelievable task. We have learned much from the Commuters, a small group of herdsmen beyond the western mountains."

"The Rockies."

"Yes. That's it. They called them that. I have been thinking. Would you agree to help establish a school, or as they said in Innanigan, an academy, at Pelbarigan? We need a center for the reassembly of knowledge."

"You have none?"

"We have always had our schools, of course. But only recently have the various surviving groups begun to talk seriously to one another. We have—" Jestak broke off. Looking over, he had seen that the old man was asleep.

Butto, meanwhile, dug into his third helping of stew, asking Stel about various things in it. Stel was amused. It reminded him of his own son, Garet, several years ago.

"What is this?"

"Thistle root. It gets tough this time of year, and so it is pounded and cut."

"And this?"

"Wild potato. They found a small one. Sometimes they are gigantic."

"Gigantic? A term subject to errors semantic."

"Don't be pedantic."

"I'm too tired to be romantic. Or frantic. What's this?"

"Milkweed buds. There aren't many—the reason? It's late in the season. Buds are decreasin'."

"You are amazin'. Such elegant phrasin'."

"Your praisin' is raisin' my self-esteem."

"Surely I dream. I hear a ream of rhyme by this stream, it would seem."

"Stop or I'll scream," said Ahroe. They looked up and laughed.

"What's this?" Butto resumed.

"Cattail root. The Shumai pulled some up when we passed through the marsh. That is what they were pounding and rinsing."

"It doesn't taste very good."

"It's food. If you're in the mood. I wouldn't exclude it brewed with whatever else we have stewed."

"The vicissitudes of our fortune preclude that I should exclude it from the amplitude of the dinner I've chewed, and, my dear fellow, my remarks mustn't be so construed."

"Whew," said Stel. "You're beyond me, I see. Vicissi-what? Ampli-what? I can see you will be pressed into service as a linguist."

"That will be fine, but not tonight," said Butto, leaning back. Stel took his bark dish and put it in the fire.

"Well, Eolyn," said Dailith. "It would appear that they are both of the same species."

"You mean they are both crazy."

"If Butto is half as effective as Stel, he must be a great asset to you."

"He's all emotion and little thought. Would you mind sleeping here with me and the comps? I don't understand why Ahroe won't stay near here. I am afraid of those wild men."

"You are safer with them than without. Ahroe is with Stel because they are married. But I will stay here. The Shumai live a wild life, but they are people of honor."

"Married? Do you mean it? I thought that was an ancient custom."

"It is practiced by all the peoples I know, though in different forms. It seems to work fairly well, though there is some trouble."

"Then they practice sexual loyalty?"

"Absolutely. The Heart River peoples are all extremely strict about that."

"Poor Ruthan."

"What?"

"Nothing. I am pleased we all speak enough alike to be understood. I am tired as a dog, as we have always said. But that's only the second dog I've ever seen. I'm amazed how he lives with the people."

"Dusk? He is Blu's dog. The south Shumai train their dogs strictly."

"Blu's dog? Why isn't he with the other group? Isn't that Blu with them?"

"At least two reasons that I know of. For protection. They have Raran. This is wild-hog country. Hogs will attack without warning, and the dog senses them first."

"And the other reason?"

"Well, forget that one. I'm sorry I brought it up."

"No. What is it?"

"You will be angry. See? You are already."

"No. That is too irrational. I sometimes get frustrated, I admit. Tell me."

"Dogs sense things about people that people miss. The Shumai are using Dusk to size you all up."

"To size us up?"

"Dogs respond to fear, love, coldness, kindness, indifference. It would not hurt to reach toward him with your inner warmth."

"I reached toward him, but he growled. He seems to like Butto well enough. Perhaps bumblers are more his type."

Dailith didn't answer. They settled down, though the Shumai, being still fresh, had removed themselves a little way to play the star game. Eolyn lay awake in her fatigue, feeling surreal, listening to them laughing and calling their strange names for the stars. Eventually, two of them came to put fresh smudge on the fire to discourage the mosquitoes.

One said, "I saw how polite you were. You washed your arm before you retrieved the stones from the stew."

"What about you? You made a bark dish for Dusk so he wouldn't eat out of the pot." Both men laughed quietly and returned to the star game. Eolyn shuddered a little. This was all so strange. Looking up the hill she saw the dim outline of a Shumai guard. He stood very still, leaning on a long spear with a short crosspiece tied on it. Something shifted in her mind, and she felt safe. Reaching out, she touched Dailith on the one side and Comp 12 on the other. Eventually she went to sleep. Dailith lay very still, staring up at the stars.

By the time Eolyn's party reached the river, two days later, they were footsore, filthy, and scratched. One of the Shumai sounded a horn as they trudged through sodden bottomland, and a long answer came from ahead. Offshore, out of the shallows, they saw an old Tantal ship, manned by a large body of Pelbar guardsmen. Oet stood on the deck by the ladder to greet each small boatload as they came up over the side. Cohen-Davies was charmed, since the ship, wooden, with lateen sails and oars, and a high prow shaped like a mythical animal head, reminded him of the tapes of the ancient medieval period. Only after peering all around the ship did he turn and look out across the great stretch of river. He caught his breath. There, rolling placid and muddy, draining the whole upper continent, lay a stretch of water he hadn't imagined possible.

Dailith nudged his elbow. "Like it? It's the Heart. We are about nine hundred ayas from its mouth, so I'm told, and several major rivers have yet to empty into it. Look there. The teal and woodies are flying south already." He pointed out three small flocks of ducks, far and tiny, out over the water. "Down there are fish as big as a man," the guardsman added. Far out, a whole tree floated downstream, slowly, its branches leading, the disk of its big roots standing high out of the water behind. A small, black bird rode on the highest root.

Before the introductions were completed, another horn sounded from the bottoms. It was answered from the ship, and soon Tor's party arrived. The axeman seemed stronger, but moved in a deep gloom.

After they came aboard, Ruthan whispered to Ahroe, "He has hardly said anything today. He seems far off."

"He might well, Ruthan. He feels lost. Let him alone. But not too alone."

As the ship got underway, Stel moved over to Tor, nudged him, and held out his left hand, palm up. The axeman slapped it down gently. Stel caught a ghost of a smile. "If I'm not mistaken, Stel, you're going to be a father again," he murmured, then moved off to stare at the river.

Stel, whirled. Ahroe? Pregnant? Did she tell Tor before him? She had been close enough to hear and came over. "How did he know? I didn't tell him."

"When did you know?"

"About six weeks ago I was sure."

"You had no business coming. Don't you know—"

Ahroe put a finger across his lips. "I wanted him—or her—to have a father after all."

Stel grinned and put his arm around her, Ruthan watching, quizzical and downcast.

"Is it that easy, then?"

"I haven't observed that—"

"Stel!"

Stel laughed, and Ahroe walked to where Tor looked out at the water. She took his arm. He didn't move or turn. She held it for some time, as Oet commanded the ship out into the water and turned north, and the shipmen set the bellying, striped sails. They began to glide upriver, the guardsmen at the oars chanting, sunset catching the sail, glorifying it with ruddy light, Ahroe holding Tor's arm, until finally, at twilight, food was brought from the cooking fire aft, and the axeman turned, reaching first with his bound right arm, then with his left hand, taking the bowl.

"Stel," he said, "can you make me an axe sheath for the left side?"

"I had been designing one," Stel said. "Yes, of course. I have been thinking of a new axe as well. I think you will like it."

The big Shumai looked at him silently, then sat on the deck to eat.

Near midnight they tied up to the foot of a small island, and everyone but four guardsmen bedded down. And Tor. He sat in the bow watching the night.

Eventually, Ruthan reached over Dusk and nudged Blu. He stirred. "Look at Tor," she whispered. "What is wrong? What can we do?"

"Go to sleep. He is doing it. Don't worry. He is thinking it all out. You can't do anything. He is far away from us all now."

Ruthan didn't sleep. Eventually, she nudged Blu again. "How can you be sure?" she asked.

Dusk sighed deeply, then slowly got up, stretched,

walked around to the other side of Blu, and flopped noisily down against him. Blu chuckled lightly. He reached for Ruthan's hand. She pulled it away, then put it back and slowly went to sleep. When she awoke at dawn, Blu and Tor stood together in the bow talking in low tones. The guardsmen had cast off, and the shipmen hauled on the big lines, raising the sail again.

It was near sunset again when the guardhorns from Pelbarigan's towers sounded, and much of the city came down to the bank to greet them. Ruthan could see Celeste, standing with an older woman on a platform. She looked filled out, tanned, and healthy. Then Ruthan saw her hands go to her face and heard her shriek above the crowd. She had seen Tor. Ruthan watched the girl turn and run but quickly was herself caught up in the tumult and novelty of welcome, and looked up at the pennons hanging from the high walls of the great stone city, its windows and towers crowded with people, almost all dark-haired, with maroon tunics. In the middle of the whirl, the old woman on the platform stood calm and still, flanked by four guardsmen. Ruthan could see that she too looked grave. Following her gaze, she saw that the old woman was also looking at Tor.

 XII

PELBARIGAN staged a welcome ceremony for the dome people in the great chapel. Ruthan noted with interest that Celeste sang in the choir, her mouth moving in perfect unison with the others. Once when Celeste caught Ruthan watching, she faltered in her singing and sent the older woman a look of metal coldness. She knew about Tor. Ruthan felt the steel point of her own remorse glide into her again. Would she never be rid of it? Where was Tor? Inexplicably, he came beside her and put his arm around her shoulder. The Shumai running band stood together to one side, under the row of columns. Ruthan saw

Blu watching. She couldn't read his expression. Tor kept his arm around her for the rest of the ceremony, until the newcomers were introduced and asked to step forward. As she turned back, she saw Tor's face still hollow and haunted, but as she turned, his arm came around her shoulder again. So that was it. He was saying to everyone that he would not desire any ill will directed toward her on his account. Looking again, Ruthan saw Celeste's face still cold.

"Ruthan," Tor said. "That is her problem, not yours."

How did he know? "It will always be mine," she said.

"It is not mine. Less and less. The one puzzle for me is why Eolyn killed Dexter."

"You are absolutely sure it was Eolyn, then."

"Of course. I have been in enough fights to know where the missiles are coming from."

"It was an accident, then. She was aiming at you." Somehow the thought of Dexter had lost its anguish, though she missed his openness, his humor, his resourceful and quirky behavior.

"An accident. Perhaps. Everything happened so fast. But then I saw her shoot the end off Ahroe's horn."

That was true. But Ruthan's thoughts were caught up in a new Pelbar hymn, with instruments, flutes and pellutes. She saw Susan Ward rapt with the music. The old woman's dulcimer sat idle in her lap.

The ceremony was followed by a meeting with the council. Eolyn's sense of an agreement was presented. The council, Ruthan could see, was puzzled and taken aback, though eased when she, Butto, and Cohen-Davies simply volunteered their services as a matter of joining the community. Royal would have as well, but Eolyn insisted, as the price of his instruction in chemistry and medicine, that she and the comps be housed in a new facility, outside the city, high on the bluffs to the north. She would set up a school for the study of mathematics, electricity, electronics, and mechanical design.

Unsure of what all that meant, the Protector agreed, to the limit of the contribution Pelbarigan's economy could make at harvest season, when all were preparing for winter. Eolyn was unsatisfied by what seemed to Ruthan to be generosity. For the time being, the whole group from the dome would be housed together in a family complex, with their own common room. The comps would serve the principals. It seemed agreeable.

Almost a week later, as organization and adjustment were still taking place, a general session for information was held in the chapel rather than the judgment room, so as many of the city as desired could listen in. The session was protracted.

One subject that the Jestana brought up was the nature of the time of fire. "We know it involved terrible weapons, fire, and meteors," she said. "Or so we would gather from evidence here and Ahroe's trip to the west. But beyond that we know little or nothing. What can you tell us about it, Thornton?"

"Our knowledge may add something, but it is also incomplete. Apparently it began with a catastrophic shower of meteors, not only as large as or larger than the biggest in ancient record, those that landed in Arizona and Siberia, but these came in large numbers, accompanied by innumerable small ones. Their sudden arrival convinced some nations that they were under nuclear attack."

"Nuclear attack?"

"Yes. Attack by the weapons that made what you call the empty places, at their worst, weapons which explode with a heat more than that on the surface of the sun. They could destroy a large city almost instantly, and the whole region around it."

A general murmur rippled through the crowd.

"The two principal nations with many such weapons, the United States, which was where we are, and the U.S.S.R., knew, of course, of the approaching meteors. They had been tracking them. They made a hasty agreement not to take advantage of the catastrophe. But smaller nations, more volatile nations, also possessed many such weapons and what they called delivery systems, and they were of course sure that they were being attacked. Especially in the Middle East, which lies far across what Jestak calls the Eastern Sea, they began hurling nuclear weapons at each other, over hundreds of kilometers, using great rockets. Soon the hostile exchange spread.

"That's about all we know because the dome was sealed and the area hit by a nuclear device. Oh, yes. A few other things. The U.S.S.R., commonly called the Russians, had lofted enormous laser satellites, devices much larger than this city, which circled the earth like low moons in space, and they had the capacity of lighting fires below by carefully calculated bursts of concentrated energy. At the time they were threatening the United States with them."

"What did the United States do about that?"

"Nothing. At the time they were in great disarray. During the twentieth century, the United States was a great industrial power, but one basic source of its wealth lay in a very efficient agricultural system. However, pressure from the industrial sector, both from workers and management, for greater and greater rewards for less and less production, coupled with a concerted attack on the traditional agricultural systems, by a refusal to reward agriculture adequately, and some incredibly poor, chemically disastrous farming methods, crippled the system. The loss of the best agricultural lands to spreading housing, and to salinity from unwise irrigation methods, helped. A collapse in agriculture occurred, with some famine, from which the nation had not fully recovered at the time of fire.

"The government, too, had become incredibly top-heavy, with a bureaucracy absolutely insistent on great rewards for few services. This included earlier and earlier retirement, and all sorts of benefits not available to the other citizens. The bureaucrats were able to retire at age fifty, with large pensions. This finally took so much of the tax money, with a grinding national debt, that the national defense faltered badly. The social security system, which was a tax pool to provide for elderly private citizens, ceased altogether, all funds being absorbed by the bureaucracy and the enormous number of its projects and regulations. The citizenry revolted, but they were put down by the army."

"Why didn't these Russians take advantage of this situation."

"They might have, but they also had deep internal troubles. Central control of their economy, and disaffection among the populace, grew steadily worse until they were very unsure that they could take advantage of their towering military superiority. Apparently they feared that any move on the part of the government, despite despotic control over the people, would touch off forces they couldn't control.

"Besides that, by the time of the disaster, new nations of real power had arisen, including the Central South

American Republic and Panafrica, which took in everything on that continent south of the Sahara Desert."

"Thornton, we have no idea about where those places are."

"We will have to write it all out and draw maps at our leisure. At any rate, judging by the small fragments of reports I have been given, including Stal's account of the record of Ozar, it would appear that the Russians did indeed activate their laser satellites. The curious thing is that they are not over here. Something must have gone wrong."

"Protector," said Ahroe. "Something has puzzled me. Thornton has said that the dome was originally a drug-manufacturing facility which demanded a sealed-off environment. I just cannot imagine, though, that it would have been so well-equipped for such a long survival. Eolyn said that the rod for testing for radiation had been added later, but Stel affirmed that he was sure it was built into the original structure. I don't understand."

"As far as I know," said Cohen-Davies, "it was indeed a drug-manufacturing firm that needed a sterile or controlled environment to manage its tests. The Brimer-McKenny Corporation, to be exact."

"Wait," said Susan Ward. "I know that is the official history. I hope you will forgive my breaking in. To explain to you Pelbar, I have been compiling an unofficial but more accurate history of the dome and levels for some time. What I learned about that is that it was indeed apparently a drug-manufacturing company, but it was really constructed to withstand just the sort of event that occurred. It was designed to shelter federal government officials in the central region. When the catastrophe came, though, none of them ever made it to the shelter."

"You mean they made secret shelters to protect themselves while providing none for the populace?"

"That is correct. Documents I found showed that it was the brainchild of Senator Daniel Dresser-Choate of Missouri, put in his state near his own home. Dresser-Choate had investments in a nearby military manufacturing facility, so he was rather worried about his own safety."

"Amazing. Thornton, I am sure that most of us have only the foggiest notion of what you have been talking about. I trust the secretaries have been busy. We will have to question you in detail and annotate this material, and then add to it your other recollections. Now, does anyone know what has happened to the rest of the world?"

"Only that our early generations were unable to receive radio messages on any frequency from anywhere and after a century gave up."

"Radio messages? Another wonder?"

"Perhaps I can explain," said Eolyn. "We have several miniature transceivers with us, two built into the pulser helmets. Comp 6 is working on my new facility. See this device on my wrist? I shall talk to him." She touched a switch. "Comp 6? Comp 6? Are you awake?"

A tiny voice came from Eolyn's wrist. "Comp 6 awake, Principal Eolyn. What do you wish?" The audience stirred and murmured.

"Just testing the system, Comp 6. Thank you. Asleep now." Eolyn then said, to the general audience, "If we can get the materials, we can be building simple devices like this very quickly." The audience murmur rose to a running exclamation.

The Protector's guardsmen rapped for quiet, and rising, the Protector said, "Thank you very much, all, and I believe that will be enough wonders for now. We need to digest and sort these things. Now it is time for a closed council meeting." The gathering broke up, with the Protector greeting all the dome people individually. It was plain she and Cohen-Davies already were fond of each other.

Later, once the council was gathered, as the Protector had expected, opposition arose. The new Northcounsel, Rickor, spoke at length to the point, opening, "Protector, it was, I believe, a concession on our parts to allow the pursuit of contact with these dome people in the first place. It was undertaken on humanitarian pretenses. It has involved considerable resources. It cannot, we feel, be construed as a prelude to creating an academy dominated by an alien group, a group so far as we know without theology, let alone the true worship of Aven, without a body of law, without a system of marriage, without the common skills needed to survive in the world as we live in it today.

"Furthermore, as we have just heard, the ancients developed a world which did not work, a world full of horrible devices of destruction, a world at odds with itself to such a degree that the purported arrival of these meteors touched off a destruction such as we cannot imagine.

"For these reasons, the north quadrant asks that the dome people, except Celeste, who is very young, and Susan, who is very old, be given whatever supplies they may desire and be asked to remove, with our aid of course, in spite of the fact that this is the harvest season, to whatever location they may find to their best advantage."

"May we hear any other opinions on the matter?" asked the Protector. "Eastcounsel. We recognize you."

Sagan, the Eastcounsel, arose, smoothed down her robe, and began. "I would like to speak in opposition to what has just been said. I have several points. The dome people are us. We must never forget that. We are all the same people. The fact that we can talk together is proof of this—after so many centuries of separation. If we cast them out, we cast out our own sisters. And brothers.

"The dome people represent no threat not already present. If we assume that they come from a world of terrible weapons, while ours is peaceful, we ignore our own history, which belies that notion. None of us pretends that we would harm the dome people. Hence if we exile them from us, as is suggested, we simply hand all their technology over to others, perhaps to the Sentani, who would probably share it with us. Perhaps to the wandering and marauding Peshtak we have been hearing of this past summer. Perhaps even to the eastern cities, if by some miracle they got that far. If that technology is helpful, we are robbed of it. If it is dangerous, then others have it and we do not.

"As to theology, we are already aware that a number of theological systems exist. Ours is not the only one. We are aware that most of them seem to spring from one root. Ours has the beauties that others lack, depths that others ignore. For that reason, we ought to spread it. Already Celeste sings with our choir. Tor reads our rolls more incessantly than almost anyone not in the ministry. He is a Shumai, but he quotes the writings of Pell and refers to Aven with reverence. We should invite others in, not shut them out."

At this point in Sagan's narrative, Tor was wandering up to the new structure the comps and Pelbar masons were erecting on the hill. He caught sight of Eolyn's back on the hillside above, and ran up to her so lightly that she never heard him. She was listening to her wrist cube. Tor heard Sagan's voice.

Close by her ear, Tor said, "I thought the council meeting was a private one."

Eolyn whirled around with a light scream. "You. What? You've no right eavesdropping on me like that. Now get out of here."

Tor laughed. "We should sit down together, Eo, until the council is over, so I can be sure that you will allow them their privacy. How can you manage this, anyhow?"

Eolyn shut off the receiver. "There is no use of their building up here, is there? When you tell the Pelbar, that wretch from the north quadrant will have her way. I knew we should have left here earlier for the eastern cities."

"I will never tell. I want you people here. If you knew the country the way I do, you would know well enough that this is by far the best place for you—unless it is Northwall. Here is far better for the Pelbar, though. This city needs a new function. Northwall has found one. Here you would be honored and cared for."

"And opposed. I heard the things that old ratskin said about us. Here, you listen." Eolyn played the council meeting back for Tor, from her microtape.

"Now what do you say? See? I feel entirely exposed. I don't know what I expected from such primitives. And you are the worst, sneaking around like a . . . a . . ."

"A mouse?"

"No. Like one of those long things."

"A weasel." Tor stood up and laughed. "Now that you are out of the dome, your analogies, at least, will improve. Now don't leave just yet. Listen. What I just heard from the Northcounsel was little more than a concession. They all know that anyone could answer all their arguments. They are in bad odor now because of some recent events. They know this venture to help you has gone well. All they can do is to present an array of arguments against it so that if anything goes wrong, then they can gain in influence. That should be obvious. Even in Shumai councils, scant as they are, we do the same thing. Our ancestors did the same thing. Ours, Eo, because yours and mine came from the same society. I lost the technology, and you lost the poetry, the family, the free air, the—"

"Stop."

"All right. I'll stop. I won't tell them, either." He looked up at her, higher on the hill, grinning. "You look nice in that Pelbar outfit. But then you'd look nice in anything. Or even——"

"Stop. Go away. I have to reason this out."

"Soon. You haven't told me how you managed to work this miracle."

"Why should I tell you?"

"I'm curious. I won't tell. I won't even tell what you overheard."

"It doesn't matter. I put a small transmitter in the hem of Ahroe's tunic. The cloth is thick. She would never find it."

"Amazing. I would like to contribute to your reasoning, if I may."

"I suppose you must."

"Just a few things. Celeste has found a home here. I doubt that she will leave. Butto would leave with you. Even though you see little use in him, he is loyal to you—and loves you."

Eolyn snorted.

"Thornton and the Protector are already so struck with each other that I am sure he will never leave."

"No loss."

"Royal would leave if you said to, but he would very likely not manage to make the whole journey to the eastern cities. He is too old and frail. Bill will stay. The other comps would likely go with you, though some might not agree. It is hard to say."

"And Ruthan? She would stay because of you, you think."

"No. I will not be here that long. But she will stay. Probably because of Blu."

"Blu? The wild man? The other axeman? What are you talking about?"

"Here is a secret for you so you won't think I have an advantage over you. Will you keep it?"

Eolyn hesitated, then shrugged. "It doesn't matter. I won't tell. Who would I tell?"

"Of course it's only a surmise. I think Ruthan will become the resident botanist, or . . . what do you call it?"

"Taxonomist, geneticist, horticulturist?"

"Yes. One of those. I think Blu will marry her within a

year. Don't sneer. Just watch. Please? I want you to see something."

"What?"

"That there are other ways of knowing than your equipment. Dusk told me."

"The dog? You're making fun of me again. Dogs pick the people you marry?"

Tor laughed again, though the melancholy never left his eyes. "You will see. You have your radios. We have our dogs."

"Ruthan is so in love with you she looks cross-eyed."

"No. I inherited the pity she would have poured out on Dexter. You, Eolyn, you and I share a common problem. We are extremes. They're the people in the middle. Do you understand?" Tor looked at her almost like a child looking at his grandmother. She recoiled inside.

"I haven't the slightest idea what you mean," she said.

"So, another secret, then. That will reveal itself more slowly. Good-bye, Eo." Tor turned and walked down the steep hill, waving his arm and his ruined stump for balance. She could hear him joking with the comps below. An extreme? Surely he was one. Eolyn could see nothing extreme about herself. Perhaps intellect was extremity, though, in this bizarre society.

That afternoon Tristal knocked on the door of Celeste's workroom.

"Come in," she said. Her back was to him. She sat at a bench crowded with pieces of glass, sandboard, fragile tubing.

"Hello, Celeste. What are you doing?"

"Tristal? Is that you? I'm glad you came. I need Stepan. Get him for me. He should have my new calipers ready by now." She continued to rub something slowly and carefully. Tristal could see only the top of her head as she hunched over, her elbows working. Then he turned to get Stepan. Raran followed him out.

By evening, the assembled dome people were told that the council had recommended the founding of a Pelbarigan Academy, to focus their presence, Eolyn's project on the hill, and whatever other sources of knowledge they could gather. By spring invitations would be sent throughout the Heart River, as far east as the Long

Lake Sentani, if possible as far west as the Commuters, even including the ambiguously inclined Emeri. Pelbarigan, it would seem, was committed to a new course as an educational center. Yet the day ended without ceremony, as evening came, announced by the tower horns, accompanied by the pouring of the radiance of a cirrus-rich sunset across the river waters.

Less than two weeks later Celeste triumphantly showed off her microscope, set in a southern window, horrifying whomever looked at the microorganisms bumping like aimless boats in a drop of swamp water. Royal was especially pleased, and anxious to establish species, habits, dangers, anatomies. For him it was the first step on a long road to sound genetics, medicine, microbiology. He began to train Celeste to succeed him, though she showed little aptitude for teaching.

As Eolyn's building progressed, in the cooling fall weather, Stel questioned her often about its strange design, with its spaced triple walls, its raking, south-facing roofs, and its large south windows painstakingly glazed with small panes of Pelbar glass. Her answers were revelations to him. The Pelbar, who for so many centuries had to conserve heat energy and live close to necessities, still had little idea of the basic principles of insulation, heat distribution, humidity control, solar absorption, and energy usage that she brought to the project.

Blu's hunting band had departed south at the beginning of Colormonth, but Stel was surprised one day, while working on the building, to hear the Rive Tower horn. Shading his eyes, he saw the same six canoes returning upriver. Tor saw them, too, from his now habitual reading place at Hagen's grave. He met them at the river bank with the guardsmen. They palmed, then embraced.

Blu stole a glance at the axeman, but saw no change in his troubled face. "We went south," he said, "into Sentani country below the Oh. We found an entire band, Sentani, with women and children, all slaughtered and left on the ground."

"How many?"

"Forty-nine, including all. Sark and Krush have gone to Koorb. We have warned Threerivers, though they seemed not to believe us, the louts."

"The Peshtak, then? So far west?"

"We think so. Three of them were there, dead. They

didn't even bury their own. Swarthy men, with some horrible disease."

"Disease?"

"Their bodies were all eruptions. Of course they had been there awhile." Blu shuddered.

"Come. We will need to tell Oet."

Soon a hasty council was called. A message bird flew off toward Northwall. Guard parties were sent to the rush-gatherers, eastward toward the country of the Tall Grass Sentani, who had already suffered from the Peshtak marauders. Blu sent two men across to the Isso, to warn the new farmsteads as far as Black Bull Island. A river patrol was set up, using the largest Tantal ship.

Two evenings later, the Protector summoned Eolyn to her quarters. The young woman was ushered in by Ahroe, who was invited to remain.

"Eolyn, I am afraid that your project on the hill may have to wait awhile. This new crisis has strained our resources to the limit. We are a rather small community, and this incursion has come during our most pressing season. It is a new thing, and we have no system for dealing with it."

Eolyn sat silently for a time, then said, "I thought you would come to that in one way or another. We had an agreement. Now you are violating it."

"We intend to maintain our agreement, but it will have to be put off. You seem not to understand the severity of the emergency."

Eolyn stood. "I'm not sure of your motives. I have been thinking about all this, knowing some such thing would come, and I have decided to go to the eastern cities after all."

"How? We can't spare any transport now, and even if we could, it is a journey of incredible length and danger."

"I've seen your maps. I can go downriver with the patrol, then head eastward until I strike the Oh. With the help of the pulsers, and the comps, I should make out all right."

"It is nearly Buckmonth. You have no idea what you are suggesting."

"Of course I know it is difficult. But we have the resources."

"You would pass directly through Peshtak country."

"Of course, and yet unharmed. You forget the pulsers.

They are equipped with heat sensors. They can sense a presence in total darkness, aim, and destroy it without human aiming. We will be left alone."

"It would be dead winter before you got there."

"No matter. Here I feel stultified by all your rules and your dictations. I am a free being. I wish to live reasonably."

"What you suggest is not at all reasonable."

"Nonetheless, it is what I intend," said Eolyn. Then she turned and left.

The Protector looked at Ahroe. "What is the cause of this? What has happened?"

"I don't precisely know, Protector. Perhaps it is just what she has said. Clearly she feels we are backward. She feels she will be better off elsewhere. She has some myth about the east, as if she will be made a queen when she arrives there. I think she is vain about her looks and troubled by the fact that few seem deeply struck by them here."

"Did Stel tell you that?"

"Yes, and since I've noticed. But she is also used to ordering everyone, the way she did in the dome. Royal seems always to have deferred to her. She isn't used to working in a larger community, and compromise. She arrives at a conclusion, declares it reasonable, and then proceeds. Let's hope she will change her mind."

But Eolyn did not change her mind, though only the previous morning, Blu and his remaining men had happily begun a long run downstream in search of the Peshtak. They wanted Tor to lead them, but he had simply refused, looking supremely indifferent. Blu was angry. Some of the men looked at Tor in disapproving silence.

He had raised his arms, the whole and the truncated, and said, "Think what you wish. It seems right for me not to go now. I can't give you a reason."

Blu had turned and left without a reply, the other men following. Tor watched them go in gloom. Stel was coming up the hill, panting, standing aside for the Shumai, joking with them and receiving little response. But Tor could see them glance with interest at something he was carrying. When Stel came up, and they palmed, he held out the new axe sheath he had promised, and with it a new axe.

"Here. This is a new design. I think you might like it. It has a longer handle, which might make it a little more

difficult on your hip. We can always shorten it. See? The
handle has whip in it, and the blade design is not for chopping wood. It is mainly for fighting. Look. The wide arc
of the blade is unsupported at the tips. But that makes it
lighter and gives it more reach." He extended the handle
to Tor, who took it in his unaccustomed left hand and
gave it some tentative swings. It seemed new and strange.
He wasn't sure he liked it.

"I think you will find it has some of the virtues of our
long swords," said Stel. "At arm's length, swinging in
quick arcs, the way you have seen our guards train, it
ought to combine the purposes of both."

"I'm not sure I can throw it at game, Stel. It certainly
is a handsome axe, though, and I thank you for it," Tor
finally said. He flicked out an arm and took the branch off
a dogwood sapling, then whistled. "It seems to leap out.
It has an incredible reach." He turned and grinned.

Late in the day, when he heard that Eolyn intended to
leave, Tor was not surprised. Ahroe told him at her house,
where Tor was practicing with his new axe, splitting kin-
dling, seeking for the quick, exact stroke he would need
if the axe were to be of use. Garet sat on a stump, watching.

Tor's reply to Ahroe was to reach out to the hem of
her tunic and feel the material until he noticed a tiny
bulge. Then he removed a small, metal button.

"What is it?"

"Something of Eolyn's. She left it there so she could
listen to the council through her radio."

"You didn't tell. Why, Tor? You should have."

"I caught her at it. I'm almost sure she didn't use it
again. I promised not to tell because I thought that might
make her leave then. She was ready to. She has been
looking for a reason. She's restless here. I think she wants
to simplify things again, with herself as the chief person.
I know how she feels. Pelbar society is complicated. You
mustn't tell anyone about this device. But you should ask
her if she wants it back. See what she does."

Ahroe did that and found Eolyn matter-of-fact and un-
repentant. At that moment, Eolyn had been trying to convince Ruthan to go, but after Ahroe gave her the
transmitter, Ruthan would not even listen to her dome
fellow any further.

Ahroe tried once more to point out the danger of the

Peshtak, but Eolyn remained curt. "How do you expect them to find us in that vast expanse. They have no radar. If I spend my life here, I will get nowhere. We didn't store all that knowledge through so many centuries just to waste it."

"I hope you won't be disappointed. We know little of the eastern cities, and what we do know is not encouraging."

"Pelbarigan is not encouraging, either."

Butto entered. As Tor had anticipated, he would go because Eolyn was. By this time, he and Stel were good friends, perpetually bantering, and Ahroe could see he deeply regretted leaving.

"All fall, and I have never seen a snake. I wanted to. The tapes had a marvelous snake."

"They are all denned up now. Wait until spring. Stel will show you knots and ropes of snakes."

"There will be snakes in the east," said Eolyn.

"For your sakes, I hope there are snakes," said Ahroe.

"And plenty of aches, I undertake, from betaking our way through quaking brakes, forsaking Pelbar cake to take a hike."

"Whew. I'm glad Stel isn't here. That would have rendered him unconscious in the strain to match it. You can beat him at his own game. His fame will never be the same since you came." Ahroe hugged the heavy man and left.

"What is the matter with her?"

"We are friends," said Butto. "I have bounced her boy on my knee, big as he is, you see."

"Don't start that with me," said Eolyn, shaking her head when Butto laughed.

Two mornings later they left on the Tantal ship used to patrol. The Protector arranged a special farewell, with music and presents. Eolyn thought it was a gesture of surrender, but in actuality the Protector was establishing a feeling of warm hospitality in the hope that the dome people would feel no reluctance to return. As Tor had surmised, of the principals only Butto wanted to accompany Eolyn, but after much hesitation Royal decided to go, too, for solidarity. All the comps but 16 went along. Bill, of course, remained. Tor was not at the bank. Eolyn found herself looking for him. Dailith, who was nearly as tall as the axeman, stood gloomily on the bank staring at her.

As the ship moved underway, the Protector's elbow was nudged. Turning, she saw the Northcounsel, who said, "It has turned out badly, Protector. We will await your promise to resign."

"You will have it, Rickor, but let us first see how this turns out. There will be time. You will not have long to wait." As she turned to go, she leaned on the Northcounsel, breathing heavily.

Tor had gone to Northwall, taking Tristal, who ran easily behind his uncle now. He was nearly as tall, and filling out rapidly. Tor found the northern city prepared for more than was likely to come. Tag had designed a communications system that would warn the whole community of attack at any point.

The two men had a long conversation about Eolyn's departure. "I have been reading too much Pelbar scripture," said Tor. "Before, I might have taken the whole bunch and destroyed those weapons."

"Maybe you should have. How many do they have?"

"Two helmets and one hand-held unit. Without them they are nearly helpless."

"With them?"

"It is hard to tell. They might withstand an army—if the army was walking across a field. These Peshtak have been drifting westward all season now, and the only people who have seen them have been killed by them. They are like smoke."

"Perhaps we should overtake them even now."

"I don't think Eolyn would tolerate it. I don't understand her. She is without pity."

The two fell into silence. Tia and Tag came in bringing Stantu to see Tor. The axeman was surprised to see how much Stantu had failed. As they embraced, he saw death in Stantu's eyes. He also saw resolution.

"No matter what they do to us, they never touch the spirit, Stantu," Tor said. He found himself wishing he fully believed it. He knew that Stantu fully understood that side of the question.

"The core of the spirit, anyhow," Stantu returned. "I am resolved. I only regret leaving Tag alone." Looking, Tor saw resolution in her eyes as well. "It is strange being killed in a war fought a thousand years ago or more," Stantu added.

The friends all talked awhile, then saw Stantu and Tag home. There the failing Shumai gave Tristal a folding knife, worn but sharp. "It was given me by Sima Pall, the former Protector here," he said. "It has been to Emeri country twice. It has drained the heart's blood of bulls and carved the lintels of my home here. It is full of use and hope, as you are." He smiled faintly as he said this. Tristal was embarrassed, but took it and embraced first Stantu then Tag.

Soon everyone could see that Tor was restless. Finally, he said, "I think I'd better go back to Pelbarigan."

"Now? It is almost high night."

"Yes. But now I've seen your map, with the four previous Peshtak raids. It makes a pattern. The attacks are near rivers. Then they vanish. Given the patterns of search, they must have moved west from the Gray Ash River, and now north from the Oh. That would put them, now, perhaps, close to Eolyn's path, unless they have turned south and west again. I can almost taste trouble. Can you lend us an arrowboat?"

"Of course. Just take one. I will come to the bank with you. How will you paddle?"

"I have a strap Stel made for me."

Later Jestak was frowning in bewilderment watching Tor and Tristal drive out into the current, with the dim shape of Raran between them in the dark.

"Something is going to happen," said Tia.

"You, too? Look at them. He paddles well for a one-handed man."

It was nightfall the following day when Tristal and Tor arrived at Pelbarigan. Tristal was completely worn out, but Tor seemed untouched by fatigue. He mounted the hill to Stel and Ahroe's, entering with only a couple of knocks. The couple looked up, startled.

"Do you still have that pointer of Celeste's?"

"Tor. Back so soon? Yes. What is wrong?"

"I don't know. Something. Let me have it. I want to find out how to make it work."

A moment later, Ahroe watched him trot down the path with it. She was puzzled. She decided to follow. Tor trotted up the main front stairhall in the city, ran to the dome people's quarters, and knocked.

Ruthan opened the door. "Tor. What is it?"

"Ruthy. Do you have that radio? Can we contact Eolyn?"

"It is extremely far. We can try." She turned and went for her wrist transceiver. They clustered around the center table in the commons as Ruthan tried repeatedly to reach the travelers.

Finally, Eolyn's voice, dim and crackling, came back. "Eolyn awake here. Ruthan? What is wrong?"

"Listen. Tor wants to talk to you."

"Tor? That great heap of surmises? What does he want?"

"Listen, Eolyn," Tor began. "I have been to Northwall. I have seen a pattern in the Peshtak raids. They have all occurred near rivers. Then they have vanished without a trace, only to reappear. Given the patterns of search, and the latest raid, I am worried. If you are traveling eastward toward the Oh, you may be in their area."

"Is that all? We must be far north of them. I have seen the maps, such as they are. They have been moving westward. I suppose you want me to come back and be a Pelbar servant. Miss me, eh?"

"What sort of a place are you in? What kind of guards have you?"

"We are in a valley, a stream valley, with high protecting walls cut in the limestone. It is long, mainly east and west. A lot of rock has fallen—big rocks—from the cliffs." Her voice faded away, then came back: ". . . are safe enough."

Tor groaned. "Safe? I hardly think it. I am coming. I will bring Dailith."

"No need. We won't wait, either. What is it, 11?"

They heard some muttering about the sensors, then the signal faded out and they could not recover it.

Tor sat down with a sigh. "Celeste, how do you work this thing? I am going to take it along."

"My pointer? Then you found it. You should have given it back."

"Yes. It seems like such a weapon for a girl. Stel blew a hole in his wall with it."

Celeste laughed. "He should be careful." With systematic precision, the girl explained the operation of the ultrasonic pointer. They then tried it out, carefully, on someone by the river bank, activating it just enough to make him scratch his leg. Celeste was amused by this, but she pointed out that unlike the pulsers, it did not work well at a distance. "Some forms of energy can be pulsed straight out, but this is really nothing but sound, and it can be shaped and directed only in a limited way." She handed the pointer back to Tor.

"Do you really think they're in trouble?" Ruthan asked.

"They well may be. If those weapons fall into the hands of the Peshtak, and so far west as this, then we are all in trouble. If they find out how to use them. And if they keep any of your people alive, believe me, they will find out. They could dominate the whole Heart River."

There was a silence. Finally, Tor stood. "I have missed a night's rest. I can't start until morning. Ahroe, try to get us some horses—three of them."

"What can you do? There will be a lot of them," said Ahroe.

Tor's look sent chills through Ruthan. "There will be something," he said.

At daybreak, Celeste saw three riders trot away down the river path, Raran following. "Who is the third?" she asked.

"Tristal," Ruthan replied. "He has more experience with horses than either man. He is going for the sake of the horses."

"It can't be Tristal. He is too big."

"It is, though."

Celeste continued to squint in disbelief.

That day they made forty-three ayas before sundown. At dusk the horses moved with complete weariness. When the small party finally dismounted, Tor said, "You two bring the horses after. I will leave a marker where to turn off the trail. It will not be for some time. I am going to run."

"No, Tor. You—" Dailith began, but Tor already was moving down the dim river trail. "What's the use of that?" he continued.

"Plenty," said Tristal. "By sunup he will be at least another thirty ayas, and he will keep going."

"No one can do that."

"Tor can."

"Well, let's get these horses unpacked."

"I will do that. You cook." Tristal set about unsaddling

and caring for the horses with a sense of total authority. Dailith was surprised, but said nothing.

That night neither could sleep until late. Both were thinking of Tor, running in the dark, and were excited and tired. Raran alone curled up in comfort.

It was nearly noon the next day when Blu's men came out on the river trail. They had swept an arc but found no trace of the Peshtak this far north. "Tracks," said Vult. "A single man, running. Look, he is Shumai."

Blu looked. "It is Tor," he said. "Look. Short steps. He must be running in his sleep. See if we can find when."

"Look here," said Ubi. "A worm cast. Last night."

"I think we should follow," said Dard. "He must know where he is going."

Blu began trotting down the trail, the others falling in behind. "Move, Dusk," he said, nudging his big dog out of the way with a knee. "So soon after eating. Tor, you'd better know where you are going."

"And I hope it's no social visit," said Vult.

A morning quadrant later, they hit Tor's marker and turned off the trail, running southeastward, straight as sunlight when the land permitted. At sundown, as the Shumai strung out wearily, he was still going, leaving a clear trail.

"We'll have to stop," said Dard. "Blu, you're the axe-man. What do you say?"

"I'm not sure. I think he is heading down into the hill forests, though. He seems to know where he's going. I think we should mark stars and continue. He means to be followed. If we have lost him in the morning, we can run arcs and pick him up again."

Far behind, Tristal and Dailith had also left the bank trail. Tristal knew several of the pairs of tracks, and knew Blu was following Tor. He was restless.

"How can you be sure of the tracks?" Dailith asked.

"Do you know your family's faces? I know their tracks. You know all your friends' voices without looking. Dailith, I am going on. You will have to manage the horses alone tonight." Tristal ran on in the dusk, Raran, head lolling low, following. Dailith stood watching, holding the halter ropes, frustrated, thinking about the undependability of the Shumai.

It was early the next morning that Tor struck the trail

of the dome people. He knew the place. Ahead was a valley like that Eolyn described. Yes. Here were other tracks, Peshtak, surely. Tor smelled fire. He left the trail and worked up the north side, low and silent.

He was a full quarter of the morning in moving close through the freshly fallen leaves, sometimes, it seemed to him, as slowly as the shadows moved on them, but at least as silently. He encountered one Peshtak sentinel and killed him silently. The man crumpled like a rag in Tor's hands. His body had open sores. Revulsed, Tor rubbed his hands in the dirt.

Coming in behind rocks, he saw the open space where Eolyn's party must have camped. A cluster of people stood below near a fire. Tor heard someone shrieking. They were torturing a comp. Tor could see Butto there, surrounded by Peshtak, but neither Royal nor Eolyn. Farther east, near an outcrop, he saw a rough shelter of heaped and woven brush, heavily guarded. That is where they would be. He worked in closer. What would he do? One of the Peshtak stood holding a helmet weapon near Butto, watching the torture. Tor gave Celeste's pointer a little power and drew a circle on Butto's back. The heavy man started and looked around. Tor waved one hand slightly, hoping Butto wouldn't give him away. Butto seemed gloomy, depressed, but when he saw Tor he started slightly, recovering himself by rubbing his head. Then his head sunk back on his chest. Tor could see they had been beating him.

Suddenly, Butto announced in an oracular voice, "He was right, the ancient poet, Jeffers, when he said,

Happy people die whole, they are all dissolved in a
    moment, they have had what they wanted,
No hard gifts; the unhappy
Linger a space, but pain is a thing that is glad to be
    forgotten; but one who has given
His heart to a cause or a country,
His ghost may spaniel it a while, disconsolate to
    watch it. I was wondering how long the spirit
That sheds this verse will remain
When the nostrils are nipped, when the brain rots
    in its vault or bubbles in the violence of fire
To be ash in metal. I was thinking—"

Butto's Peshtak guard, who had been watching him with increasing bewilderment and anger, turned and knocked him down, hissing, "Quiet, pig."

Butto stumbled up. Tor drew a slight line down his leg with the pointer. Butto nodded twice, looked around, then turned, as if absently, toward the man with the helmet, jerking his thumb slightly toward him. Tor aimed the pointer and hit the Peshtak with full power. He screamed and grabbed his ears. In a flash, Butto had reached over and touched several buttons, then yelled, "Pray like Stel," clapping the heels of his hands to his eyes. Tor understood, rolling behind the rock and burying his eyes in his left forearm. He felt a rush of heat and saw red light through his arm and eyelids as the helmet bloomed up and out in a sudden, huge ball of roaring white fire that set the whole center of the valley ablaze, instantly roasting the whole crowd of comps, all the assembled Peshtak, and Butto himself.

Tor looked up, stunned. Turning, he saw the guards by the shelter had been blinded by the flash. They were standing in burning grass, holding their faces. The whole front of the shelter was smoking and flaring. Tor raced through burning leaves and grass and felled the seven guards with quick, whirling strokes of his new axe. He could hear Eolyn inside screaming. He dashed around the back, encountering three Peshtak, killing all three in a whirling flurry.

He ripped off mats and bark on the rear of the shelter, hacking at saplings and bindings. Diving in, he felt a knife slash into his right arm. He whipped his axe around again in the smoky dark, felt it bite and slice deep, and re-sheathed it. In the smoke he saw Eolyn lying bound. He slipped his truncated arm under her shoulders and ran out the hole in the back of the shelter.

Eolyn looked up, dazed. "Royal, Royal," she said. Tor turned back and found the old man in the blazing structure, then dragged him out. Then he sliced their bonds with his axe edge and brought them back away from the shelter. Turning, he saw the fire creeping out, southward, but slowing in the dampness. He shuddered and shrugged away his gaze.

"Eo," he said. "Where are the other weapons?"

"Both helmets were together. Probably they both exploded. I don't know where the hand pulser is. My God, how did you get here?"

"Dailith and I rode horses the first day. Then I ran."

"That is impossible."

"Tiring. Let that be. Where are the others?"

"Others? These were all."

"Never. Ah, here comes one."

"That's the handsome one, Kubra. He is the leader of these horrors."

A man of middle height came walking slowly from the rocks, clearing his eyes. Tor advanced on him, kicked his legs from under him, tossed aside his knife, and stood him up.

"Over here," Tor said, leading him toward Eolyn and Royal. "Stand there."

The man was slightly swarthy, with an extraordinarily handsome face, apparently beardless. Tor looked at him closely. He still appeared to be clearing his eyes.

"Where are the others?" Tor asked.

"Tor, your arm. Let me bind it," said Eolyn. Tor knelt on one knee while Eolyn ripped strips from the lining of her coat and bound the knife wounds, which ran down to the stump end of his right arm.

"I am sorry for you," said the Peshtak. "That knife was poisoned, of course. You have not long to live."

"Where are the others?"

"There are no others. I alone remain. You have defeated us totally. Unfortunately, you will soon weaken, and won't enjoy it." The man shifted his feet slightly, squinting in the sun, adjusting his coat with its large silvery badge.

"You are Kubra? Why have you come here? Why have you been killing the Heart River peoples?"

"We were attacked. In every case, we were attacked. Even here we meant no harm until these people started killing us with their terrible weapons."

"Don't listen to him, Tor. They came in the night. The heat sensors read them. We told them to get back, shouting it. They simply hid for a time. We held them off for a whole day, but they crept in on us like the darkness itself."

"Ah, good woman. You know that was not the way it was. We came in need of food."

"What is wrong with your face?" Tor asked.

Kubra started slightly, then said, "My face? Nothing. It may be a little flushed from that terrible heat. My eyes are still dazzled."

Unaccountably, Tor lifted his horn and blew five short blasts, then five more, then three rising notes twice.

"What on earth are you doing?" Eolyn asked. "Here, hold still."

"Just proclaiming the victory this Kubra has admitted, before I sicken and die," said Tor.

Suddenly, in one motion, Kubra lunged for Tor. Tor hit him across the face with a quick twist of the flat of his axe, stood, grabbed Eolyn with his ruined arm, and ran for the rocks to the south. As she was swept up, Eolyn saw in a fleeting instant that Kubra's face had been swept aside. It was a mask. Beneath it lay the ravaged face, with no nose and shriveled lips, that she had seen on a few of the others. She shrieked.

Tor dumped her by a giant rock, then clambered silently up over a large fallen stone mass ahead. Eolyn lay frightened and panting, hearing fighting sounds behind the rock. Soon Tor reappeared. "Go around the rock and stay," he said. "I have to get Royal."

She did, finding there five Peshtak bodies, one still twitching. She screamed again, and drew back, as Tor reappeared, carrying the old physician over his left shoulder. Royal hung limp and dazed.

"We have to stay here. The others are across the valley. At least two groups. We will hold them back with the pointer. Did you find the other pulser here?"

"I didn't look," said Eolyn, shuddering. "But one of them has it."

"That is bad."

"How do you know there are more? That are over there? Don't tell me you felt all this, too."

"I did, partly. I could feel them behind me. That man, Kubra, confirmed it. He was lying about everything. I thought I saw him signaling behind his back to these. I saw him shift in the sun to signal people behind us with his metal badge—those over there. Some of them may still be blinded by the blast. But they will be coming, especially if they have the pulser. But Blu will take care of them."

"Blu? I thought you were alone."

"I was. But I heard Dusk barking. That's why I called

and warned them with the horn. They will be coming on the high ground behind the Peshtak. If the Peshtak hide from Blu's men, then we can sting them with this pointer."

"Did they hear? How do you know?"

"Dusk stopped barking."

"Look. They are coming."

A line of Peshtak, about forty, spread out and began walking across the valley, recurved bows nocked. Some looked ill. Others seemed dazzled. A number were women, and several no more than boys. Tor let them get so close that Eolyn grew very nervous. Then he swept the ultrasonic pointer slowly across them. As he did, they screamed and ran, but as they neared the south rocks, arrows flashed out, killing a number. The others turned and ran back. Tor picked them out one by one, focusing the pointer, dropping them. They turned again. Blu's men remained under cover, but more arrows flicked out as the Peshtak came close. Tor advanced across the valley. One man shouted orders, and they all turned and rushed at Tor. He stood his ground, raking the pointer across them. But only a few wavered, and none made a move to surrender. Those who drew and shot at him were too far away to be effective. Soon they were all on the ground. Tor sighed in deep distaste.

"Shut that thing off, Tor," Blu shouted, faintly, from across the valley. Tor waved. The Shumai emerged from cover.

"Don't touch them," Tor shouted back. "They are all diseased with something."

The two men met in the middle, plainly glad to see each other, though unsmiling. "I am worried," Tor said. "The hand-held pulser is nowhere around. There may be more. They are tucked in the rocks like snakes."

Blu looked at the still burning valley and whistled. Tor explained what happened as they walked back toward Eolyn and Royal. The Shumai spread in a pattern, watching. Plainly they had been learning from the Sentani. Eolyn was kneeling over Royal. He too had been beaten by the Peshtak, and only now was he getting any comfort.

The Shumai posted guards and began to relax. The strain finally showed on Tor, but he remained wary. "I don't know," he said. "There may be more. And that pulser."

Dusk bristled, ears pricked, then rushed toward Dard,

who was standing guard near the south valley wall. He turned to see the dog explode in a pulser blast. Then Dard, drawing his bow, also blew apart. All the others were in the open, but instantly running.

A Peshtak emerged on a rock, holding the pulser. He aimed among the group and blasted, but only exploded ashes. He fired rapidly at random as the Shumai ran, killing one more man, then, unaccountably, fired twice high in the air. He slumped, an arrow sticking through his chest. The pulser tumbled down the rocks and landed hard, firing one more energy blast as it hit, scaling some rocks off the valley wall.

"Get the pulser," Eolyn yelled. But no one moved. They heard a yell and growl, and another Peshtak appeared high in the rocks, running, Raran behind him. Another arrow flashed over the dog and into the man, who fell.

"It is Tris," Tor yelled. Still no one moved for a few moments. Then, as the Shumai began moving slowly and in utter silence back across the valley toward the rocks, they heard another yell and growl, and silence again. Eolyn watched them seem to dissolve into the rocks. Left alone, with Royal quietly panting on the ground, Eolyn heard the sibilant moan of the November wind and smelled the sharp smoke, with a horror of burnt flesh in it.

Finally, Tor's horn sounded, and the men reappeared and walked back. They were sober and grim. The loss of Dard, and the other man, Cruw, had hurt them all; the burnt valley littered with Peshtak and the still, black limbless mounds dazed them. Blu had retrieved the pulser and brought it to Eolyn.

"Take this thing apart," he said.

"But . . ." she began, then looking at him, deactivated it, disassembled it, and gave him the pieces, one by one. He handed each piece to a man until finally only the heavy power pack lay in his hand. He hefted it.

"Be careful," Eolyn said. "By itself it won't hurt anything. In fact, if you keep it and take it to Pelbarigan, we can use it."

Blu handed it to Tor. "Come," he said. "We have men to bury. And a dog. A good, good dog." The Shumai took their dead to the high south outcrop, up in the woods above the sheer rocks, and sent the rest of the day in burial ceremonies, erecting one stone slab over the mound heaped on the two men and Dusk.

Late in the afternoon, Raran growled, facing down the valley, and a party of men appeared.

"It is Sark and Krush with some Sentani," said Tor. He blew his horn, one long, almost endless blast, the tone of greeting in sadness. A horn returned the note, echoing it off the valley walls. The men looked at each other. Dard was Sark's son. Tor looked at the ground, then pulled himself up and ran down to meet them. The others watched the tall axeman talking with the men, who formed a small star, sentinels looking outward in seven points, down the smoking valley. Then Sark came up alone, climbing slowly.

Standing by the rock-topped grave, they waited for him, and, as he arrived, Blu gestured. Sark's nostrils flared. He stood by the grave unspeaking, then finally sat down, throwing his coat up over his head. At length the other men sang in unison the song of Sertine, whose voice is heard in the prairie wind, whose voice has always been heard in the grass, at all seasons, in all years, whether "we walk in the grass or lie under its roots—Sertine, the abiding and just Governor of all."

Their deep voices came down to the valley in unutterable sadness, and at last Eolyn, who had been listening in fear and uncertainty, surrounded by silent Sentani, caught something from the song that touched her. She looked across the ruin of the recently beautiful wooded valley and fell into sobbing.

Royal reached out and touched her arm. "It is all right, Eo. You didn't know. We will go back to Pelbarigan and try to make it up. In spite of everything, we do have a great deal to teach them."

She nodded, not believing this, crushed down with loss and guilt.

The Sentani moved up the valley and set up a camp, using the center valley floor. They set out sentinels and prepared a meal, using meat and wild food they had brought with them.

Eventually a young man came to Eolyn and Royal, who were still alone in the dusk. "Come," he said. "Mokil says to come inside the guard star." He lifted Royal up and carried the old man like a child.

Mokil was waiting for them. He was a short, white-haired man, looking straight-mouthed. "Over there," he said, gesturing. "There will be food soon." Then he turned. "Logi," he said. "I hear horses."

Dailith rode wearily into the firelight, leading the other two mounts. "Where?" he said. "What happened? Where are the others? You. You are Mokil?"

"We have met?"

"At Northwall. At the fight. You wouldn't have known me. I am Dailith."

"You were at Northwall? You must have been a boy."

"Just about. What has happened?"

"Come. Get down. Rewe, you and Chog take these horses. Here, give this man some tea." The Sentani immediately accepted Dailith as a brother, as they always did anyone who had been at the fight at Northwall. They told him what they knew of what happened. Soon the Shumai straggled wearily into the circle of firelight. The Sentani fed them, almost wordlessly, and the running band settled down to sleep. Sark remained on the hilltop, with one man. Another man took them some food, setting it by Sark, nudging him, but he never moved.

Dailith brought food to Eolyn and Royal, then sat with them. "Will you come back?" he asked.

She looked at him, red-eyed. "How can I? I am ashamed."

"Come. Tell them you made a mistake. Come with me."

"With you?"

"Dailith looked at her. "I . . ." he said. He looked at Royal. "This is going to sound stupid, but . . ."

She looked at his weary face, guileless, with its strong chin and warm brown eyes. She caught his unspoken meaning. Her eyes swept the fire circle for Tor. He wasn't there. "Why? Why would you do that? Look at them all. Look how they ignore us, hate us."

"They don't hate you. They don't blame you for the Peshtak. After all, you destroyed them. Or poor Butto did. They are angry with you for what they see as bullheadedness. Give them time. They are shocked by what the pulsers did. They fear you. You are unknown to all of us. Look. All their lives they have avoided the empty places. Now, today, for the second time since the time of fire a new one has been made."

"That is not an empty place. It is only an energy flare.

There will be some radiation, but not much. The second time?"

"They have heard of the explosion of the dome."

"Oh. What shall I do?"

"Admit you were wrong. I will stand by you."

"Wrong? How was I wrong?"

"You assumed you could go safely to the eastern cities. You endangered the whole Heart River by nearly placing these weapons in the hands of the Peshtak. They could have stood across the river from Pelbarigan and systematically destroyed the city."

"Why did you let me go, then?"

"What could we do? You are a free woman. You can do what you wish. The Pelbar all think that. But the Sentani, if they had been there in force, might have simply killed you all, knowing the immense danger you brought. They have suffered from the Peshtak—four raids now, this making five."

"What would you have done if they did that?"

"Done? What could be done? The Shumai would not have bothered. You rejected us, but still you put the Pelbar in a bad light because of this. We let you. Enough, though. You see how it is. I will stand by you, and I am sure Tor will. He is that large. He was worried. He somehow knew. He got Ruthan to radio to you and came all the way here from Pelbarigan."

"He did that for me—for us? Tor?"

"He did it for the Heart River peoples, Eo. He was afraid of the weapons."

"Then not for me."

"For you? Good Aven, woman. What have you ever done but scorn and ridicule him?"

"He is inexplicable."

"He is valuable. Listen, Eo. Neither one of you will ever be truly happy. Like most of us, I mean. You are opposites. You are both driven inside, somehow. But . . . I would like to try to make you happy. Live with me, Eo. Marry me. I mean it. I will be everything I can for you. Come back with me. It will be all right."

"Marry you. I thought that's what you meant." Again she looked at his frank, strong face, with its dirt and beard stubble, its young, innocent sturdiness, its freedom from the slight, athletic arrogance with which the Shumai all carried themselves. "I . . . all right. I will. Are you sure you want to get into this? You say you know I will never be happy."

Dailith gave a nervous laugh, then dropped his eyes. "Yes. I'm sure. I knew it when the dome was still burning."

Slowly they settled down for the night, Dailith by Eolyn and Royal. Eolyn could not sleep. She heard the Sentani signal the guards and quietly change them. She heard a Shumai quietly get up and go to sit on the hill near Sark, then another one return a short while later. Once she heard the barking honk of a flock of geese flying south in the dark—Celeste's birds, which she had drawn on the light screen that spring, so long ago, it seemed. Everything had a rhythm to it. All these people fit into the rhythm. She felt wholly left out of it. Perhaps something had been omitted from her makeup. Perhaps she too was a comp of a different sort. No. That was not so. She could feel—at least now she thought she could. Surely Dexter had had less feeling all along, damn him. Was Dailith accepting her for love or out of duty? What was she getting into, promising she would marry him. Only months before, she thought that was an ancient and outworn custom. It seemed to work well for Stel and Ahroe, though. They functioned as a unit. They had sympathies that united them in an uncanny way. Perhaps it would work for her. She would try.

As the first light of dawn began, Eolyn heard Sark and another man come into the camp. He walked to the far rim of the dim firelight. "Well, Tor, was it worth it?" he asked.

"For you, no, Sark. For the rest of us, yes."

"Better those people all crumbled with their dome. You would have your arm and I my son."

"That couldn't be, though, could it. And if that were the way, all those Peshtak would still be loose, murderous as ever. The dome people took much of the loss. Butto was a fine, fine man."

Sark's voice changed. "Tor, what would the words of Aven be for this? I can't get outside it."

"The words of Aven are that the body's life is not our life. Our life is what we do, what we think, how we come close in our actions and our motives to the pure life of Aven. For if we are so made, we have affirmed our understanding of eternal identity, as ones not needing flesh but needing only to know the will of Aven and follow it, knowing that this will preserve us in the thought of Aven forever."

Sark considered this. "But Dard, he was preparing to kill. What good would these Pelbar ideas do him?"

"No, Sark. Dard was loyal to his friends. He was self-less. He stuck with them in the hopes of preserving life. He didn't plan to get any personal gain from it. That is love, Sark. I think we must believe that that is goodness."

"What do you really think of these words of Aven?"

"I don't know, Sark. I really don't know. But think of it this way. This was like the time of fire all over again, but small. Except for Dard and Cruw, who are our sacrifice, it might have gone on and on, bringing its fire, its emptiness, its lack of life, so long as the Peshtak had the pulser. The Shumai have always been close to life. We have never denied it with walls or domes. Dard is in the middle of this life. If you come back here in the spring, you will find the mound of their grave scattered with flowers. The ferns will uncurl there, and wind sound in the trees overhead. When the sun sends light shafts down through the young leaves, it will strike the marker stone, and the stone will glow with its affirmation of their worth. It is not like the rod in an empty place. They will always be a part of this valley, that hill, as long as the leaves reach for light. That is the Shumai view, and the Pelbar sees their immortal part as rising beyond and above all that, as I have said, affirming them when there are no leaves, no light. The sharpness of our hurt will heal, and heal the quicker when we make these larger thoughts our medicine. It is hard, but that is what we have to do."

"So. Is that what you have done about your arm?"

"That's what I am doing, Sark, and trying to do. It is not done."

"Will it ever be accomplished?"

"I don't know, Sark. I don't know. But I do know Dard and Cruw have given us a strong declaration of human worth. They came defending all of us. The Sentani will pass this way often enough, and they will clear the mound through the years, as we all will, if we come. That doesn't give Dard back to you. But you have given him to all of us. We are a togetherness, and if they have died for us, we have to live well for them, illustrating their own sense of life, since they can't."

"I will have to tell his mother. I wish you were there to say all these things."

"Ah. Who can tell a mother these things about her son? Her son."

"I am going to the prairies, Tor. I will winter on the Isso. I will need to face Flayer and tell her. But I can't do that now. I can't even tell myself. I think I am through with the running band, Tor."

Tor grunted and stood up. "I will go with you to the river," he said. "But we will have to walk."

"We are all stiff, Tor, and we haven't been knifed. We will walk."

As it turned out, six of the Shumai went with Sark, in addition to Tor and Tristal. The six would cross with the old man and winter on the Isso, near one of the farmsteads. Blu and the rest would accompany Eolyn and Royal back to Pelbarigan. Eolyn remained under her furroll as the casual good-byes were said. She tried not to move. Someone shook her shoulder, and she turned and looked up. Tor was kneeling by her. "Good-bye, Eo," he said.

"Your arm, Tor. It may become infected. Be careful of it. Keep it clean."

"It will be all right, what there is of it. Don't worry. Dailith and Blu will take care of you." He stood and joined the others. She watched him, moving stiffly among his men and the Sentani, all in awe of him, friendly but deferential, as if he were a moon in a cloud of stars.

Tristal stood with them, head down, cleaning the last flecks of dried blood from the pivot of the locking clasp knife Stantu had given him. He had killed the third Peshtak on the hill with it. The others looked at him with a new respect as one of them to be proud of. Eolyn saw a residual trouble on his face. He scrubbed at every corner of the knife with dry leaves, now even trying to remove old stains from Stantu's use of it on the plains and at Northwall, as if he hoped to restore it to fresh clean metal just from the forger's shop, bright and smooth.

XIII

THE trip back to Pelbarigan was difficult for Eolyn. At least she was on a horse, but the persistent silence of the Shumai, and of Royal, who was suffering, wore on her.

The evening of the second day, she confronted Blu. "If you won't talk, why don't you leave us? I'm sure we can get back alone."

"What is there to say? And we are going this way any-how."

"That isn't a frank answer, Blu. I overestimated my-self. I didn't create the Peshtak. If you had encountered them without me, or us, maybe you would all have died."

"True. It is the shock. We are used to fighting, to hard living. But to burn a whole valley at once, like snapping fingers, with all the people in it. I suppose we fear you."

"Fear me? What of me? How do I feel with eight silent men, all armed, hating me, all with me for days on end?"

"We don't hate you. We don't understand. The whole world has been changing. We are in the middle of it."

"You can always go out onto those empty plains and be the way you always were."

"No. Not now. Something has broken. I am going to Pelbarigan."

"What for? To marry Ruthan?"

Blu stood still, startled. "I will ask. How did you know?"

"Tor said you would. He said—he said he saw you would by watching your dog, Dusk."

Blu considered that. Behind him, Rawg began to laugh. Blu turned on him. "No, Blu," said Rawg, holding up his hands. "I saw it, too. On the ship. But Tor had his back turned. He must have listened to Dusk's claws clicking when he walked around you."

Blu was embarrassed. But he turned back to Eolyn. "Well? What do you think? What will she say?"

"I? I don't know. I have none of your gifts. It would seem a logical choice, so long as you don't drag her around the wilderness."

"I won't. I won't, though we may take some trips. I hope."

When they arrived at Pelbarigan, they found that Tor had been there and gone again, upriver. He and Tristal were to visit a logging site, perhaps to stay awhile. He said he wanted to strengthen his left arm with heavy work.

Surprisingly enough, soon after the return of Eolyn and Royal, the Protector called a council. "This will be rather short," she said. "I have two announcements to make. The first is that I made an agreement with the northern quadrant before we undertook to breach the dome. I said that if it did not turn out well, I would resign. I have considered it, and decided that it has indeed not turned out well enough. My fault was in not prevailing on Eolyn's party not to leave. Therefore I am now resigning and ask you to hold an election tomorrow at this time." A murmur rose through the room, and a number of people stood to protest. The Protector stood up to leave.

"Wait, Protector," one of her guardsmen said. "You did not make your other announcement."

"Oh, yes," the Jestana said, turning. She raised her hands, and the guardsmen thumped for silence. "The other thing. Tomorrow at the first quarter after high sun, there will be three weddings in the chapel. Only one will be a Pelbar-type wedding, though our ministers will conduct them all. I hope you approve. The first will be of the guardsman, Dailith, with Eolyn. The second, of Blu, the Shumai, to Ruthan." Another murmur arose. "The third—the third," said the Protector in a raised voice, "will be mine. Thornton and I will marry. He has asked me and I have accepted, in what he assures me is the ancient manner. We will move to Northwall so I can be with my son. We will be sure you receive all the information about the ancient world he will generate." She turned and departed by the door behind the Protector's chair. The whole council was stunned and stood silent for a time. Then the murmur rose again as they left.

As the Protector had surmised, the council and city did not think she had misjudged the matter of Eolyn's departure. The chief loss was to Eolyn's own party, and to the Peshtak. The Shumai were not from Pelbarigan, and the loss of Dard and Cruw was never sharply felt. They were also relieved that the pulse weapons had been destroyed. The Shumai had thrown each piece separately into the river, ayas apart, except for the power pack, which Blu kept.

Their sympathy in this matter offset the shock of her marrying Cohen-Davies. But as they thought that over, they knew that she had been the Protector a very long time, had served faithfully, and had wanted to be free of the position for a while, though it had never seemed opportune. As the northern quadrant came to feel, they had been outflanked. Feelings went against them. No chance of electing a conservative Protector seemed possible. When the time came to vote, Sagan, the former Eastcounsel, Stel's mother, was elected. It was a bitter defeat for the northern quadrant, and again they talked of withdrawing to Threerivers. But even they saw the new promise of a Pelbar Academy, and a hope of the city's regaining the prominence that the rapid growth of Northwall had taken from them.

At the weddings the chapel was crowded almost to overflowing. Dailith and Eolyn were married in traditional Pelbar style. This was distinguished chiefly by the bridegroom's complete self-surrender to his bride, as old Pelbar custom had it. Dailith accepted this as a matter of upbringing. Both of the other weddings came from Cohen-Davies' memory of taped weddings from ancient times. As he and the Jestana kissed, a spontaneous cheer rose from the assembly, merging with the beginning of the concluding hymn from the choir. Proceeding slowly down the side aisle of the chapel, the old newlyweds had the nearly unified sympathy of the entire community, to which Cohen-Davies had endeared himself by his perpetual stories.

Soon after, a Tantal ship arrived for the Jestana and her goods, which were considerable. It flew a black flag. Everyone knew immediately from this that Stantu had died, and the crowd was hushed as the ship drew up to the bank wharf and Jestak's family stepped off.

Near the shore, where Stel was supervising the erection of an ice ramp, one of the workers stopped and looked. "Bursting bees' nests and flowering cows, will you look at that!"

Ahroe, who was near, whirled to reprimand his lan-

guage. Garet was near. Then she followed his gaze to
Jestak's daughter, Fahna, walking with her family to the
main city entrance. "You," she said. "Glan. You have no
business . . ." The four men turned to her, all grinning,
including her own husband. "Stel, I can't believe it."

"I can't believe it either, Ahroe." The men laughed.

"How can anybody—" she began. Then she looked,
too. "Well, what can I say? Forget it. Forget it." She
turned away.

Fahna walked in her freshness through the early-winter
chill, as if shedding flowers. She was looking around,
though only she knew it was for Tristal. He wasn't there.
A slight flush heightened her beauty. The gate guard
never raised a hand in salute, but Jestak merely rolled
his eyes at Tia and continued inside to find his mother.
She was a private citizen now, free from the politics that
had filled her life, first as a family head, then as a coun-
selor, finally during her years as Protector. Oet would not
awaken her in the night anymore to tell her of some crisis.
She would never have to sit up and immediately decide
the correct thing, with a city waiting to second-guess her.
Nor would she be in a dull retirement. She would direct
the flow of information from her new husband, guarding,
as she thought, his privacy and hers in the process. She
was sorry her old friend and sometime adversary, Sima
Pall, would not be in Northwall to greet her. But life
would still be full and worthwhile. She looked forward to
riding up the river on the big ship, even with the chill
from the north bringing stray snowflakes already.

Stel visited Tor and Tristal at the logging camp late in
Lastmonth, paddling upriver alone in an arrowboat. He
walked into the camp blowing a song on his flute, roughly,
with his mittens on. The two stooped through the low
door of a small log hut to meet him. It was gray and
snowing, almost the shortest day of the year. Both seemed
contented. Stel was surprised at how Tristal had shot up.
He stood only a finger's breadth shorter than Tor, though
still slender.

"Ho, Stel," Tor said. "What is it? Is there a war to
fight?"

"No. Hello to both of you. The others told me you
would be over here. I brought you some things—from
Ahroe, mostly, and from Ruthan and Eolyn." Ahroe had

sent honey candy and rabbit-skin socks, with the fur inside. She included a roll of Aven, copied out for Tor, in book form, and a book of riddles for Tristal. Ruthan sent new fish hooks, some seed cakes, and small bags of herb seasonings. Eolyn sent her first mathematics pamphlet, designed for teaching, along with a slide rule, made as the ancients had before electronic mathematics. She also included a small stoneware jar of sour-apple jelly. Celeste had made the pot in the Pelbar ceramics shop. It was neat and exact, with a top sealed on with beeswax.

Stel stayed a day, meeting the mixed crew of nine Shumai, an old Sentani couple who cooked and did camp chores, and four Pelbar, who worked and represented Pelbarigan, where the logs would go. The Sentani had a pellute, and much of the evening was taken up in accompanied singing.

The second morning Tor stood in the wet snow as Stel pushed his arrowboat out into the gray river. Stel turned and waved when he had glided out into the current, and Tor merely jerked his head in reply. What was the axeman thinking? Stel saw no motivation in him, no direction. He seemed to be waiting.

The Pelbar artisan paddled south near the east bank, where the channel ran, carrying him with an unobtrusive swiftness. Sun struck the sheet of ice that lay thin over most of the river. Stel squinted against it. He would be with Ahroe by afternoon. Her pregnancy was very evident now, and, like some other women, she was made radiant by it. She had been given officer's duties in the guard until parturition, but Stel saw it as a permanent step upward. He was concerned. He always liked a little freedom of action, hoped for another trip. She would be in the council, and in a difficult time, with change and new problems.

As Stel watched a flight of scaup sweeping overhead on their way to feed, a rush and jar made him turn his head. He looked through the dazzle of light at a spear protruding from the arrowboat ahead of him. Water was rolling up around the shaft. Instantly kneeling, leaning over, he stuffed a skin into the hole and turned toward shore. A group of Shumai stood there, with an older axeman, laughing and jeering. They looked rough, dressed all in skins and furs. Stel saw no bows.

Deciding without thought, he paddled right toward the

bank. He knew they expected him to turn away, but he rode within easy spear range. He would never get away.

"What on Sertine's green plains is wrong with you?" Stel said, feigning anger. "That water is cold. I do my swimming in the summer." He imitated Shumai dialect, from years of hearing Hagen daily. They looked nonplussed, but some mocked him. He drew the boat up on the bank in the face of spearpoints, but turned his back on them, stooped, took the spear out of the boat, and held it out, saying, "Whose is this?" A man took it.

Stel swept his eyes across the men, who had fallen silent. "You must be looking for Tor. He is over an ayas upstream, on this bank. He is logging for the winter. I've just come from there. Here, perhaps he will hear a horn yet." Stel took his horn, but felt it jerked from his hands. "All right," he said. "You call." He felt his legs kicked from under him. Sitting in the snow, he said, "Where have you been? We have been at peace for years. What's the matter with you?"

"Pelbar fish vulture. What peace?"

Stel looked up. "Good Aven, man. After the fight at Northwall. The whole Heart River is at peace."

"Peace nonsense. What have you done to the Shumai? We crossed the whole upper plains and never saw a trace of a running band."

"Then Tor was right."

"Tor, who? Right about what? Talk fast now, before we give you a ride on some speartips."

"Tor is an axeman who lost an arm last summer getting me out of the dome. His running band has broken up. All the bands are. They are settling along the Isso and at Northwall. They are farming, logging, herding. Don't fool with me. Surely you know this."

"Lies, man."

By the boat, another man called, "Ho, Ilder, he's got Shumai noggins and bowls in this bag." The men turned, all but one walking over. Stel saw the man turn. He thought he heard a dog. Raran. He knocked the man down and ran, thinking, I am a fool, dodging behind trees and brush as the Shumai yell went up. They would try to run him down, Stel thought. They would, too, he knew, but not easily. They were all older men, older than he, though rangy. One nearly had him. Yes, he heard Raran nearby now. The man grabbed his collar. Stel twisted free and ran on, as Raran flashed past and hit the man in the chest, carrying him down.

Stel never turned, but yelled, "Raran, come on, girl," thinking, If she runs with me, they will spear me. He glanced over his shoulder. Raran wasn't coming. She stood over the man she had knocked down. All the hair on her back stood up in a ridge, and her head was at the man's throat, teeth bared. Stel stopped and turned. He couldn't abandon the dog.

"Call your dog off, fish guts," the axeman yelled. "We will give you a quarter sunwidth head start."

"She's Tristal's dog. If you want your man alive, blow the horn for Tor."

"No need if that is him coming."

Stel flashed a look backward. It was Tor, with Tristal and four other men. Now it was a matter of waiting. Tor stopped at Stel, who said, "They speared my boat. They don't even know there is peace." Tor walked forward at the raised spears, left hand up.

"Tor Vison of Broadbend, originally," he said. "What's the matter. Stel attack you?"

The axeman stepped forward. "Disdan. We are come from the ice country."

"Ice country? No matter. Tristal, call Raran. You'd better come with us. Wherever you've been, you seem not to know we are at peace. We have a stew cooking. Send somebody to get Stel's boat. I suppose he will have to fix it." Tor turned his back on the Shumai and walked upriver, joining the waiting loggers, Stel following. Stel could hear the snow sloughing behind him as the Shumai followed. Raran walked beside him.

They did bring the boat, with everything repacked in it, piled also with their own backsacks, dragging it on the snow. They were surprised to find Sentani and Pelbar with the Shumai. Tor sat them down and fed them, talking all day, while Stel cut out the broken slats of the boat and shaved down new ones to fit, gluing it all fast, letting it dry, pouring on melted beeswax.

Disdan had not known about the peace. He and his men had been gone from the country for fifteen years, far to the north and west. They told Tor of a country full of flat-horned deer, of mountains of ice, with narrow valleys between, of herd animals and wolves, and great white beasts. Ilder's coat, thick and large, was made from a part of one skin.

"It sounds like what the Commuters call bears," Stel called over. "I met one in the western mountains."

"No mistake," said Tor. "Stel has been there, and beyond. It is a changed world. Now, tell me more about this country of ice."

Stel saw Tor's eyes light up. Disdan's men talked into evening about the area. No people lived in it anywhere. On the west, a range of great mountains, always snow-covered, blocked the way. They had never traversed the mountains. They had lived in careless abandon, free from anxieties, they said. Tor knew they were holding something back.

Finally it came out after sunset, when they were again eating stew. "The truth is," said Disdan, "that our axe-man was a man named Uchman."

"Uchman? The one who fired the prairie upwind from the Kan River Camp?"

"That one. He fled, and we went with him. He died this spring. We decided to come home."

"He killed a lot of people," Tor said.

They fell into silence. "He always claimed," Disdan said, "that he lit the fire to drive a herd of black cattle, but when it came out from the lee of the hills, the wind took it."

"Well, that was a long time ago. There have been other fires." Tor looked at Tristal. "We had one this fall that no one would believe. Tell me about these mountains. You say no one has crossed them?"

When Stel went to bed they were still talking. In the morning, when he left, two of the men who nearly killed him the previous day dragged his boat to the river across the snow. This time he paddled well out on the water, knowing it was foolish, but feeling better. He was glad to hear the Rive Tower horn at dusk announcing his coming.

Ahroe and Garet were down at the bank awaiting him. "What happened?" Ahroe asked. "You're late. We waited last night well into the fourth quadrant."

"The boat was speared by a gang of wild Shumai, all dressed in skins. They didn't know about the peace."

"What? Be serious, Stel. We were really worried."

"I am." He laughed. "They are with Tor now. They say they are going to come here, and I have promised to take them all up on one of the towers. You'll see. Here. Presents from Tor and Tristal."

"Were you scared, Father?" Garet asked.

"Stel put his arms around the two. "Gar, I was so scared, I—I—"

"Never mind," said Ahroe. "You're here. Put the boat back. Know what? A secret. Ruthan is going to have a baby."

☐ XIV

NOT long afterward, Disdan's running band did come to Pelbarigan, trotting down the frozen river edge like shaggy beasts. They stayed through the winter festival, hanging about, staring at everything, becoming a nuisance. Blu finally told them it was time to work and suggested returning to help Tor, or else cutting wood at Pelbarigan. They decided instead to go to south Shumai country to find relatives.

Using a telescope from Celeste's optics shop, Eolyn watched them leave from the tower. She shuddered.

"Cold?" Dailith asked, putting his arm around her.

"No. Look at them. Their ancestors might have been accountants, or computer experts, or federal bureaucrats. There they go running like beasts in the snow."

"We have the accountants, computer experts, and federal bureaucrats to thank for that. They made the mess."

"It was a failure in the system somewhere."

"Was it? Tor says the failure lay in the human heart."

"Tor. He is another wild beast. Why do you always bring him up?"

"I don't know. He haunts me. He isn't stupid. He is extremely effective, as you ought to know. I know he feels that the deepest human problems are solved inside, and the solutions don't lie in technology."

"He doesn't have to avoid it so completely, out there chopping with his axe instead of devising some simple machine to do the work. What solutions will he find in his endless 'words of Aven' or Shumai songs? I understand that now he wants to read about the Sentani god, Atou."

"It is all the same, Eo. It is one God by different names."

"In the dome I always thought God was only an expletive."

"I wonder. Are we turning our backs on where our study should really lie? Are we starting down a long road to technological wealth again, and leaving the search for religious insight, or what the Haframa calls spiritual perception, behind?"

"Religious insight won't feed you and keep you warm and free from disease, Dai. Be serious."

"I wish I could be as sure as you are."

On a misty morning early in Windmonth, the great log raft drifted slowly downriver, bearing the entire work crew. In its center, mounted on a bound square of rock, the stewpot of Souf, the Sentani woman, still cooked. It seemed never empty, only taken from and added to.

Tor and Tristal came ashore, walking up to Ahroe's house. They moved briskly, refreshed and contented. Talking that evening, Tor asked about his boat. Had Stel stored it anywhere? Was it in good shape?

"Yes," Stel returned. "We caulked it well and put it in the storage caves. Are you going so soon? You just got here."

"We are going to Disdan's ice country, Stel. We are going to cross the mountains where no one has been."

"Tor," Ahroe said. "With Tristal? When are you coming back?"

"Back? I hadn't thought. Perhaps never. It depends what is on the other side."

Talk turned to other things, but Ahroe said little. Finally, she went to the back rooms and would not come out.

"What did I do?" Tor asked.

"You said you were going away and maybe not coming back," Stel said. "And taking Tris."

"It is a good thing to do, Stel. You will see it is, maybe."

"I hope so. I really hope so. Tris, will you come home?"

"Home?" His face lit up. "I don't know, either. Someday, maybe. Home is with Tor, though."

A little later, Tristal took Stel's pellute and sung them a song, his own song. He had been practicing at the logging camp, and sung in the Pelbar manner, in his new deep voice:

> Good-bye, my favored stranger.
> Now I let you go.
> Some tangled strands of you are caught
> in memory's branches, though.
>
> Forgetfulness is like a blade
> We sharpen on a stone,
> But when we test it with a thumb,
> we cut it to the bone.
>
> Dark blood wells out along the cut.
> Eventually it seals.
> Wrapped up in distance, thought, and time,
> the deepest wound still heals.
>
> The sun will rise across the plains.
> Its light will flood the soul.
> And floating down its brilliant stream,
> our spirit's strength grows whole.

Stel was touched by the song, and got Tristal to sing it again so he could learn it. On the third time, Ahroe appeared in the doorway. She was near her term, leaning back to balance her swelled womb. Her eyes were red. "Can't you be quiet?" she said. "Garet is trying to sleep."

A voice came from inside. "No, I'm not, Mother. I'm listening."

"Be quiet. Lie down and be quiet."

Soon after, they all went to bed.

Morning came foggy. At dawn, Tor and Stel got out the boat and stocked it with provisions. Blu came down to the bank with Ruthan, both looking happy. He and four of his men were laying out garden shops and what Ruthan called "an experimental plot for agricultural research."

When they were ready, Tor asked, "Where is Ahroe?"

"She wouldn't come. I suspect she is on one of the towers if the both of her could get up there."

"Why? Won't she even say good-bye?"

"No. She couldn't, Tor. You are going away, that far, taking Tris, and maybe never coming back."

"Oh. Well, tell her good-bye, then. I wanted to give her this from us." He handed Stel a small disk, as big as two thumbnails, of silvery metal. The top read LIBERTY in an arc around the edge. Below, a woman's face, in low relief, looking right, came faintly up from corrosion. "I thought it looked a little like her. Not so good-looking, of course. I found it in some rocks this winter."

"It is a coin, an ancient coin," said Stel, turning it over in his hand. "They used it for exchange. The Commuters had some."

"Oh. Please ask her not to be angry. We have to go."

"I know. She knows."

They pushed the bow out into the water, then Tor embraced the men and kissed Ruthan. She set her jaw and said nothing. Pushing out farther, they got in, with Raran, and Blu shoved them out into the current.

Ahroe was on Gagen Tower, Celeste with her. Looking down, the girl asked, "Who is that? In the river. It isn't Tor. Oh. There's Tor in the bow. It looks like two of him."

"It is Tristal, Celeste. They are going away."

"Tristal? No. This one is too big. Away? For the summer?"

"They are going to the ice country. Farther than you dream of distance. They hope to cross some high mountains into unknown country." Ahroe's voice was tight.

"Why would they do that?"

Ahroe didn't answer. Eolyn, who had also come, looked at her. "You will miss them, then? That much?"

"Miss them? Yes, of course. Look at them in that eggshell. Tris is a true poet. Did you know that? He is not really equipped for this. Damn them both. Look at Tor, with his one arm. Stel tells me he spent most of a day last winter chopping geese out of the ice and letting them go free. He fell in the river twice doing it. I know he has found mice in his food stores and carefully covered up their nests again, with their naked young. Look at them.

They have no idea what they are in for. They find no dimension here for them. They are thinking to find freedom. Tor wants to be rid of you. . . ."

"Of me? Tor? Of me?"

"Of course. For yourself and for your power. He told me he can't get that burst of fire out of his head. He says he thought he would never fear anything, but he wakes up sweating thinking of a whole valley of burning men."

Eolyn snorted. "Butto did that. I would have tried to reason it out somehow."

Ahroe stared at her. "Butto was a brave and good man. And Tristal. It is possible for someone so young to love, you know. Stel and I did. We had troubles, but we did. He found in Celeste somebody like himself, alone, walking in the mud and rain, without parents. He felt somehow—I know it is irrational—that they were meant to come together and heal each other's loneliness. He is not going for Tor's sake. He is going for himself. She never even saw him. Look at them, courage and ability aside. A couple of boys. They aren't really tough like Stel and me. Or even like Blu or Dailith. They won't measure out their happiness in human handfuls. They want something beyond that, and it doesn't exist."

"You make it sound dire," Eolyn said. She took the long telescope and watched them in the morning mist, Tor standing, watching ahead for snags, Tristal in the stern, stroking, stroking, even and strong, Raran standing amidships, looking back at Stel, wagging her tail. She watched Tristal whack the dog gently on the shoulder with the paddle and saw Raran plump down and drop her prick ears. A bank of fog rolled downriver and the two headed into it. At last it seemed a solid wall, slowly taking the bow, then Tor standing erect, then Raran, then Tristal, and at last the flash of his paddle.

Celeste let out a murmur and reached for the telescope. It slipped, spun on the parapet, and fell to the stone pavement of the tower, the eyepiece shattering. The girl stooped, then knelt and took the pieces in her hands, cutting a finger. Eolyn looked down at her, shaking her head. Celeste looked up, her mouth open, trying to speak, trying, but again finding that no words would come.

From high overhead, perhaps above the mist, came the calling of geese, snows and blues, flying north, loosing their glad and desultory cries as geese have always done, raining them down on Pelbarigan, on the mist, somewhere out there on Tor and Tristal, flying their instinctive routes, high and free, migrating as they have since the Pleistocene, before and after America, and through all the times of the Heart River peoples.

About the Author

A native of New Jersey, Paul O. Williams holds a Ph.D. in English from the University of Pennsylvania. Following three years of teaching at Duke University, he settled at the tiny Mississippi River town of Elsah, Illinois, where he is currently a Professor of English at Principia College, teaching American literature and creative writing. He and his wife, Nancy, have two children.

His response to his small community has been varied, including helping to found Historic Elsah Foundation and direct its small museum, and serving as the president of the local volunteer firefighters. His poems, essays, reviews, and articles on literary subjects and Midwestern history have been widely published. While he has written largely on nineteenth-century America, and served as a president of the Thoreau Society, he has also developed a deep interest in science fiction and fantasy.

The Breaking of Northwall and *The Ends of the Circle,* his first two novels, are set against the same background as *The Dome in the Forest.*